ALONG
THE
WATCHTOWER

ALONG
THE
WATCHTOWER

———

Constance Squires

RIVERHEAD BOOKS
New York

RIVERHEAD BOOKS
Published by the Penguin Group
Penguin Group (USA) Inc.
375 Hudson Street, New York, New York 10014, USA

Penguin Group (Canada), 90 Eglinton Avenue East, Suite 700, Toronto, Ontario M4P 2Y3, Canada
(a division of Pearson Penguin Canada Inc.)
Penguin Books Ltd., 80 Strand, London WC2R 0RL, England
Penguin Group Ireland, 25 St. Stephen's Green, Dublin 2, Ireland (a division of Penguin Books Ltd.)
Penguin Group (Australia), 250 Camberwell Road, Camberwell, Victoria 3124, Australia
(a division of Pearson Australia Group Pty. Ltd.)
Penguin Books India Pvt. Ltd., 11 Community Centre, Panchsheel Park, New Delhi—110 017, India
Penguin Group (NZ), 67 Apollo Drive, Rosedale, Auckland 0632, New Zealand
(a division of Pearson New Zealand Ltd.)
Penguin Books (South Africa) (Pty.) Ltd., 24 Sturdee Avenue, Rosebank, Johannesburg 2196,
South Africa

Penguin Books Ltd., Registered Offices: 80 Strand, London WC2R 0RL, England

The author gratefully acknowledges permission to quote lyrics from "Peace Frog." Words and music by The Doors. Copyright © 1970 Doors Music Co. Copyright renewed. All rights reserved. Reprinted by permission of Hal Leonard Corporation.

Copyright © 2011 by Constance Squires
Cover design by Kelly Blair
Cover photograph copyright © by Richard Kolker / Getty
Book design by Tiffany Estreicher

First Riverhead trade paperback edition: July 2011

Library of Congress Cataloging-in-Publication Data

Squires, Constance.
Along the watchtower / Constance Squires. — 1st Riverhead trade paperback ed.
    p. cm.
ISBN 978-1-59448-523-7
I. Title.
    PS3619.Q57A79 2011
813'.6—dc22

2010046877

PRINTED IN THE UNITED STATES OF AMERICA

10 9 8 7 6 5 4 3 2 1

To Steve

"Ghosts crowd the young child's fragile eggshell mind."

JIM MORRISON

PART ONE

Grafenwoehr, West Germany

1983

ONE

Lucinda Collins was the type of girl who noticed things, the trail-her-fingers-along-the-banister type who would usually have lingered at the unfamiliar stairwell window to wonder about the quaint church just visible on a distant hill, how old it was and how far away. But not today. Today her foot-falls sent a flat tattoo echoing down the stairwell as she took a corner and bounded down the next flight two steps at a time. She didn't even glance out the window. Instead, she watched her black high-top Converses as they came down hard onto the dirty tiled steps. The sound of her stomping boomed against the walls like something she had thrown in a fury. She could be quiet if she wanted to, but she didn't want to. Why should she?

The stairwell was noisy, anyway. Kids' voices floated up to her from below and a television laugh track came through the door of an apartment on the fourth floor. Lucinda trotted down another flight, smelling dirty bleach water and burning coffee. She reached the final flight and looked down at the chief source of noise, a circle of kids, driven indoors by the snowstorm outside, playing jacks on their bellies in the tiled foyer.

All five of them looked up at her. They were between her and the front door.

"What's your problem?" a gap-toothed boy with black hair asked. He stood up and brushed off the front of his corduroys. "Sounded like Godzilla coming down the stairs."

She wanted to ignore the kids and head out the door, but she took a deep breath and stopped. You don't blow off your new neighbors the first time you meet them—she had moved too many times not to know that. Besides, that boy had called her Godzilla, a better-than-average insult that made her think of her old neighborhood in North Carolina. The teenagers who lived next door had played that song in their garage a dozen times a day. Lucinda had always wondered whether it was really just about Godzilla, the movie monster, or if Godzilla was some kind of code for drugs, like "Lucy in the Sky with Diamonds" or one of the zillion other songs with secret meanings. Before Lucinda could really consider whether it was a good idea, she found herself humming the surly guitar riff and singing out loud the chorus of the song, a silly song—even a thirteen-year-old could tell that. "Oh no!" She stomped a foot. "There goes Tokyo. Go, go, Godzilla!"

A stunned silence followed. She had meant to defuse the boy's criticism by showing she had a sense of humor. That usually worked. Lucinda studied her high-tops. What was wrong with these kids? Come on! Why didn't they know the song?

Trying to sound like a DJ, she said, "That was Blue Öyster Cult."

They continued to stare at her. Finally the black-haired boy broke the silence with an appreciative whistle. "Who are you?"

"I'm Lucinda."

"Are you living in the attic?" a girl asked, scrutinizing Lucinda with round eyes like a doll's. She wore a Philadelphia Phillies stocking cap, the wings of a Lady Di haircut curling around the edges.

"Just temporarily," Lucinda said.

"Rats live in the attic," the girl said. "You're a rat."

"It's just temporary."

"Temporary rat!" the girl said. The others all laughed.

"What rank is your dad?" one of the boys asked. "I bet he's a privRAT!" They laughed harder.

She tried to step around the girl in the Phillies hat, who looked up at her, those round doll eyes sizing her up. Lucinda got past her to the door. "He's a major," she said. The kids quit laughing and looked at her anew, reassessing her in the light of her father's rank. It wasn't as if her father was a general or something, but major was miles from being a privRAT, that was for sure. She had gone to a civilian school back in North Carolina and nobody there knew or cared about rank, but here, Lucinda could see things were different.

"Snob," one of them said, and they all returned their attention to their game.

She pulled open the door and slid out sideways, blasting them all with snow. The gap-toothed boy with the hair, who had been leaning against the banister smiling at her the whole time, grabbed the door when she let go of it and joined her on the stoop. "Anybody ever call you Lucy?"

"No. I have to go," she warned him. "It's an emergency."

He stood squinting into the snow, which hit his hair like stars flashing into a dark night. "An emergency, huh?"

Lucinda didn't want company. Her family was in the midst of a full-on meltdown, DEFCON 1, and she was the only one who could switch off the reactor. She gave him a quick nod and stepped around him. "I'm in a big hurry here."

"Okay," he said, appearing at her side as she headed down the sidewalk. "But where are you going?"

"My dad's office." She glanced around at the rows of gray stucco apartment buildings with letter-coded stairwells, unmistakably Army. "I don't know where it is, but I'm going to find it. I have to."

"He's working on a Saturday?"

"I guess. Yeah."

"What's his battalion?" the boy asked, assuming the air of a tour guide. He wore Army-surplus boots, thick-ribbed brown corduroys, and a dark blue wool coat. No hat, but a red sweatband covered his ears and protected his forehead from the full force of the snow. His face was fine-featured and open, almost beautiful.

Lucinda told him what she knew. He said, "I know where that is."

"What's your name?" Lucinda asked.

"Sydney Greenstreet Eliot, but you can call me Syd."

"Syd." She grabbed his gloved hand and shook it. Friend making was one of the recurring hardships of being an Army brat and Lucinda had learned to rush through the process like ripping off a Band-Aid. "Friends?" she asked. Syd gave her a quick grin. She sized him up. He was taller than she, and super skinny. "Are you twelve? Or thirteen?"

"Thirteen next week," he said, straightening.

"Me, too," she said.

"Next week?"

"No, I mean now. I'm thirteen now."

"Just a minute." He ran back to the foyer and reemerged with an umbrella. It was Army green—the color of uniforms, tents, jeeps, tanks, floors and walls, bombs and socks. All her life, everywhere she went, that olive-drab color had made every place the same place. It told her she was home. Her mom thought it was ugly as sin, but to Lucinda that kind of thinking was like taking exception to the air.

The umbrella easily covered them both, and they took off up the long boulevard, each with one hand around the stem.

"We really have to hurry," she said. "My mom told me to be back in an hour. She thinks I'm looking for the library."

"HQ," he said, picking up the pace, "is at the top of the hill. I think your dad is there."

Lucinda looked ahead and saw the wide, imposing head-quarters building about a quarter mile up a gentle incline, rows of wet, twisted flags flapping in front of it. Traffic swept past them in both directions, some civilian cars and many Army vehicles, Humvees and jeeps, and even a couple of tanks powering down the road like poisonous toads. The snowstorm didn't seem to be slowing things down much. "Thanks for helping me," she said. "We just flew into Frank-furt yesterday."

"So what's got you out in this snow when you don't even know where you're going?"

Lucinda dug her hands into the pockets of her coat, a blue peacoat that had looked warm when she bought it in September, but which now felt inadequate. She wasn't sure she could make him understand how very wrong things were. He would know from his own experience what it felt like to lose everything, again—friends, home, school—just as soon as the scars of the last move had healed. But she doubted he knew what it was like to find nothing, not even the pretense of a new home, at the end of the journey. Her mother's motto as they drove onto a new base was always "Bloom where you're planted," but this time her father hadn't even bothered to plant them. They were just sup-posed to bloom in the emptiness. She took a deep breath and tried to stick to the facts. "Well, my mom's already mad because my dad didn't get us on the family housing list until last week even though he's been here two months in bache-lor quarters and he was supposed to get everything ready. So we show up last night and he tells us we have to live in those crappy temp quarters. You ever been up there? It's like Anne Frank up there."

She gestured back up at the building, pointing at the dormer windows protruding from the roof like ship's portals. That morning, she had looked out of one of those windows while she listened to her mother slamming cabinet doors, hunting for food that wasn't there. She wondered if her mother was watching from the window now. That would be good news. That would mean she had stopped streaking back and forth barefoot along the spine of the attic room, trailing vapors of black fury like a crashing plane. But Lucinda didn't see anyone looking back, not even Jacob or Erin, her six-year-old twin siblings, who were surely dying to get out of there.

"My place is way nicer than where you're staying," he assured her. "Temps suck."

She told Syd about the worst part: how her dad had also forgotten to buy them any groceries, to leave them any money or a car. "Airplane peanuts," she said. "That's the last thing we ate, and that was yesterday. That's why I'm out here," she explained. "To find him. So he can fix it."

Syd shook his head. "He can't fix all that."

"Yes he can," Lucinda said, eyes on the dirty snow along the sidewalk. She believed it. "He's just really busy with his job." Her dad had survived Vietnam, killed people, could name all the U.S. presidents in order, and had once almost dated Tina Turner. Surely he could fix this.

"He sounds like a rat fink," Syd said. "My dad's a major, too."

"And a rat fink?"

"No," Syd said. "No way. He's just a butthead. Where are you from?" The inevitable question. Where were you *born*? was a question for which she had an answer. Everybody was born somewhere. But where are you *from*?

"Shiloh. Shiloh, Texas. We have a family home there." The syllables of the name stretched like roots into the bedrock of her imagination, the house and land she would inherit from her dad one day, after it passed from her grandma Esmé, who owned it now although she was scheming to sell it for a condo in Galveston. But Lucinda had never been there. Most of the time she felt like sand blowing across the earth, particles of something that hadn't been whole in a long time and never would be again. But that was just a feeling, because in fact, she owned a pond ringed by tall cottonwoods and a white house with columns on a hundred acres of land. The house grounded her in time, too, built in 1869, more than one hundred years old. One hundred years and one hundred acres. Take that, Sydney Greenstreet Eliot. Temporary rat indeed!

"Shiloh—that's a battlefield," Syd said. "You can't live on a battlefield. It's in Tennessee, anyway, not Texas."

"My great-great-grandpa just named his place Shiloh. He built it with his Civil War pension," she said, stepping around a fire hydrant. "He fought at Shiloh. In Tennessee."

"He must've been Union."

"Why?"

"Government pension."

Lucinda had never thought about that. She looked at Syd. "How do you know?"

"I'm from the Heart of Dixie. Where the stars fell. Alabama." He said this in a weary, elegiac voice, like he had personally reconstructed the South and had the blisters to show for it.

"Have you ever lived there?"

"No." He shrugged. "But my family practically owns the whole coast down there. Got cousins all over, aunts and uncles, we go way back in that area. Got a county named after my kin. I know all about it."

Lucinda nodded her head vigorously. She knew all about her family place, too. "Bet you know more than they do—your relatives that live there."

"Bet that's right."

Slushy water splashed her leg from a car that had pulled alongside and was keeping pace with them. Lucinda looked and saw that it was her father's dark green Opel.

Lucinda's dad rolled down the window and stuck his head out, his bald head gleaming. "Lucinda?"

The sound of her father's voice startled her and it took a second for her to realize that her search for him was over. "My name is Lucy," she said, eyes on the ground. "I'm a rat. This is Syd." Syd bowed his head, staring at Major Collins from under the umbrella.

Her father reached out of the window and waved for a jeep coming up behind him to go around. "What are you doing out?"

"Going to get you."

"Get in," he said.

"Are you sure you want a rat in your car?"

"Lucinda, get in."

She and Syd squeezed into the front seat, snow sliding from the collapsed umbrella and melting all over her father's mint-green upholstery. Major Collins pulled in his lips and looked them both up and down, his blue eyes backlit against the cold light. Relief hit her and she wanted to hug him, but she was too frustrated. Frustrated and bewildered. When she was small, her bedtime ritual had involved kissing him on the forehead and each cheek, followed by a hug. Then her father would say, "Good night, Irene." A character in a song, he told her. She wanted something solid and predictable like that now, some kind of assurance that he was still a part of her life: kiss, kiss, kiss, hug, Good night, Irene.

Behind them, another car began to honk, so Major Collins put the car in gear and returned his attention to the road. "Now, why were you coming to get me? Everything okay?"

Lucinda heard the mild curiosity in her father's voice and began to sob. He had no notion that anything might be seriously wrong. Even as she cried he only patted her on the head and said, "You've got jet lag, kiddo."

She reined in her crying as best she could. Syd patted her leg and she latched on to his hand and felt his brown cords rubbing against the slick surface of her thin jeans. She looked at their entwined fingers and a weird giddiness came over her. In that moment Syd became like a location, X marks the spot, a lighthouse beam flashing across a dark and choppy ocean surface. She breathed in the foreign smell of diesel fumes and knew she was, somehow, exactly where she was supposed to be.

Lucinda looked up at her dad's composed face, his attention fully on the road. "I love Syd," she said.

Her father let out a snort. "So you were coming to ask my permission to marry? That it?"

Beside her, Syd began flipping the air vent open and closed. He looked a little startled by her announcement but didn't loosen his grip on her hand. She said, "You took the car. There's no food and no way to get food. You bought yourself cereal but you didn't buy anything for us. I hate Grape-Nuts!"

Her father blinked rapidly, looking away and out the window. "Oh, holy shit." He turned back to Lucinda. "What's your mother doing right now?"

"Pacing. She broke some stuff."

"Goddammit." He slammed the steering wheel with the heel of his hand.

"Did you forget?" Lucinda asked.

"I just . . ." Her father shook his head. "I never thought about it. I thought she'd take care of things. She always takes care of things."

"Dad? We don't even know where we are."

"Okay, okay. I guess this looks pretty bad for me."

"You bought cereal for yourself!"

"No, no. I just carried that over from my bachelor's quarters. You can have some, if you want. It's not just mine— we're a family, you know."

"Dad!"

"Okay, help me here, baby. We need a plan."

"It's easy," Lucinda said. "Food, money, car."

"Yeah, okay," he said. "Let's get the food first. How about some fresh brötchen?"

"What's that?"

"Bread," Syd and her father both answered.

So they started with the bread, heading off post into the old German town that had been dark when they arrived the night before. A minute after they passed through the gate, they drove past bars, strip clubs, massage parlors, and pawnshops lining the road beyond the gate, the neon signs, all in English, dingy-looking against the bright snowfall. Except for the twins' birthplace, Saudi Arabia, where the local government frowned on sex, drugs, and rock and roll, every base where Lucinda had ever lived had such a strip, catering to what her mother called the GIs' leisure-time needs. But soon the strip gave way to more proper businesses and they were driving through the old German town of Grafenwöhr.

The streets were lined with whitewashed stucco buildings, many with dates chiseled in stone above their low doors: 1521, 1684, 1710. "It's all so old!" Lucinda said.

Grafenwöhr's cobblestone streets showed in places through the snow, which was banked on the sides of the road from earlier storms, almost as high as the car. "Look," she said, pointing at a pair of old women in head-to-toe black, the tops of their heads barely clearing the snowbanks. "Witches!"

"War widows," her dad corrected her. "There are a lot of them still."

"They're still wearing black?"

"Looks that way, doesn't it?"

"World War Two was over forty years ago!"

"The dead are still dead, honey."

Lucinda looked back at the women, who were laughing and talking. "Do you think they ever wear colors?"

"I don't know."

"I hope so," she said. "Pink and green and electric blue."

The main road led to a central marketplace where a town hall, a four-story square building with a steep roof topped by a bell tower, loomed over a public fountain. A string of cars was parked along the street in tight spots chiseled out of the still-falling snow. Her father parked the Opel and ran into a bakery. Lucinda followed with Syd.

As she stared at the pastry case, it really struck her that she was in a foreign country. The pastries here looked like art. Each tart was surrounded by wax paper, arranged on brightly lit glass shelves in a display case low enough for her to see it all. The bread was piled high in deep wicker baskets behind the counter. The smell of baking thickened the air, like a soft bed you could lie back on.

"They make this stuff fresh every day," Syd said, his voice low with awe. "No preservatives."

"Are you serious?" Lucinda thought of the vanilla wafers that were a ubiquitous feature of her family's pantry. Her dad joked that they had a half-life of a thousand years.

"Those things," Syd said, pointing to tarts covered in

strawberries and kiwis covered with clear gelatin, "are my favorite. We get them every Sunday after church. Those, too," he said, nodding at a cream-filled puff drizzled with chocolate. "My mom loves those the best."

"Come on," her father said. He was holding a bag of brötchen, hard rolls.

"Dad," Lucinda said, "look at these! Could we have some of these?"

Her father glanced down at the pastry display. "Junk food," he said. "You don't want to develop a taste for it."

"But just this once?" Lucinda said. Syd stood next to her, hands stuffed into his coat pockets, surveying Major Collins.

"Looks good, but it'll make you fat," he said. "Fat people give in to stuff like this. That's the difference between us and them. Don't you think I'd like to eat that? Sure I would!"

"Mom would like it," Lucinda said.

Her father dismissed the idea with a wave. "Are you weak or are you strong? That's the only question." He smiled at the rosy-cheeked woman behind the counter and handed her a sheaf of bills. Lucinda knew she couldn't argue. Weak or strong—one of his formulations that stopped all discussion. Because who wanted to be weak?

Syd had pulled his red sweatband taut between his fingers and was aiming it at her dad. "Rat fink," Syd said. The hair stood up on her neck. She looked at Syd, following his disgusted gaze to her father. Syd's family came to this bakery every Sunday and picked out pastries, everyone getting what they wanted. A crack opened in a door of her mind. Syd wasn't fat—not even close.

Her father unlocked the car doors for them and walked next door to a liquor store. Lucinda and Syd stayed outside on the sidewalk. "Just a minute," Syd said, and ran back into the bakery. He returned a minute later with a small paper sack and handed it to her.

She opened it. Inside, nestled in pink tissue paper like a diamond, was one of the chocolate-covered cream puffs she had been admiring. She pulled it out of the bag and held it on her wet gloved hand. "It's too pretty to eat."

"Eat it."

She inhaled it in two bites while Syd looked on. "Well?" he said. "Nothing wrong with that, is there?" Still chewing, sweetness suffusing her mouth, she shook her head. It was too late, but she wished she had saved some of it for her brother and sister. Her mom, too. But she had wolfed it down. Weakly and selfishly, just like her dad had said.

Before she could ask Syd to spot her another few pastries to take home, her father swung out of the liquor store with a six-pack of beer in dark amber bottles. "First time we were stationed over here," he said as they got back in the car, "when you were a baby, your mom and I loved this beer. She wasn't legal yet back in the States, but she could drink here. This will cheer her up." He handed Lucinda the bottles to hold. "I came straight here from Vietnam pretty spaced out. Main thing I remember was this beer tasted like some stuff they had in Xuân Lôc. You remember anything?" he asked her. "Anything from that first tour?"

"When I see pictures it seems like I do." Lucinda knew well the slides and photographs, hundreds of them, that her parents had taken of their first European tour of duty. They had gone everywhere and seen everything and loved every minute of it. There were pictures of Lucinda toddling in the Roman forum, the ruins of Crete, the snowy precipices of alpine lookouts. They had camped, and each series of vacation photos included a shot of tiny Lucinda smiling from the bucket they used to bathe her in, her blond hair streaming into the sudsy water. In every picture her parents grinned behind cool shades like champions.

Major Collins reached over Lucinda and snapped Syd's headband. "What's your story, little man?"

"I'm the Crimson Tide," he said, jutting out his jaw.

"Oh, you are. Never could give a crap about football, myself. You belong to anybody?"

"Eliot," Syd said.

"Shane Eliot? Yeah, you look like him. We're waiting on your quarters. Why don't you hurry up and leave?" he said, laughing.

She looked at Syd, betrayed. "You're moving?"

Syd kneaded his forehead. "Yeah, in two months. Either Bliss or Benning."

Lucinda looked at her father and then at Syd. She would be living in Syd's quarters, which meant that Syd would be gone. And the sooner he left, the sooner her parents would make up. She could hardly take it in.

"You'll probably get his old room," her father said, patting her on the shoulder. "Leave it nice for her, okay, my man?"

Lucinda slid her hand out of Syd's. She closed her eyes

and leaned her head back, acute pain surging behind her eyes.

"Lucinda?" said her father. "You okay?"

"Yeah."

"You with me?"

"Yeah." Her father probably thought she was having one of her epileptic seizures, but that wasn't it. A seizure would have been a welcome relief. Sometimes the seizures deleted pieces of short-term memory. Maybe she would come out of it and not remember meeting Syd at all. How perfect. Syd! She felt his warmth and the solidity of his body squeezed next to her, saw his silky hair curling into his ears. Yet he was vanishing. At the same time, she winced at the news of two more months in temporary quarters. Two months! It was grievous either way—such a short time to spend with Syd, such a long time to wait for quarters.

This was just how it went. She always lost her friends— she had parted tearfully from her best friends, Audra and Simone, in North Carolina just two days earlier. At the beginning of each new posting, she always vowed she wouldn't make new friends, but she always failed and wound up with fresh grief. And it was getting harder.

Lucinda opened her eyes and saw that they were approaching the gate. Striped barriers lowered across the blacktop and two guards emerged from the gatehouse. Arched across the road, a latticed iron banner spelled U.S. ARMY TRAINING AREA GRAFENWOEHR in letters dripping with ice.

Her father brought the car to a stop, unrolled his window, and leaned out. "What's going on?"

A young black face hovered outside the window. The guard saluted. "Hello, sir. Sorry about this."

"What's up?"

"A bomb threat, sir. We're checking all cars."

Her father said, "I haven't heard anything."

"Just came in, sir. Don't know if it's really the Red Army Faction or a prank, but we've got to take all threats seriously."

Lucinda's father pulled out his wallet and handed his ID to the guard, who looked at it and returned it with a nod.

"Please pull the vehicle to the side, sir. We'll do this as fast as we can."

"Hells bells," her father said.

"A bomb threat?" Lucinda said. "Really?"

"This happened one other time when I was here," Syd said. "It's the Baader-Meinhof Gang. They suck. We had to evacuate the school buses and stand outside while they checked for bombs and it was cold—I mean really cold. This one kid turned blue—like actually blue."

Lucinda thought of her mother back at the apartment, waiting. "Is this going to take a long time?" She stepped from the car, pulling her coat around her, and stood with her dad and Syd on a short strip of sidewalk in front of the guardhouse while two privates got down on hands and knees on the slick street and pointed flashlights at the green Opel's undercarriage.

"Goddamn terrorists," her father said.

"Why do they hate us?" Lucinda asked. "These terrorists."

"We're imperialists," Syd said. He began jumping up and down like he was on a pogo stick. It was freezing.

Lucinda thought about the word. "Like *The Empire Strikes Back?*"

"No," her father said, "not like *The Empire Strikes Back.*"

From the top of a jump, Syd said, "Maybe a little."

Lucinda started jumping, too. It really warmed her up. She watched as one of the guards knelt on the ice and peered under the back bumper of the Opel, and tried to fit the comparison together. The Germans were good guys, the Communists across the Iron Curtain were bad guys, but then there were the bad old Germans, the Nazis who weren't around anymore except in their long shadow. It was hard to figure—Lucinda was fuzzy on the difference between Communists and Nazis. Neither had freedom of speech; that much she knew. And it went without saying that the Americans were the good guys. "We're the rebels?"

"We're Darth Vader," Syd said, punctuating each word with a bounce.

"Don't be an idiot," her father said. "Most Germans love us. We're protecting them from the Warsaw Pact. Pouring millions into their economy. I can't believe I'm explaining this to two jackrabbits."

They watched as the guards took the insides of the car, which they had piled onto a soot-black snowbank, and began putting them back, wet and dirty. "You're good to go, sir," the black soldier called out.

Lucinda and Syd stopped jumping. As they hurried to

the car, Lucinda stepped off the curb and sank her high-tops into icy water. "Oh no," she said. "Oh, man!"

Her father stopped and looked at her feet. "Why the hell are you in those flimsy shoes?"

When they were in the car her father reached down and took her by the ankle. "Let me see those feet," he said. "Your mother would just love it if you lost some toes on your first day here."

Lucinda twisted toward Syd and raised her foot. "My lucky shoes," she explained. They were more than that, though. They were talismanic, emblematic: they said the magic word.

"What's this?" her father asked. She watched him read what she had written in black permanent marker across the whitewalls along the rim of her shoe: CROATOAN.

He let go of her foot and started the car. "You should know, Syd, that Lucinda has an overactive imagination. Since you two are in love and everything. Last summer she decided we were all descended from Virginia Dare."

"Who's Virginia Dare?"

"First English baby born in the New World. She vanished with the rest of the Roanoke colonists."

"I just said we *could* be," Lucinda said, scowling up at her father. "She might have survived."

They had visited the site the previous summer and Lucinda had become intrigued with the story of the colonists who vanished. Her mother said Lucinda's fascination showed she had empathy, and her father said she was feeling sorry for herself—they had just gotten orders for

Germany—by feeling sorry for everybody who ever had a tough time relocating. In the museum, Lucinda had studied the models of the settlement and felt herself walking among those rough dwellings, smelling the sea and the pines, feeling the precariousness of their lives. No net, no friends—she knew that feeling. Those colonists were away from home and there was no one watching when they vanished. No video surveillance cameras to replay; history had closed over them like a wave. CROATOAN. The final word, the only clue carved into a tree. *Come and find us*, it said. *This is what happened*. Whoever had carved it had thought readers would understand what it meant—that was what Lucinda couldn't get over. Nobody knew what it meant. Nobody. There were lots of theories, but no one knew anything.

"Those people were probably slaughtered by Indians, honey. I'm sorry, but that's probably all that happened. There's no mystery."

"I do not believe that," Lucinda said.

"So don't, then."

Lucinda's foot was so cold the pain felt like needles. She pulled it into her lap and unlaced the sodden shoe, prying it off with the wet sock and stretching her leg over Syd's lap to press her marble-white foot against the heating vent. Syd picked up her shoe and read it. "Croatoan. That's cool," he said.

"I kind of feel like we're colonists here, you know?"

Syd narrowed his eyes. "Hmm. No."

"Like we've come back across the ocean to this settlement."

"To the wilds of twentieth century West Germany?" her father said.

"I know it's not the same thing," Lucinda shot back. "I just mean how it feels."

Dawning pleasure had spread across Syd's face as he listened to the exchange between father and daughter. Lucinda could see that he really liked her, Syd did. He was a bright spot. But she had been thinking, since they got out of the car, that the bomb threat was a bad sign for her family's stay in Germany—there were mean omens like this sometimes when they rolled onto a new base. There had been the hurricane that hit the night they got to Fort Bragg. And the way they had arrived at Fort Bliss the day in early spring when all the cottonwoods dropped their cotton, sending her mother into anaphylactic shock from an allergic reaction. The bomb threat seemed on par with these bad omens, but this time the bad news had come before the sign arrived. She had met and fallen in love with Syd and learned that she would lose him all in one busy morning.

They headed for the base commissary to finish buying groceries.

"We should get back to Mom," Lucinda said, pulling her shoe back on.

"We'll make it fast," her dad said, sliding the car into an icy parking spot. "Just get whatever your mom usually gets. No junk."

So they rushed up and down the aisles, tossing groceries into the cart. Back in the States, they usually shopped in civilian grocery stores, which were much bigger, brighter, and more interesting to look at. There were no advertisements here—no Green Giant, no Hey Kool-Aid, no Charlie the Tuna with a fin full of coupons and tuna salad recipes. Instead, the products sat in dusty cardboard boxes on the Army-green metal shelves. They had to dig around to find what each box concealed.

As they cruised to the checkout lane, Lucinda looked up at the clock above the front door. It was quarter to eleven. She had left the apartment a little after nine. She turned to her father. "Dad!" she said. "We have to go! Right now! I told Mom I'd be back in an hour."

Her father, standing in line with his wallet out, dropped his arms and stared for a long second at the fluorescent lights suspended from the ceiling. "Shit," he said. "Goddammit, Lucinda. Why didn't you say something?"

On the sidewalk outside the commissary, as she and Syd waited for her father to finish up at the register, Syd knocked snow from tree limbs with his umbrella. "Yeah, right. How could *you* forget. He's the one who forgot to get you a place to live and food to eat. Rat fink."

Intense irritation pricked Lucinda. She liked Syd, but her mother was stranded, mad as hell and rightly so; her little sister and brother were starving, and here Syd was, this extra person, talking about her dad like he had the right. A stranger, really. Who was this guy? What had she been feeling? Something wonderful, sure, but wasn't it also a weak feeling? Weakness usually felt good, didn't it? Her family

was at DEFCON 1 and she was holding hands with some
guy who wore a sweatband in the middle of winter. It was
like he was a spy sent in to keep her from completing her
mission. What did they call that? A honey trap. She'd heard
that in some spy movie. Syd was a honey trap. She wanted
him out of her sight—for now and forever. She walked away
from him and stood by the car.

Besides, even if he wasn't a stranger, wasn't a honey trap,
he was leaving. Going stateside. She had to shut him out; she
simply had to. He would understand; he knew the drill.
Weak or strong—in this she could be strong. She had to be;
otherwise it was just too hard.

When her father came tearing out of the commissary,
tossing groceries into the trunk of the Opel, Lucinda jumped
in the front seat and locked the door behind her. Syd stood
outside and knocked on the window, saying something she
couldn't hear through the glass. Lucinda saw his gap-toothed
smile and the look of bewilderment in his eyes, but she
looked down at the gearshift until her father, watching her,
finally started the car and drove off, leaving Syd standing in
the parking lot shivering in his coat.

Lucinda stared at his figure growing smaller in the rear-
view mirror. Syd who had fed her. Syd from Alabama. Stars
fell. She wondered what that meant. She had never been to
Alabama and she doubted it had its own special sky. But
maybe it did.

"You'll forget all about him," her father said, giving her
knee a squeeze.

"Are we close to housing?"

"He's got about a five-minute walk." He laughed. "Little man should've worn his lucky shoes."

"He called you a rat fink."

Lucinda and her father burst into the attic apartment at eleven, nearly tripping over the twins, who were playing with a deck of old-maid cards on the floor. They yelled when the door opened, jumping up and down to see the grocery bags, which Major Collins set on the kitchen counter and began emptying. Lucinda looked around the room for signs of destruction, broken dishes strewn across the dark, overstuffed couch and big-armed chairs against the walls, but everything looked in order. Lucinda's mom, however, was nowhere to be seen. The apartment was nearly dark, lit from the yellow glow of one floor lamp and reflected light coming from the snow outside the dormer windows.

"What did you get?" Erin asked her father.

"You hungry?" He picked her up and ran his index finger down the slope of her nose. "Where's your mommy?"

"Sleeping," Jacob said, pointing to the closed bedroom door.

Their father set Erin down and asked Lucinda, "Can you cook?"

"Kind of," she said, not sure it was true. She could do sandwiches.

"Make something," he said. He grabbed the six-pack of German beer and stared at the bedroom door for a minute before he depressed the handle.

When she heard their voices from behind the door, Lucinda switched on her father's transistor radio that he had carried in Vietnam and found it tuned to the AFN station and the hourly news that began with a bass voice saying, "It's eleven o'clock in Central Europe. The news is next on AFN. Do you know where your children are?"

Lucinda found some beat-up cookware in a bottom drawer and used it to boil water for the bag of rice they had just bought at the commissary, following the directions on the bag. It had a recipe for some sort of casserole that she tried to make as best she could, combining cans of Campbell's soup with the rice.

AFN yielded up some music in the form of Lucinda's favorite Blondie song, and after a few minutes the smell of warm food began filling the apartment. Erin and Jacob were less starved than she had feared. They were behaving like it was all a great adventure, wolfing down brötchen with noisy approval.

Finally the bedroom door opened and her parents filed out.

"What's for lunch?" her father said in a loud, shaky voice, clapping his hands together. "Smells great in here!"

Her mother looked sick, shoulders stooped and face drawn up. The wings of her auburn hair were flattened against her head, her eyes red from crying. "You cooked?" she said to Lucinda.

Lucinda nodded. She set a stack of metal bowls on the table as Erin and Jacob climbed into their chairs, ready to eat.

"You didn't come home," her mother said, taking a seat in one of the straight-back chairs at the table, moving stiffly.

Lucinda peeled the wax paper from a stick of butter. "I'm sorry," she said.

"I told you I didn't need any trouble from you, right?"

"I was trying to help."

"That's what I hear," her mother said, glancing at her husband.

"It was that crazy bomb threat, Faye. We'd have been home much sooner," her father said.

Lucinda ladled the stew or whatever it was into bowls. The twins accepted theirs and the table fell silent as they all began to eat. In a minute Erin shrieked and Jacob spat out his food onto the table. "Gross!" he said. They all looked into their bowls at what was floating to the surface—tiny bugs. Cooked bugs.

"Boll weevils," Major Collins said.

Lucinda's mother flattened a hand against her chest, red fingernails, polished especially for the flight to Germany, spread like a tight firing pattern. "The groceries," she spat, "must be ancient. Old and ancient and shitty and not fit for use, like everything else in this shit hole." She pushed her palms into her eyes. "A new low, Jack. This is a new low."

"No, honey, look. Faye, kids. This is fine," Major Collins said, looking around the table and smiling. "Like what we ate in Ranger school. It's a good reminder."

"Of *what*?" Lucinda asked.

"We eat to survive."

Lucinda stared at her father.

"Really, gang," said her father. "You're just jet-lagged. It's okay."

"What's okay, Jack?" his wife said between sobs. "What the hell is okay?"

"Lucinda's meal." He looked into his children's faces. "Bugs are a good source of protein!" He ate a heaping bite, watching his wife, and said, "Mmm. That's just fine. I like it fine. Come on, everybody. Eat up, eat up."

If he was wrong, if everything really wasn't okay, Lucinda didn't know how her family could survive the hour. DEFCON 1. But he sounded so sure. And he was her dad. Without looking again into her bowl, Lucinda lifted her spoon and tried to swallow without tasting.

TWO

It was summer, finally summer, and Lucinda was at the commissary with her dad. He was shaking his head at the broad, freckled back of a young woman in a sundress smoking a cigarette just ahead of them.

"Wide load smoking," her father said. "Would you just look at that?"

The woman heard his insult, and she took it like a bullet, her body stiffening as she dropped the vegetable can she had just pulled from the shelf. She stooped to pick it up, and Lucinda saw that she had begun to cry.

Lucinda ran ahead and intercepted the rolling can, holding it out to the woman, who looked at her in a kind of daze, wincing when Lucinda apologized. "He doesn't mean anything," she said, trying to press the can into the woman's hands. "He just doesn't know how people feel."

The woman wouldn't take the can. "Why don't you tell

him to go to hell?" she hissed, taking a fast drag on her cigarette and rushing from the aisle behind her shopping cart.

"Dad," Lucinda said, walking back to him, "you hurt her feelings."

He shrugged. "I'm sorry about that, baby. I didn't mean for her to hear me."

Lucinda looked down at the can she held. Yellow hominy. What was hominy? Bloated corn. Her father had taught her the word *bloated* a couple of years earlier when he showed her pictures of corpses on battlefields in the book of Matthew Brady photography he kept on the coffee table. The book was full of pictures of Civil War dead and her father had pointed out the way they bloated, bursting the seams of their clothing after they died.

"You weren't even trying to be quiet," Lucinda said.

Her father, in a white T-shirt and khaki shorts, was eating a handful of cereal from a box he had taken out of their shopping cart. Lucinda watched him, her natural adoration for the man troubled by his harshness. The sweetness in him that was, for her, his real self was hard to keep in view sometimes.

"Truth hurts, Lucinda. There's nothing more revolting than a woman who smokes. Except a fat woman. But do you know the grossest thing in the world?" he asked her, leaning his face close to hers. "A fat woman who smokes!" He made a gagging gesture. "Don't ever smoke. Or get fat. I don't think I could take it. I couldn't be your old man anymore. I'd have to disown you, baby, even though it would make me really sad, and I'd miss you."

"Your dad smokes," Lucinda pointed out. "And Grandma Esmé is pretty fat. You never disowned them."

"My mom's not fat," he said. "Is she?"

"She's squishy when you hug her."

He considered this, twisting his hands over the slick metal of the cart handle. "You can't really disown your parents," he said. "Remember that, kiddo."

They moved through the checkout line, and the cashier, a German woman with eggplant-colored hair, gave her father the total. On the checkout counter a cardboard display held a multicolored population of tiny rubber trolls with bulging eyes and tall stands of neon hair only slightly more artificial-looking than the cashier's. Lucinda grabbed one, hot pink with orange hair, and slipped him into the front pocket of her shorts. She didn't know why. She didn't even like the troll. But her father said life was for the taking, and only the strong ever realize it. Lucinda realized it.

The day was bright and breezy. They got in the car and drove across Grafenwoehr by gray stone buildings that looked odd without a dull gray sky behind them, like bugs made to stand away from the bark or leaf with which their bodies camouflaged. Outside the buildings, GIs in sneakers, cutoffs, and dog tags played baseball and soccer.

"There they are," Lucinda said. Beyond the water tower and generals' quarters they passed a soccer field where she saw her mother kicking a ball while a phalanx of six- to eight-year-olds, including, somewhere, Jacob and Erin, followed her like magnetic filings.

"Look at her go," Major Collins said. "Exercise is a natural mood elevator."

A couple of blocks later, her father pulled into the parking lot of the base pool. "How about a swim?" he asked.

"We don't have our suits," Lucinda said, turning in the passenger seat to look at him.

"Ah, well," he said, opening the car door and getting out. They met at the front of the car. "These shorts will work. Yours, too."

"But what about a top! I need a top."

"Aren't you wearing a training bra?" he asked, putting finger quotes around the word *training*.

"I can't swim in my bra." Lucinda looked down at the not-quite-flat surface of her green T-shirt.

He laughed. "Sure you can," he said. "We'll put one over on them."

"What about the pool rules?"

"Rules are mostly so stupid people don't wander around lost. I know a lot of dead boys would still be around if they'd followed rules, but that's war. You sure don't want to lose your ass or go to jail, but other than that"—he thumped her chest—"rules are for other people."

Lucinda followed him into the pool area, where her father kicked off his sandals, pulled off his T-shirt, and dove in. After stepping out of her flip-flops, Lucinda looked around. How could anyone mistake her bra for a bikini top? They couldn't. They wouldn't. It was white and plain and probably see-through when wet. Down at the shallow end she saw a bunch of boys playing Marco Polo and knew if she got close enough, they would probably recognize her from school. She knew their voices; they had ridden the same bus to school all spring semester, immature jerks that popped bra straps by way of checking to see who was wearing them. If they saw her actually in her bra with nothing on over it, her life would be over. She dove into the pool in her shirt and shorts.

She swam to the bottom and touched the drain with her foot before pushing back up. There were a lot of rules. Today had brought a heavy new one: he could disown her but she could not disown him no matter what. That rule wasn't for other people—it was for her. She broke the surface and gasped for air.

The lifeguard, a German girl with stringy blond hair and gigantic boobs, pointed at her and whistled. Pretending not to hear her, Lucinda dove underwater and tried to assess what was going on above by watching the submerged half of her father. She could tell only that he was facing the lifeguard and was making no move to exit the pool. She came up for air and saw the lifeguard standing at the edge of the pool saying something to him. Her father was treading water on his back, grinning at the lifeguard, so that he managed to look like someone in a big easy chair with his arms thrown around the sides and his feet on an ottoman. Lucinda thought she detected flirting. She had seen him flirt with waitresses and the wives of his friends, often with her mother right there, her features strangled in mortification while he bantered. The special phoniness of it, the face he presented to the women he flirted with, filled Lucinda with shame.

He laughed, and the sound of his voice echoed off the tiles throughout the pool area. The lifeguard blushed and looked down. Yes, definite flirting. Lucinda dove underwater again and came up for air between them, splashing water on the lifeguard's feet.

"Ten more minutes, Major Collins. You *und* your girl can with proper swimming suits later return." The lifeguard barely registered Lucinda, who feared the way the German girl's eyes were lighting up. Lucinda dropped back under and came up, this time with a huge mouthful of warm chlorinated water that she aimed at the lifeguard's pixie face. Although the spray she aimed at the lifeguard didn't even clear the pool, she felt her father's calves clamp around her middle and pull her under.

"Be nice," he said, laughing when he brought her back up. "Gertha here is going to let us swim for a few more minutes. Say thank you."

She looked Gertha over. Gertha was pimply and had a heavy accent. Gertha had hairy underarms and legs. Gertha was not her mother. "My dad says German women all get fat," she said. Her father's legs tightened around her and pulled her under again. This time when he brought her up, he kept his legs tight around her until she apologized to Gertha.

When he let go of her, the orange-and-pink troll popped out of the front pocket of her shorts and bobbed to the top of the water. "Hey!" her father's voice boomed. Lucinda made a grab for the troll, but her father already had it. He swam to the edge of the pool and motioned her over.

"Where did you get this?"

Lucinda looked down, focusing on the bug corpses trapped inside a pool light.

"Where?" he repeated.

"You said we should take what we want out of life."

"Lucinda," he said. "You know good and damned well that's not what I meant."

THREE

"This is just a straggler," her father said. "Their glory days were years ago."

It was the next morning and they were listening to the news over breakfast. Expecting an unpleasant talk about her fate as a troll thief, Lucinda was surprised to find her parents occupied with crimes of a greater magnitude. Some offshoot of the Baader-Meinhof Gang had detonated a bomb and her parents were talking about it.

"You can kind of see where they're coming from, though," Faye said.

Major Collins stared at his wife across the table. "Can you? The Baader-Meinhof Gang?"

"They're murderers," Faye said quickly, "horrible murderers, but you know, these are the kids of the Nazis and they just don't want to be like their parents, going along and being quiet when they feel they need to speak up."

"They've killed over thirty people," her father said.

Faye made an expansive gesture. "Think how you feel about your father."

"What does my asshole dad have to do with anything?"

"Grandpa Ted?" Lucinda said, pouring a bowl of cereal. "The one who stank?" She had met her grandfather, who had abandoned his wife and child early on, once in a hotel in Beaumont, Texas, where he came in a cloud of cigarette smoke bearing a one-pound bag of clementine oranges. Except for the blue eyes, her father looked nothing like the old man, whose skin was yellowed from nicotine and who wore cowboy clothes even though he didn't look like he ever went outside. He had hugged her and called her "Belinda" and imprinted her cheek with his belt buckle, the stars and bars on heavy brass. After he left, Lucinda's father lobbed the oranges one by one out the window after the old man's disappearing pickup, muttering "I don't even know that man," through clenched teeth as he reeled back and aimed.

Faye, dressed in a red Adidas tracksuit for another day on the soccer field, said to her husband, "Imagine the way you feel about your dad times ten. A thousand. The shame these Germans must feel about the Nazis. They must feel *contaminated*, like it's *inside* them. Like the only way to get it out is to—"

"Kill Americans?"

"Listen, Jack, I'm just thinking about their initial impulse. I'm not saying I sympathize with them."

"It sure sounds like it."

"Skip it," Faye said.

Silence filled the room and Lucinda considered bringing up her own imminent punishment just to break the impasse.

Lucinda's father dragged his butter knife across a piece of toast and gave his wife a slow smile that worked like the opening chords of a sunny song. "I should have let you keep on going to that hippie commune."

Recalling how they met was a cooldown tactic she had seen him use before and it usually worked, her mother slipping into a skin she seldom wore, a flower child, a hitchhiker staring into a limitless horizon. Watching her slide into that self was like watching cake rise from batter in the oven. She became, if only for a few moments, what she was probably supposed to be. Her mother and father had met at a diner in Tucumcari, New Mexico, when Faye was on her way to San Francisco to "be a hippie." She had run away from a foster home in Broken Arrow, Oklahoma. Fresh off a Greyhound bus, she sat at the counter next to young Jack Collins, who was taking the scenic route to basic training. The opposite direction from Faye in every way. But it was a love-at-first-sight thing, so Faye never got to San Francisco and was here instead, an Army wife on a U.S. Army base half an hour from the Czech border.

Faye leaned back and looked at him over the cup of coffee she brought to her lips. "I'd have made a great hippie."

Lucinda's father chuckled, his eyes merry.

"What's so funny?"

"You're wound way too tight for that, baby. You'd have

been out on your ear in a week. Booted from a commune."
He brought his hand down on the table. "That's my woman."

Sometimes Lucinda wished she could be the girl she
might have been if her mother had made it to San Francisco.
A hippie kid with a different name. Sunflower. Or Argosy.
There was a character in a book with that name and she
liked the sound of it, like a big boat, an ark, carrying people
to safety.

But what about her dad? Maybe he could have come to
San Francisco, too. Gone AWOL, worn sandals. She had to
admit it was hard to imagine her father living any other life,
especially now that their day-to-day existence was running
smoothly again; they had moved into permanent quarters
and their furniture had arrived. Inexplicably, as happened
everywhere they were stationed, they were settling in.

"And you, my little thief, you're going to Vacation Bible
School," her father said. He held up a hand. "Don't even
start because you're going and that's that."

"Vacation Bible School?" Lucinda said. "Come on, are
you kidding? I'm too old."

"They have a teen class," her mother said. "Besides, back
in North Carolina you wanted to go. That girl down the
street wanted to take you with her."

Janice, the girl in the house two doors down, had talked
about Vacation Bible School like it could answer all her
deepest questions. Lucinda had had a craving, for as long as
she could remember, for some sort of framework for talking
about things unseen. Anymore she found rock and roll
starting to fill that spot, music and lyrics like spirit and

word, but earlier, she had thought religion might have a vocabulary to help her put voice to her questions and longings. But her parents thought Janice's parents were "creepy, bug-eyed hill people," and wouldn't let her go to church with them. It was just as well.

"You could ground me," she offered. "For two weeks, three. You could ground me for a month. Come on."

Lucinda looked from parent to parent. Often, she could divide and conquer, but she could see they were a united front on this topic. They had been happy to let her skip the religious education until yesterday.

"Are Erin and Jacob going?"

"They're in soccer camp with me," her mother said. "Maybe next year."

"We can't have you going around stealing stuff, Lucinda. You're going to learn some goddamned morals. End of discussion."

"Yesterday you said rules are for other people."

"Sure, but what else did I say?" He aimed his fork at her. "Don't get your ass shot off or wind up in jail. This could land you in jail," he said, pointing at the troll, who stood in front of the salt and pepper shakers like the demon of dissent driven from her breast.

"Nobody goes to jail for stealing a troll," Lucinda said. "Besides, we never go to church."

Her mother said, "I pray for you every morning and every night, sweetie."

"Look, Lucinda," her father said, "I'm not saying I want you to believe any of this stuff. You know I think religion's just another set of rules to keep stupid people in line. But we live in a Judeo-Christian society, so you need to know the stories. Our culture's founded on them. Noah's ark and all that. If you don't know the stories, you may as well be a damned Jap or something."

"You really don't believe in God?" Lucinda said. She asked him all the time, always hoping for a different answer although she didn't know why.

"Nope."

"Then how can you believe in ghosts? I heard you talk about them to Major Reno at the officers' club, remember? Back in Fort Bragg? You were laughing, and you said, 'We sure made a lot of ghosts.' I think you were talking about Vietnam."

"That's just a turn of phrase," her mother said. "It's just the way soldiers talk when they're getting drunk. It doesn't mean your father believes in ghosts." She gave her husband a sharp look.

"Is that right, Dad?"

Her father stared down at his plate. "Religion has nothing to do with ghosts."

Vacation Bible School was held in a building now used for the base grade school, but which had been built as a hospital for the Royal Bavarian Army in 1907 and used for that purpose by Weimar troops in World War I and the Nazis in World War II. It was hard to figure how the building ended up as a grade school, but Grafenwoehr was full of such anomalies, layers of intentions left by the different armies that had used the base over the course of the century. Lucinda's teacher told her class the history of the building offhandedly, adding, "And this room was the morgue. That's where they prepare bodies for burial."

Lucinda had a hard time paying attention as her teacher, Mrs. Harner, the wife of a sergeant in her father's battalion, talked to them about Adam and Eve and the dangers of sex. Part of the distraction was periodic muttering by Liz Frye, who sat next to Lucinda doodling Philadelphia Phillies logos on a piece of paper. She was the doll-eyed girl Lucinda had met in the foyer her first day in Germany. Now that Lucinda was in new quarters, Liz was her downstairs neighbor, and the two were becoming friends.

Instead of paying attention, Lucinda read every scrap of brightly colored cardboard lettering on the bulletin boards that lined the walls. Bored out of her mind, she let her eyes go out of focus, her classmates becoming fuzzy forms of muted colors. Then she saw someone standing in front of one of the bulletin boards. He was young and handsome in the blue-eyed-blond way that Hitler had so admired. He wore a hospital gown and stood in bare feet with his hands loosely clasped behind his back. Part of her felt muffled, unable to register what she was seeing. But another part understood quietly and without fear that she was seeing a ghost, a Nazi ghost. He turned and, it seemed to Lucinda, he knew that she could see him.

He stayed there, shifting his weight from foot to foot, staring at the bulletin board, all morning. In stories, people were always hysterical when they saw ghosts, but Lucinda felt only wonder and elation. He had appeared to her and no one else. She felt chosen. She never took her eyes off him, but he never looked at her again.

After lunch he was gone. When she got home, Lucinda deliberated over whether to tell her parents. She was dying to, but she knew that they would think her imagination was running away with her. How strange that she had seen her first ghost the very day her dad had told her he believed in them.

"Tell me about the ghosts you see, Dad. What kind of ghosts?" she asked him later that afternoon as they climbed the stairwell to their quarters.

"My ghosts," he said, mulling the question. He grabbed her around the waist and swung her around the corner of the third-floor landing, "are people that won't go away. They're in my head."

That night, while her parents went to the movies, Lucinda babysat Erin and Jacob and read one of the dozens of mysteries that had made the trip with her from Fort Bragg to Grafenwoehr. Lucinda sometimes spent Saturday afternoons at the theater. One Saturday, back when her family was still in temporary quarters, Syd had been there with friends. Lucinda had pretended not to notice him, focusing instead on the decor of the Baroque old *kino* hall, regal with velvet curtains and the amused gaze of frittering figures in bas-relief panels. She had been standing in line for popcorn when Syd appeared at her side and said hello. "I don't see you," she said.

"You do, too."

"Go away."

Syd had put a hand on her shoulder and said, "It doesn't help, you know."

"What?"

"Ignoring people. I tried that last time we moved."

"When do you leave?" Lucinda asked, trying not to look at him.

"Tomorrow."

Lucinda slammed shut her eyes. Then she felt a kiss on the cheek and heard him walk away. He said something at a distance that she didn't catch—a final good-bye, she guessed.

Her father hated all Vietnam movies; they never got it right. He had only ever liked one, *The Deer Hunter*, and he had spent a few days in a hotel after seeing it, "processing," as her mother had explained. Yet they went to see *Apocalypse Now*, which had at long last made it into Department of Defense circulation.

They returned home a little before ten o'clock. Her mother went directly to bed and her father headed for the hall closet, where he kept his slide projector and his box of slides. Lucinda had never been allowed to see them, but she knew they were of his tour in Vietnam. Bringing the slide projector over to the coffee table, he only noticed her, under a blanket on the couch, after he almost sat on her. "Hey," she said.

"Hey, baby." He moved so she could sit up. "You okay?"

"Yeah."

"You didn't have a seizure, did you? Why aren't you in bed?"

She had not been able to get the Nazi ghost out of her head. The more she thought about it, the clearer certain details became. He had a dimple in his chin, stubble, and a pale fuzz of chest hair showing above the collar of his hospital gown. "I was reading," she said, lifting the book from her lap.

He picked it up and looked at the cover. "A ghost story, huh? Is it any good?"

"Not really," she said. "It's not realistic. How was the movie?"

"Your mother thought it was great." He snorted. "Damned civilians. What do they know? You should have seen it. There's that sweaty fat ass Marlon Brando playing Army. Absurd. He was bat shit in Cambodia. I was there, let me tell you, and I didn't run into any Colonel Kurtz."

"It's just a movie, Dad," Lucinda said, patting her father's arm.

After he put her to bed, Lucinda crawled on her stomach from her bedroom, down the hall, and behind the couch. A few inches from her dad's feet, she peeked out and watched the slide show projected onto the wall. Her father drank a Pabst and flipped the controls, lingering over some slides for long minutes and speeding past others. The first few were slides Lucinda had seen before, pictures of her mother standing in front of a hangar in a red minidress, long auburn hair pulled over her shoulders, holding an infant Lucinda.

The next slides were of street scenes in a big city, Saigon, she guessed, many slides of Vietnamese women in doorways, shots taken from the air, of air strikes in progress, smoke rising from holes in the dense canopy, shots of her father and other men in a room, posing in front of maps scrawled over with grease pencil, shots from a gunboat riding through the jungle, with her father on deck, shirtless with an AK-47 strapped across his chest. M-16s were U.S. government issue in Vietnam, she knew, but most soldiers preferred the enemies' AK-47s. She had seen such guns before. If you had one, you had probably killed to get it. She knew this the way she knew two plus two is four. Then there was a slide of two Vietnamese men on the ground, clearly dead, the head of one cocked at a sharp angle. Their guns were at their sides. Even in the dark photo you could tell they weren't bloated yet, so Lucinda knew they hadn't been dead long when the photograph was taken. In the next shot, her father was posing with the dead men's guns. Her father got up and went to the refrigerator for another beer. He stood in the living room and stared at the projection of himself, holding the weapons of his dead opponents, for a long time.

FOUR

The ghost was there again the next day, staring at the wall in his hospital gown while Lucinda's Bible school teacher told the story of Lot and his wife, fleeing from Sodom. She knew she should listen, but she heard nothing and let her eyes go out of focus again until the ghost became clear and sharp, the way the slides grew sharper the night before, each fuzzy until her father had turned the focus wheel. "Lucinda?" Her teacher was asking a question. "Lucinda, why was Lot's wife turned into a pillar of salt? Do you know?" Lucinda shook her head. "Does anyone else know? Julio, how about you?"

"She looked back and she wasn't supposed to."

"That's right."

Lucinda returned her gaze to the ghost but couldn't find him. She tried to relax and let her eyes go out of focus again until finally she spotted him. He seemed a little closer to the hallway. He stood exactly as he had before, just looking, shifting from foot to foot. Lucinda was afraid he might leave. Without thinking, she stood up and began to excuse herself. "Lucinda, where are you going?"

"I have to go to the bathroom."

"Our bathroom break will be in fifteen minutes. Can you wait?"

"No, ma'am."

"Well, okay. Hurry up." Lucinda walked to the door where the ghost stood, sidestepping carefully to avoid him before she passed through the doorway, and ran down the hall and out of the building. She needed to show the ghost to someone; someone who could help her make sense of what she had seen. She thought of Liz first, but she liked Liz and didn't want to risk the one friend she had in Germany thinking she was crazy. She thought of her mother, just a couple of blocks away. Her mother might be easier to talk to than her father, but she was busy with a dozen little soccer players and wouldn't be able to leave them. Besides, her mother would think Lucinda was just trying to get out of Bible school, which she wasn't. Her father, on the other hand, was the one who said he believed in ghosts. Maybe he would come.

She could see his office building on top of a hill overlooking the rest of the base. It was a fifteen-minute walk and she was hot and sweaty when she finally stepped into the air-conditioning. The Seventh Army Training Command insignia, a blue star shining out from behind a yellow, stair-stepped triangle, was tiled into the floor. She headed for the stairs. She was familiar with the building and found her father's office down a long tiled hallway, olive-drab cinderblock walls decorated with a picture of Ronald Reagan and aerial photographs of the region. Sergeant Oakley looked up from his gray metal desk when she entered. "Hi, Jimmy! Is my dad here?"

"Sure, Lucinda. What did you do, walk?" She nodded, and he gestured to the opaque glass door with her father's name and rank. She walked through and only then thought about how she would explain herself.

Her father, behind a larger version of Sergeant Oakley's gray metal desk with an American flag and a map of West Germany behind him, looked up when she entered. He was on the phone and writing something. Lucinda noticed the pink-and-orange troll standing on his desk in front of an Olan Mills family photo they had taken a few years earlier. "I have to let you go, sir. Emergency. I'll call you right back." He stood up. "What's wrong?"

"I need to show you something."

"What? Why aren't you at Bible school?"

"That's where I have to show you something."

"Lucinda, goddammit." He ran a hand back and forth through his phantom hair.

"You need to see this. If you can."

"What do you mean, if I can?"

"It's a secret. May we take the car?"

"A secret?"

"Dad, I'm telling you the truth."

They rode silently in the Opel to the Nazi hospital-turned-school until, while they sat at a light, her father asked her about Syd. "What do you hear from your little fellow?"

"My what?"

"Your one true love. That Eliot kid. Has he written?"

"Dad, I quit talking to him."

"I know, I know. But I told him not to give up."

Lucinda punched his arm. "Oh my God! You did not!"

He laughed. "I did, too. Told him you were just scared."

"That explains it."

"What?"

She thought of his kiss in the movie theater the day before he left. "Nothing. I haven't heard from him. He gave up." She felt a little sick. He was gone for good. Lucinda turned to her dad. "Does Mom know about the guys in the slides?"

Her father's hand came across the seat and squeezed the top of her thigh. "You weren't supposed to see those."

"Were those guys dead?"

Her father nodded.

"Are they your ghosts?"

He downshifted and turned into the parking lot of the school. "I don't know. Killing them just wasn't that hard, honey. Everybody says it is, taking a human life, you know, but . . ." He shrugged. "It didn't bother me that much."

"Then why do you look at those slides?" Her father had stared at the projections on the wall as if they held a secret he wanted to know. "Why do you look at them?"

Her father turned off the car and sat concentrating for a long minute on the heavy front door of the school. He said, "I guess I want to know what they say about me."

"Come on," Lucinda said. They got out of the Opel and Lucinda led her father by the hand toward the old morgue where her classes were being held.

"Won't you tell me what we're doing here?"

"No."

"What is it I'm supposed to see?"

"You'll know it when you see it."

Mrs. Harner was walking among the tables. "Lucinda—oh, Major Collins, hello. I was just about to call you. I didn't know where Lucinda had got to."

"No sweat," he said. "She's got some kind of bee in her bonnet, Maureen, bear with us."

"He's going to join our class," Lucinda said, pulling an extra chair to where she had been sitting.

Her father sat down and attempted to fold his legs under the table. The other kids laughed and stared as Mrs. Harner started describing a hypothetical moral dilemma. "You have a friend who you know is taking drugs . . ."

Lucinda nudged her father and whispered, "What would you do?"

"Court-martial his sorry butt." He gave Mrs. Harner a harassed look like a kid dying for recess. "All right, Lucinda, what are you trying to show me?"

Lucinda picked up a piece of pink paper and began tearing it slowly. "What color is this paper to you?" she asked him. He'd been color-blind his whole life.

"Brown, kind of light brown." He shifted and lifted the table off the ground with his knees.

"Maybe you really see colors the same as everyone else, but you just call them different things. When you were little your parents could have taught you that red is brown and pink is light brown," Lucinda said. "They could have lied to you. We could be seeing the same colors and not knowing it."

"I really don't think so," he said. He looked at her, waiting.

She examined the doorway. She hadn't seen the ghost when they came in, but she hadn't been trying. Now she let her eyes go out of focus. Taking a deep breath, she turned her head toward the doorway. The Nazi ghost wasn't there; he was back in his original position, staring at one of the bulletin boards.

"Can you make your eyes go out of focus, Dad?"

"I don't know." He started to stand up. "Lucinda, honey, I've got to get back."

Lucinda took firm hold of his arm and pulled until he sat back down.

"There's a ghost right there," she said. She gave a forward nod of her head.

"A what?"

"A ghost."

"You're seeing ghosts? Jiminy Christ, is that why you dragged me here?" He placed his hand over her forehead, checking for a fever. She brushed his hand away, but she kept her gaze locked on the ghost, fearing, if she moved, that he would disappear again.

"I'm not sick, Dad. And it's not ghosts. It's a ghost. It's just one."

"It's that damned Dilantin. It's making you hallucinate. We've got to get your dosage changed."

He took hold of the hand clutching his arm and gently pulled to disengage it. "Listen, sweetie . . ." But Lucinda would not let go.

"He's right there. Right there! Can't you see him?"

Her father stopped trying to pry her hand loose.

"What does he look like?"

"He's in a white hospital gown open at the back. He's barefoot. Young, handsome. I think he's a Nazi soldier. This room was a morgue, you know."

Major Collins cleared his throat. "Can you see him with your eyes focused?"

"Just a shadow. But like this, he's all the way clear, like with your slides."

He patted her back. From the corner of her eye, Lucinda saw him lean forward and put his chin into his hands. He was trying.

"Baby, are we kidding around?"

"Are you?"

"No. I really see them. But you shouldn't."

"Well, I do."

"For real?"

"For real."

"I wonder why," he said, almost to himself. "Lucinda, are you sure this isn't your epilepsy?"

"Positive," she said. It was true that she saw wet-looking prisms around lights, as she was seeing now, before a seizure started, but she had never seen a whole new person.

"Well," he said, "the apple doesn't fall far from the tree, I guess. Come here." He lifted the table off his knees and stood up. Mrs. Harner looked ready to scold him, but kept talking. "Show me where he is."

Lucinda walked over to the ghost and stood close enough to touch him.

"He's right next to me. Don't stand in him." Her father stepped aside to make room for the ghost. They all three stood facing the wall. Mrs. Harner had stopped reading and she and the class watched them in silence. The bulletin board was a multicolored cardboard rendition of Jacob wrestling the angel. Jacob was midnight blue and the angel was canary yellow with chartreuse wings. "Do you think he likes this bulletin board?" Lucinda asked.

"Maybe. But do you see this seam?" he asked, running his finger along a line where brick met cinder block. The wall was whitewashed, so she had never noticed it from her desk. "I think this was a window."

"That's it. He's looking out a window. Doesn't he know it's bricked over?"

Her father shrugged. "He probably sees the room the way it used to be."

"Do you see him?"

"No," he said, "but hey, I like this bulletin board. Nice angel." Her father crossed his arms over his chest and looked to where the ghost stood as if he were sizing him up. "I'm sorry, sweetie, I wish I could see him."

Lucinda shook her head. "He's just like orange and pink; you don't see them, either." She looked at the ghost, who blinked at regular intervals but showed no awareness of Lucinda or her father, whom she saw watching her through the ghost. Her dad seemed to be waiting like a soldier at attention for her to tell him "at ease." She recognized this, and for a moment longer they stood, side by side with the ghost between them, until finally her dad took a step back and gave her a quick hug.

"See you at home."

"Thanks for coming, Dad."

He bowed and said, "Croatoan."

"Croatoan," she said, smiling after him.

As soon as he left the room, she realized that the whole class was staring at her. "Lucinda?" Mrs. Harner said, gesturing to Lucinda's empty seat next to Liz, whose doll eyes were wide.

That afternoon they watched a video of *The Ten Commandments*. It was relaxing to sit in the cool dark and not have to listen to poor Mrs. Harner trying to make her curriculum compelling. They ate popcorn German-style, sugared rather than salted, and Lucinda noticed, as the movie played, how many of her fellow classmates were squinting in the direction of the ghost, trying to see it. She was sure she would have been teased for the rest of the summer in the States, but here, on an old Nazi base, in this ancient country, they believed her. The realization struck her hard and spread through her like warm honey. Germany suited her. After being in the country half a year, it was starting to feel like home.

FIVE

Later that summer, Lucinda was rolling up her sleeping bag and tidying her "camp," as her father called it, on the fourth-floor balcony of her family's apartment, where she had slept all night alone. It was the Fourth of July, and for a long time that morning, she had lain awake listening to the apartment complex beneath her and the Army base around her come alive, from the distant call of reveille at the barracks, to the sounds of showers and radios, tanks, and the rhythmic footfall of soldiers running in formation, singing jodies, the lyrics of which she could not quite make out.

As she stood and cinched the tie around her sleeping bag, she heard the sliding glass door open on the balcony below. Probably Liz. Lucinda grabbed her spiral notebook and scrawled a quick note: "Happy Fourth of July! See you at the pavilion." She curled the note into the girls' makeshift mailbox, an empty can of peaches with a string wrapped around it, which Lucinda then lowered until she heard it land on her friend's steel balustrade. After a minute, she smelled cigarette smoke and knew she had made a mistake. It wasn't Liz who had stepped onto the balcony, but her dad, Captain Frye. Lucinda half expected him to yell up to her, tell her to use the phone like a normal person, or maybe there would be a tug on her string and she would find "Good Morning" in fatherly scrawl on a return note. But there was no greeting and no tug on the wire.

Instead she heard weeping. The sound was a ragged bark that lurched out of a throat struggling to suppress it. Such crying she had heard before through the pipes in the half bath, and told herself it was little Blake, Liz's two-year-old brother, waking from a nightmare. It hadn't sounded like a child, but her mind couldn't factor the adults into her list of possible suspects, so inconceivable was the notion. Now she knew it had been Captain Frye the other times, too. Captain Frye, who walked around always with his hands in his pockets and his shoulders slumped, like he had height to spare and nothing to do. Liz's father.

She had never heard a grown man cry. Her own father could be remote and cold, but there were no breakdowns, no tears that she knew of. She felt frozen in place as the July sun heated the face of the apartment building. She listened to Captain Frye's sobs and the occasional fierce inhalation on his cigarette. In a moment she became aware of her own immobility, like when the bugle notes of "To the Colors" came over the base loudspeakers at four o'clock. Everyone stopped with their hands over their hearts as the flag was lowered. Mid-walk, mid-stealing-second, mid-hopscotch, it didn't matter. You stopped, waited for the bugle to finish. Lucinda always wondered what would happen if she didn't stop when everyone else did, just kept moving in the statue garden that the base momentarily became. She would race ahead in the stolen time and win somehow. But not now. Captain Frye was crying, and Lucinda stood motionless, still holding her string, letting the sound of his weeping wash over her.

Down the block, she saw Captain Diego and his teenage son, Carlos, dragging the carcass of a wild boar to a fire pit already smoking on the cement patio of the officers' club pavilion. She breathed in cigarette smoke drifting up from below. After a few minutes, Captain Frye stopped crying and cleared his throat. Lucinda felt pressure on the string, and then heard the screen door slide open and the sound of cartoons coming from the Fryes' living room. Then the door closed and she was alone again on the balcony. She pulled the string through her fingers until the can clattered up the side of her balcony. A cigarette butt, uncrushed and still smoldering, was in the can, turning the note she had written to Liz into a piece of curling black ash.

When she walked into the house, her father grabbed the sleeve of her pajama top as she passed him on the couch. He sniffed her sleeve. "You're a kid, right?" he said. "A mere child?"

"What?" Lucinda said.

"When I find out a person smokes, I take whatever I thought about their IQ and drop it ten points."

She lifted the sleeve of her pajama top to her nose. "Captain Frye smokes on the balcony. Just now, he was out there."

Her mother was sitting in the recliner drinking coffee and reading the new John le Carré novel while Erin sprawled on her stomach in front of the TV watching cartoons. Without looking up from *The Little Drummer Girl*, Faye said, "I've noticed it, too. Menthols."

"Your mother's a spy, did you know that?" her father said in a stage whisper, leaning toward Lucinda and pointing at Faye. "She notices details like that so she can report back to Mother Russia. Menthols! Why do you think I don't bring home any important papers?"

Faye glanced up at him. "Because you don't have any?"

"I don't smoke," Lucinda said.

"See to it that you never do," her father said, letting go of her sleeve.

Faye turned a page. "But if you do, baby, make sure they're menthols—nobody bums menthols."

He shot his wife a look. "Ten IQ points, just remember. Ronnie Frye, now, I guess he's got worse problems than a few IQ points."

"You're such a shit, Jack," Faye said.

Lucinda sat down on the far end of the couch and tried to think of how to tell her parents what she had heard.

"I'm kidding. The man's got balls like the Liberty Bell. Of course, he's cracked like the Liberty Bell, too. He was a POW."

Her mother got up and put a hand on Lucinda's shoulder. "Honey, what's wrong?"

After a moment, Lucinda managed to speak. "He was crying," she said.

"Who was?" asked her father.

"Captain Frye was crying?"

Lucinda nodded. "On the balcony this morning. Like he couldn't stand it."

Her father set his coffee mug on the table and cracked his knuckles.

Her mother smoothed Lucinda's hair. "It's nothing for you to worry about." To her husband, she said, "Well?"

"Don't start."

"How much further will you let this go before you say something?"

Looking at his own interlaced fingers, he said, "Faye, there's nothing I can do. It's fucked up, but if the brass finds out, he'll be out with the next RIF, make no mistake."

"They would kick a man out of the Army for suffering from problems he got fighting in the goddamned Army?"

Without moving her eyes from the television, Erin scooted forward and turned up the volume.

"Zero Defect Policy. I've explained this to you before."

"I want you to explain it to your daughter."

Lucinda's father looked at her for a moment, then looked away. He shrugged, shook his head, spoke to his wife. "You're perfect or you're finished. That's basically it. The Army's still contracting from Vietnam anyway, so if you're broken, they don't fix you; they toss you. We're all keeping our heads low."

Faye said, "Survival of the fittest, right?"

"It's harsh, but the thing is? You don't want people who fall apart under pressure," her father said. "In a combat situation."

It was yet another conversation about Vietnam. Lucinda's sense of that war was of a wall cloud whose mantle the world had come out from under just before her memory kicked in. She identified it with the footage she had seen on television when she was small; Vietnam was the color war, whereas World War II was the black-and-white war. Although she was living in the European Theater, she still thought of World War II in the gray tones of its footage, while the blood and palm trees of Vietnam were supersaturated in her imagination, the second half of *The Wizard of Oz*, where the colors turn vivid.

"Just talk to him. I'm not saying you should do anything official. Just let him know he's not alone, for God's sake."

"I don't want to embarrass him."

"Bullshit, Jack. It's yourself you don't want to embarrass."

Her mother's nostrils flared. The recliner was in its upright position now, the footrest retracted. Faye had closed the book and was sitting bolt upright.

"Faye."

"So you're just going to let that man go? Jesus, Jack. Think of what could happen. Think of those two kids and poor Amy. Look at her," she said, pointing at Lucinda.

"What about the memories? You really want your kids to remember you as a spineless shit?"

Her mother was ramping up. "He's going to hurt himself or somebody else, and it's going to be your goddamned fault! You will be to blame, Jack! You'll make an orphan of those two kids!"

Lucinda's father stood abruptly and turned to look out the glass door to the balcony. "I'll talk to him, okay? I will. We'll have a talk."

"When?"

"I don't know," he said. "Soon."

"Today," Faye said. "Do it today."

"Today?"

"At the picnic, or I swear to God—"

"Yes, okay, honey. At the picnic."

The recliner reclined again and Faye opened her book. Lucinda felt the pressure go out of the room as her mother's outrage dissipated. A near miss. Her mother said, "The picnic should be nice. Girls, are you excited about the fireworks?"

Erin glanced over her shoulder and said, "Yeah!" From the bedroom hallway, Jacob appeared, his straw-colored hair wild from sleep, digging both hands into the front of his Spider-Man underwear. Both her parents laughed. "What you got in there, buddy?" Major Collins said, pulling his son to him. "If I could, I'd walk around all day like that. Keep 'em safe."

SIX

Lucinda darted in and out of the Fourth of July crowd, negotiating a path among clusters of bare legs, food-laden paper plates, and red plastic cups full of beer held aloft in the warm afternoon air. "Recon," her father called it: Lucinda's way of cautiously assessing her environment before she decided whom to hang out with. She had planned to spend the day with Liz, but now found herself hoping to dodge her friend, unsure of what, if anything, to say about what she had heard that morning. The smell of roasting wild boar turning slowly on a spit had enticed all the Collinses out of doors, and now they were dispersed among the revelers. She watched her mother carrying a Jell-O salad to the pavilion, where rows of picnic tables were set up to hold food. Faye set down the dish and waved to Captain Frye, who leaned against one of the Bavarian-style crossbeams that laced the building's open sides. He usually had a weird, fizzy energy, like he was carbonated, but today, smiling in khakis and a white linen shirt, he looked like he'd strolled out of a commercial for something clean and mellow.

Lucinda saw her dad in line at the keg and went over to him. "Dad," she said, touching his arm. "You haven't told the story yet."

He looked down at her. "What?"

"The story about the jockey."

"Jockey?"

She sighed and shifted her weight onto one hip. "The jockey at Shiloh? The one that died? You tell it every Fourth of July. It's tradition."

"Is it? I didn't know. Didn't know we had any of those." The line moved and he stepped forward and grabbed an empty plastic cup. "I'm next in line, sweetie. Can you tell it to yourself this time? I bet you know it better than I do, anyway."

The line moved again. He held his cup sideways to the mouth of the keg spout. Watching him sometimes, she could imagine him as a kid her age, sent to stay with his grandparents at Shiloh while his divorced mother "went gallivanting." He had wandered around inside the Shiloh stories just as Lucinda did now. How could he say he didn't know it was tradition?

"Hi, Janie." Her father had turned and was smiling at a blond woman in line behind him. He rested a hand on Lucinda's back. "Run along, kiddo."

She spotted Jacob standing in a sandbox. Her sister was heading down the long field between apartment buildings behind a soccer ball. Lucinda walked to the sandbox and tried to interest her brother in hearing her story. He looked up at her. "What's a jockey?"

Lucinda dug her hands in her pockets and drifted toward the fire pit, where the boar was turning on a spit. It wasn't much of a story, anyway—a jockey, an ex-slave who had just come west after the Civil War, fell off a horse during a race. He had been on his way to Indian Territory, where they were founding all-black towns, and just took the jockey job for the cash. Nobody remembered his name—Lucinda's dad knew where the grave was, though, a headstone with no name on it. 1866, it said, and REST IN PEACE. GOOD RIDER, TRAVELED FAR. While the jockey was dying on the track, fireworks going off in the sky above him, Lucinda's great-great-grandpa, a young man then, asked him where he wanted to be buried. "Right here," he said, and his became the first grave in the Shiloh cemetery. They built a church to go with the growing cemetery years later when Lucinda's granddad bought the land. But family lore remembered the racetrack and the man who had survived slavery and the Civil War just to die at Shiloh on the Fourth of July.

Lucinda heard her name and looked over to see Liz Frye waving at her from the fire pit, a ball of blue cotton candy in her hand. "What's up?" Lucinda said as she joined her.

"Abracadabra," Liz said, waving the cotton candy at Lucinda like it was a magic wand. Lucinda studied her friend's face. Liz's eyes were a little too bright, it seemed, but maybe it was just all the sugar. Lucinda decided to hold her tongue about the morning's drama and spent the afternoon trying to act normal with her friend, waiting for darkness to fall, for the fireworks. They ran all over the picnic. Worn out by the heat, she and Liz sneaked upstairs and listened to music for a little while and met her father coming up the stairs for a nap when she and Liz were on their way down. By then the sky was dimming, turning pastel, and her mother stood outside the pavilion, foot propped on one of the crossbeams, talking to Captain Frye. Both in mirrored shades despite the failing light, Faye and Captain Frye were inscrutable and somehow unified.

Coming through the crowd toward them with Liz, Lucinda waved.

"Girls," Faye said. "How's it going?"

"Hello, Mrs. Collins," Liz said. "We think you look like *I Dream of Jeannie*. We talked about it in the car the other day, right, Dad?"

Reddening, Captain Frye said, "That's right, we sure did. We love those reruns."

"Jeez," Faye said, laughing, "if only I could blink my eyes and make things happen."

"What would you blink for?" he asked her mother.

"Hmm," Faye said. "Our house back in North Carolina. A real bookstore. The produce section at Kroger's. A real damn margarita with some real damn Mexican tequila." Faye came up with her list with barely a pause, and Lucinda got the feeling she could go on and on. "How about you? What would you wrinkle your nose for?"

Captain Frye looked at the ground for a long moment. "Not a thing."

"Oh, bullshit. Come on."

Captain Frye took a pull at his beer. "Not a goddamn thing. Not a goddamn thing in this world."

Liz, who had been watching her father, looked sharply away. He smiled at Faye, but Lucinda, watching him closely, saw only pain in the look. Pure pain. And suddenly she remembered a remark her dad had made just the other day as the whole family was unloading groceries from the trunk of the Opel and Captain Frye had come out of the building and said hi before climbing into his own car. "He wants you, Faye," her father said as Captain Frye drove away. "I swear to God, old Freaky-Frye's got it bad for you." He had said it in his teasing, singsong voice, and Lucinda's mom had scoffed, but now, staring at Captain Frye's sad smile, his face twitching in the flickering light from the roasting pit, Lucinda saw that it was surely true. Captain Frye was in love with her mother.

She pulled her mother by the hand out of earshot of Liz and Captain Frye, into the pavilion. "Why doesn't Dad talk to him like you told him to?"

"Because he doesn't want to. He doesn't think it will do any good."

Lucinda watched Captain Frye talking to Liz. "He loves you and I guess you love him back."

"Of course, hon."

"Oh my God," she said. She held her breath. She hadn't really believed it could be true, but now her mother was admitting her love for Captain Frye as if it were old news. She sniveled into her hands.

Her mother knelt down and took her by the shoulders. "Lucinda?"

"What about Dad?"

Her mother cocked her head. "Who are we talking about?"

Lucinda felt like she was spinning through a meteor shower, hot sparks burning her skin. "Captain Frye?"

"Oh, Lucinda!" She laughed and hugged her daughter. "He and I were just talking. I'm trying to cheer him up."

"Yeah, because he was crying over you this morning."

"Is that what you think? Don't be silly, hon. The poor man's a trauma case. He wasn't crying over me." She stood up, patted Lucinda's cheek. "You let your imagination run away with you."

But Lucinda was feeling the effects of heat, confusion, and cotton candy. The nausea took over and she began vomiting, bracing herself against her mother's hip. When she looked up through wet eyes, the lights above her webbed in liquid patterns.

Her mother said, "Lucinda, honey, let's get you home." She and Captain Frye supported Lucinda while she found her balance.

As the three of them began slowly to limp across the wide field that spread out between the officers' club pavilion and their apartment building, Faye spotted Erin and Jacob at the kiddie table. "Ronnie, could you take Lucinda up? I'll be right there once I round up the other two. I don't know where their daddy's gotten to," she said.

"Sure, sure," Captain Frye said, giving Lucinda a reassuring smile. "It's you and me, kiddo. Just like this morning."

His words reached her through layers of gauze. "You cried," she said. Then she heard a loud explosion and saw the first fireworks blossoming overhead. Captain Frye pulled her along through the crowd as if the fireworks were real bombs going off and they had to take cover.

Once they were inside the stairwell, he shocked her by picking her up and carrying her up all eight flights to her fourth-floor apartment. He held her tight against his chest and sang a marching jodie to the rhythm of his steps. "Airborne, looking good. You should be in Hollywood." His voice vibrated against her shoulder. "Lift your head and hold it high, this platoon is marching by." He rounded the second landing in one swinging motion and hit the next flight of stairs. "Close your eyes and hang your head. We are marching by the dead."

He stopped suddenly and looked down at her, his face coloring, so Lucinda joined in with the only verse she knew. "Sound off," she said softly. "One, two."

He flashed her a smile and pushed open the door of the apartment as he boomed the ending, "Sound off, three, four."

Inside, Captain Frye set her down and reached for the kitchen light switch. He flipped it and the fluorescent tube in the center of the kitchen buzzed and flickered, a green, uncertain light.

Lucinda leaned against the kitchen cabinets. She was feeling better, but she didn't feel good. It was like what happened after a seizure—everything streaked light. A fast-rushing darkness backed everything. She wished for the clear, bright morning, when her parents had been a unit debating what to do about Captain Frye, somebody who hurt, somebody who lived downstairs, somebody they might try to help but might not. Someone with a separate fate. Now everyone was swirled together; Captain Frye was in her house and she didn't know where her father was. Captain Frye turned to her in his diffident, hunch-shouldered way and said, "Why don't you put on your pajamas and go to bed?"

"I don't want to miss all the fireworks," Lucinda said. "Hey, I was wondering. Did my dad come talk to you today?"

"Seems like I saw him."

"But I mean, did you have a talk?"

Lucinda took him in. His head came to the top of the cabinets. He really was so handsome. He seemed to glow, flickering warm light, the blond hair on his biceps catching the light like sun on snow. "What about?"

"Oh." Lucinda pulled at her hair, embarrassed. "Never mind."

Realization crossed his face and he looked off. "He was probably just afraid, Lucinda."

"You mean about the crying?"

He nodded.

"You think my dad was afraid to talk to you?" Her dad thought Frye had balls like the Liberty Bell. Did Frye think her dad was a coward? "Why?"

Captain Frye smiled at her, shrugged. "What could he say?"

"He could tell you everything's going to be okay. He tells us that all the time. Even when you know it's not really true, it's nice to hear."

He leaned next to her, placed a hand on the counter. "He didn't want to push me," he said. "Understand? He knows how it feels. Your dad knows. I really think he knows."

They were friends somehow, in a space where she could say to him what she sensed no one else wanted to say.

"Why *do* you cry?"

Captain Frye stared at his hand on the counter for a long time. Then his chest heaved once, a single, violent sob. Lucinda's hand flew to her mouth.

"I don't know. I just know I'm not home anymore."

Captain Frye's face was turning red, and his eyes were filling with water. His teeth ground in his jaw. Lucinda was getting scared. He was so close, looming over her. She was appalled at the transformation coming over him. She wanted to get out of his shadow, out of the room, but she couldn't move.

Captain Frye batted away a tear with his free hand.

"It's not home," Lucinda told him. "It's Germany."

He blinked at her, gave an odd, choking laugh. Suddenly he plucked her away from the counter and crushed her to his chest with both arms, lifting her off the ground. Lucinda was breathless with terror, but in the next instant he had set her on her feet and was halfway out of the room.

"Your mom will be here soon." And he was gone from the apartment. Standing by the kitchen table, Lucinda heard eight loud steps as he made his way down the stairwell. Eight. He had jumped each flight, six stairs per leap.

Then she slid open the sliding glass door and stepped onto the balcony. Sounds of the party below carried on the warm air. She leaned her elbows against the balustrade and looked out. The fireworks display was building in intensity, with a barrage of multicolored explosions all at once, lapping over each other like ripples from a spray of stones tossed on water. Below, the dark figures of the crowd were mostly still, their upturned faces visible with each new explosion. She saw Captain Frye come from around the side of the apartment building and dart into the field in front of the pavilion. Maybe he was crying in the dark, maybe in love with her mother, maybe even now he was seeing blood and palm trees he could not switch off. And her father—he was somewhere, too, and maybe all the same things could be said of him. Lucinda wiped her eyes with the back of her hand. The field was lit intermittently by sparklers carried through the crowd by kids who whirled them through the air, spelling out words in tall letters illuminated against the night air that Lucinda could almost, but not quite, read before they disappeared.

SEVEN

When school started in the fall, Lucinda and Liz went all out competing for the spelling bee. They tied each other for All-Eighth-Grade and had to have a tie-breaking round that Lucinda won. But Captain Frye had been crying a lot, his sobs vibrating the bathroom pipes, and Lucinda felt guilty for her victory. She and Liz never talked about it, but she knew worry was pulling Liz down like an undertow. A dirty victory, Lucinda thought. She carried her guilt to the All-USAREUR final round in November, and there, while on the stage in an old World War II hangar in Garmisch where General Patton had once addressed American troops, during the final winning round, she had a seizure.

Lucinda was standing to one side of a boy from Frankfurt while he spelled *palimpsest*, when she felt the outer perimeter of her consciousness begin to loosen—the familiar aura of an oncoming seizure. The process felt like there were rubber bands, normally drawn taut across the walls of her skull, which began snapping one by one. When the last band snapped she knew she would lose consciousness. Her entire mind began grappling with the rush of darkness.

"Lucinda Collins of Grafenwoehr," the moderator announced. Lucinda stepped onto the silver X marked on the stage with electrical tape and tried to smile into the lights. She caught sight of her mother sitting on the first row, with Erin and Jacob. Lucinda wondered if she could tell what was about to happen. "You look spooky before a seizure," Faye had told her, and at that moment, twenty feet away, Faye looked spooked, like she was leaning in to catch Lucinda as she dangled from a high window. "Empyrean," said the moderator. "Lucinda, the word is empyrean."

The rubber bands in Lucinda's brain began snapping hard. Determined not to let the seizure overtake her until she had spelled the word and removed herself from the stage, she held fast and looked at the darkness head-on, shadows spilling around every corner of her consciousness. "Empyrean," she said in a whisper. Her mother's hand came up and her index finger and thumb made a pinching motion that told Lucinda to e-nun-ci-ate. "E-M-P," Lucinda said. Then she paused. The world went fuzzy. Halos surrounded the lights at the foot of the stage, and prisms splintered across her eyes. Letters, the idea of them, seemed flimsy, their patterns difficult to trace. "Y-R," she continued, straining. Her mother leaned forward and began spinning a thick section of her auburn hair like a baton between her fingernails. Lucinda saw the letter E appear and vanish in a flash of color before she lost consciousness and dropped to the floor of the stage, her left side paralyzed, her right arm and leg banging rhythmically against the stage floor.

Lucinda came to in a hospital room a few hours later, to the sound of her mother yelling. "Where's my *husband*? That's your question while my daughter lies here in a coma? Hell if I know, you patronizing son of a bitch! Let me tell you something, goddammit. If anything happens to her, it will be because incompetent pigs like you would rather pull a splinter out of a GI's ass than take care of a little girl. Sorry, a *dependent*. There's nothing sorrier than being dependent on the undependable. You can all go straight to hell."

Lucinda heard a voice she assumed was that of a neurologist say, "Mrs. Collins, I am trying to help you. Please stop threatening me."

Lucinda's mind stuttered awake, registering more and more clearly her mom's careening voice and the sunny, sterile room with its two-tone cinderblock walls. Faye and the doctor, a short man with dry, reddish skin, were facing off at the door to the room.

"My daughter has a serious neurological condition and you tell me to buy a scale?"

"For the dosage—"

"Do any competent MDs go into the Army? You were at the goddamned bottom of your class, weren't you?"

There was something so thrilling about watching her mother go off on strangers, especially on Lucinda's own behalf. She didn't do it often, but when she let her temper out, Faye was Joan of Arc, she was David to Goliath; she was fearless and fierce. Sometimes she got herself in trouble. Sometimes her reactions, righteous and justified in their initial impulse, spun so far out of control that they were worse than the behavior she was protesting. The threat in her mother's voice now reminded Lucinda of a time in fifth grade when they had just moved to North Carolina. Lucinda was the new girl, and the teasing and ridicule had been heavy. When she mentioned it to her mother one morning, Faye had charged onto the school bus and berated the bus driver for not stopping the bullying. She had pulled the startled driver, a woman who was twice Faye's size, from the driver's seat and hissed at her a threat that Lucinda couldn't hear, then turned to the children on the bus and said loudly, "Whichever one of you little brats is picking on my daughter better cut it the hell out unless you want me on your doorstep." She then stomped off the bus, leaving Lucinda with a lonely front seat to herself that she kept for the rest of the school year.

Lucinda sat up in bed and saw her mother poke the doctor in the chest with her index finger. "She gets an EEG and a full workup every six months. If that's not enough, I want you to goddamned say so right now."

"Just increase the EEGs for the next few years until puberty's over," he said, looking back at the clipboard. "All those hormones can make things worse."

After he left, Faye turned around and smiled when she saw that Lucinda was awake. "I didn't mean to lose it," she said, "but damn, that snotty little bastard had it coming, don't you think?"

"Totally," Lucinda said.

Her mother sat down in a chair by the window and picked up her book, a biography of crazy, murdered King Ludwig II of Bavaria, the young, eccentric king who had been a rock star before there was rock and roll. He was still a ubiquitous icon in Germany a hundred years after his death, and Faye had succumbed to Ludwig fever, reading the book to see what all the fuss was about. She tucked her feet beneath her and for a few minutes was quiet. Then she looked up thoughtfully at Lucinda.

"Why does a nineteenth-century monarch remind me of you? Should that worry me?"

"What do you mean?" Lucinda asked.

"Vivid imagination, staying up late, stuff like that."

Faye slid a bookmark onto the page she was reading and set the King Ludwig biography on an end table. The cover showed a painting of a smiling teenager with wavy black hair and a narrow chin. "He thought he was Parsifal, the Grail King. You used to love those Arthurian stories, too, do you remember?"

"I never thought I was somebody else."

"No, but your best friend is a Nazi ghost," Faye said.

"He's real, Mom. He is. I wish you could see him." She had last checked on her ghost a month before, on Halloween, slipping into the old hospital-turned-elementary-school after the bus brought her home from junior high and the little kids had vacated the grade school in the afternoon. She had found him there, still staring out the bricked-up window, still barefoot. She pulled the blanket up to her chin and looked at her mother. "I wish he was here right now," Lucinda said. "What if he walked in with a bunch of flowers and a get-well card—then would you believe me?"

Faye laughed. "That might do it, yeah."

"Liz can't see him, either. I tried to show her."

"Nobody can, honey. Nobody but you."

There was no point in arguing. Imagination, reality— they were like different clubs that met in the same building, the way Lucinda's ballet classroom was used for bridge club on Saturdays. Lucinda sat up and took a sip of her Coke. "Who won the spelling bee?"

"They gave it to the boy who was winning when you fell. They stopped the contest after that because everyone was so worried about you, hon."

"*Palimpsest* boy?"

"They had to count you out."

"But I would have stomped him," Lucinda said, clenching the edge of the sheet. She blinked at the fluorescent light of the hospital room, black floaters darting in front of her eyes. She had known how to spell *empyrean*. She could have won. Instead she knew she must have fallen hard, shuddered and thrashed, looked awful, horrified everyone. Kids from her junior high school were there, and they would tell everyone. Soon the knowledge of her sickness would show on the faces of her schoolmates, keeping her separate, like a fly trapped between panes of glass. It had happened at other schools.

Outside, the Alps rose in the distance, while the grayish-green buildings of the Garmisch Army Base spread out below them. Lucinda vaguely remembered looking out a similar hospital window in Saudi Arabia, when the twins were born. Garmisch, Fort Bragg, Riyadh, Fort Sill, the base always seemed to sprawl below the hospital in exactly the same way. When Faye had the twins, six-year-old Lucinda had spent the day and the night with the nurses, sleeping on a cot reserved for on-call doctors while her mother was in active labor. Her dad had been in the field that day. Lucinda remembered the drive home with the new babies, her mother hunched in the driver's seat, her abdomen soft and big like a deflated balloon. Lucinda sat in the back between the infant car seats and held a tiny foot in each hand. When they reached their quarters Lucinda's mother had collapsed in exhausted tears at the steering wheel while Lucinda sat in the backseat crying, too. Soon the newborn twins began to cry. All four sat there in the car wailing, the air conditioner blasting and the Saudi heat beating down outside.

Major Collins did not know about Lucinda's latest epileptic seizure. Faye reached for the phone and tried for the third time to reach him. She called their house. Smiling at Lucinda while her voice went hard, she said, "Jack, it's me again. Still here with Lucinda—I'm not going to repeat the number. If you could call, it would help a lot." Then she dialed another number and left another message with her husband's commander, asking him to pass along her messages.

Lucinda's dad was not much good with her epilepsy or any sort of sickness or frailty in his children. It was like he thought they were sick or weak *on purpose*. After Lucinda's first seizure, when she was six, she awoke with him standing over her, hat in his hand, saying, "I've never seen you fail before."

"Her neurons are misfiring," the doctor had said.

Her dad repeated the word. "Misfiring?" He cupped his hands around her head and stared down at her, searching her face. "Guns misfire. Why would her synapses misfire? They only have one direction to go, one thing to do. Why aren't they doing it?"

The doctor told them then that Lucinda might have been damaged from forceps used when she was born. Maybe she would outgrow the seizures, the doctor said. In the meantime, it was a mean time. There was nothing they could do.

"Listen," Faye said, "since we're here, how about you, me, and the kids do some sightseeing before we go home. How would that be? Neuschwanstein is close by."

"Is that a castle? Which one is it?"

"You know, the one Disney used as a model. It's where King Ludwig was murdered. We'll go tomorrow morning after they let you out of here."

From the hallway, Lucinda heard her brother's laugh. A nurse had volunteered to give the twins wheelchair rides down the hall, and they had just zipped by the room.

"I would have won. He only won because I didn't get my turn."

Faye bent down and gave her a fast kiss. "No doubt about it, honey."

"Would Dad come with us?"

"Not this time."

They stood near the tour guide, who was holding up a paddle that said ENGLISH in the broad foyer leading into the castle that held the ticket booth and the guest shop. Lucinda, who felt almost completely recovered from the previous day's seizure, examined a rack of postcards before finding a Neuschwanstein snow globe about the size of a baseball, which she turned over and over in her hands. She tossed and caught the glitter-filled orb, walking toward Faye.

"Mom."

Faye looked up from folding Erin and Jacob's jackets over her arm. "No, Lucinda. It's junk."

"It's a microcosm."

"What?"

"A castle inside a castle. We're inside it, can you see us? So is King Ludwig. Look." Lucinda held the snow globe out toward Faye as if her mom might peer into the plastic castle's tiny windows.

"Can you spell *microcosm?*"

"*M-I-C-R-O-C-O-S-M.*"

"Good job," Faye said, releasing Jacob's hand in order to dig out her wallet. "I guess you deserve a little something."

As they toured the rooms of the castle in a large group led by an English-speaking guide named George, Lucinda compared Neuschwanstein to her vision of Shiloh, her shimmering mirage of home that stood at the end of her mind. Shiloh was no doubt a more modest enterprise, but both houses were built the same year, 1869. Both were one man's dream. She wondered if Jeb Parker, her great-great-grandfather who built Shiloh with his Civil War pension, had read in the newspapers anything about Neuschwanstein, or if he would have believed that his granddaughter would walk these floors before she would set foot in the house of her own kin.

They moved into the study and stopped before a life-size painting of Ludwig when he was a young king, standing in his general's uniform and coronation robe. "He was pretty like a girl," Faye said. Lucinda nudged her way to the front and stood in front of the painting.

She liked Ludwig's face—she could imagine meeting him in the long locker-lined hallway of history and showing him to his homeroom class. She would advise him against the white tights, somehow get him some jeans, let him borrow her Devo T-shirt, and warn him against all the thugs that lay in wait as he walked on down the hall: *Your advisers are going to drown you. Get outta here, fast.* But history wasn't a hallway at all, or anything straight. It was more of a swirling mass. She gave her snow globe a good shake. She imagined a tiny version of this painting inside the castle in the snow globe, with a tiny Lucinda standing in front of it shaking another snow globe with another, smaller painting inside, on and on, like one of those mirrors of infinite regression.

Erin and Jacob appeared on either side of her. Jacob grabbed the globe from Lucinda and the twins tossed it

back and forth like a baseball, unimpressed by the painting.
King Ludwig. Her mother may have been right that they
would have had a lot in common. She wished she could
meet him where they could caper unseen like ghosts
through the castle. In her imagination she felt the cold of the
marble floor against the bottoms of her feet and the crisp
chill in the air. They would hide in the Venus Grotto among
the rocks and colored lights. They would swim in the black
water. "Old black water, keep on rollin'"—that was a song
by the Doobie Brothers. Ludwig would never have heard
any rock and roll, a thought that filled Lucinda with pity.

But it didn't matter, anyway. He was dead, like the settlers at Roanoke, like Virginia Dare and the Nazi ghost. She
felt the separation of years, a dead phone in an emergency, a
channel of communication that would not yield to her.
There was nothing she could do to stop his murder. When
he posed for that portrait he had no idea what was going to
happen to him, that he would be certified insane and con-
fined, and the next day they would find his body and his
psychiatrist's body at the bottom of a lake. She wanted to
scream down the centuries, "Run, Ludwig, run!"

"Hey, space bunny," Faye said, kneading Lucinda's shoulders and turning her away from the painting. "Try to keep
up, okay? The tour's moving upstairs. Come see the Upper
Hall—you're not going to believe this." They walked and
listened for the twins, who were already upstairs, moving
securely among the rest of the tour group.

Faye and Lucinda climbed the stairs together, rejoining
the tour group where they stood in an oval room under a

canopy of stars. The domed blue ceiling was covered with gold stars—real gold, of course—filling the firmament. A pillar shaped like a date palm rose in the center, the leaves of the palm appearing to brush the sky where the column met the ceiling. From somewhere in the crowd, Erin's voice rang out. "Staaars!"

Lucinda watched Faye take off toward the sound and George paused. The crowd was laughing, so the tour guide, taking their cue, smiled and said, "Yes, stars, and aren't they breathtaking? Ludwig's obsession was to sleigh-ride at night, and indeed, he became entirely nocturnal for the last decade of his life. This is just the most striking example of how the night sky appears throughout the castle. Louis the Fourteenth was the Sun King—well, Ludwig was very proud of his blood tie to the French royals, and he took every opportunity to draw parallels. So Ludwig was the Moon King, the Night King, the Swan King."

As the tour continued, Lucinda thought about Ludwig's various titles and imagined what it would be like if everyone could identify themselves by their enthusiasms and prominent features. Her mom was easy—she would be the Book Queen, especially now that she was working at the Grafenwoehr base library, where she joked that she brought home more books than she shelved. Queen of Warmth and Beauty and Nice Things. The Queen of Frustration—she was that, too. Her dad. Lucinda stopped at an arched window and looked out at one of Ludwig's other castles gleaming on a distant mountaintop. Her dad was the King of the Code. Codes, plural: What doesn't kill you makes you stronger, adversity breeds character, you can't disown your parents, rules are for other people.

"Dad would have liked this," she said to her mother as they headed back to the gift shop at the end of the tour.

"I'm going to call him again."

Faye tried out her German on the cashier. *"Haben Sie eine Telefonzelle?"*

"Gleich da drüben," the cashier said, pointing to the back of the shop.

Lucinda stood outside the phone booth and listened as her mom finally reached her dad and described to him Lucinda's seizure, the hospital stay, and the trip to Neuschwanstein. "We did go as a family, Jack. We did. This old castle's not the only thing you missed out on, you know." Faye looked down at Lucinda and shook her head. "I bought her a snow globe. Yeah, you know, it's a souvenir. She deserved it." Lucinda leaned in, hoping to hear her father say he was sorry for her, but instead she heard him say something about Shiloh. "Oh, Jack, she's always saying that. Your mother's too disorganized—she won't do it. Besides, who would buy it? What? I just mean it's in the middle of nowhere. I'm sure it's the most beautiful goddamned place I've never seen.

"Can you believe it?" Faye asked, putting down the receiver. "His daughter's been in the hospital, he hasn't heard from his family in a day, and all he's worried about is that his dippy mother might sell the family shack. I hope she does."

Lucinda barely heard her. Her dad hadn't seemed to care that she was in the hospital.

When they left the castle, the sun was out. The alpine air smelled like ice, even with the sun shining. The Collinses walked together down the long asphalt road leading from Neuschwanstein to the lot where the car was parked. "Why do we have to go?" Lucinda protested. "There's still more to see."

"I know, but if these kids don't get a nap, we're all going to regret it," Faye said. Erin walked between her mother and sister, but Jacob was walking in front of them, tripping down the steep hill.

"Where will they sleep? We don't have a hotel room, we're a long way from home."

"We could hop a plane for North Carolina and they could sleep on the flight."

"Sure, Mom."

"We could go spend a few days in Austria. Ski a little."

"Let's stay here. The castle's gigantic. We could hide during the day and come out at night," Lucinda said. She sat down along the stone wall that followed the road. "There's food in the gift shop. Nobody would know."

"That's what you used to say when you were little when we went to the Smithsonian," Faye said. The twins collapsed along the wall under Lucinda's swinging feet. "And at Roanoke, too, remember?"

"I don't know why I always think that. It's stupid." Lucinda shrugged.

Faye looked at Lucinda closely. "You're just looking for a home," she said, sitting down next to her daughter on the wall. They could see the green Opel below them in the parking lot, full of kids' clothes and snack food. They would eventually get in the car and drive away. Erin and Jacob would fall asleep, mouths agape and arms flung wide, like dancers midleap, and Faye and Lucinda would take out the map and figure out the way back to Grafenwoehr, where Lucinda would have to tell Liz how she lost.

PART TWO

Grafenwoehr, West Germany
1985

EIGHT

Lucinda had never thought much about the GIs. They were the Army itself, the moving parts in the backdrop of her life. At Graf there were sometimes a hundred thousand of them, U.S., German, NATO, swarms, while the permanent party folk, like her family, were fewer than ten thousand. The GIs were everywhere, but she had never been to the barracks where they lived until now. As her father pulled his Opel into a parking space in front of the Kaison Barracks on a Saturday morning, she began to imagine for the first time what it would be like to be a GI. Most of them were eighteen or nineteen, which, now that she was fifteen, didn't seem so incredibly old anymore. What, she wondered, did they do when they weren't following orders?

Apparently they listened to rock and roll, just like her— or at least Private First Class Nately did.

"I'm not really supposed to bring you here, you know,"

her dad said, handing her the two six-packs of blank ninety-minute TDK cassette tapes they had just bought at the PX. "Just follow me and keep quiet. Don't be a smart-ass."

Lucinda took the tapes. She also had, folded in her jeans, a list of albums she wanted PFC Nately to tape for her if he owned them. Her appetite for rock had begun to exceed the limits of her allowance, and her parents were unwilling to add further subsidies. When Major Collins discovered that PFC Nately, a clerk in his office, was a real rock aficionado with a vast record collection, he had seen an inexpensive way to satisfy his daughter's burgeoning habit. Nately couldn't very well say no, and so here they were on a Saturday, about to intrude upon the leisure time of one of her dad's men. Nately lived in a grim, gray building with a number, 2047C, stenciled in black on the corners. Small, uniformly spaced windows lined all four floors. In fact, from the outside the building didn't look much different from family quarters. She'd heard from her dad how ugly Eastern Bloc architecture was, and that everyone would have to live in its squared-off cheerless buildings if Americans didn't fight the spread of communism, but Lucinda couldn't imagine anything much uglier than the barracks the U.S. Army had erected here on the western side of the Iron Curtain.

When she was younger and had asked about their first tour of duty in Germany, she had taken her father's explanation too literally, thought that the uniformity of the architecture was what he meant by the term *domino effect*—the windows, she pointed out, looked like dots on dominoes. She tried to imagine the buildings all falling, one against the other, tipped by some gesture from across the border, but she was unable to convince herself that this was likely.

When her dad realized how she had misinterpreted the domino phrase, he had laughed and given her a second explanation for why American troops lived in Germany, for why the Cold War had developed in the first place. "Look, Lucinda. It's just a job."

He strode ahead of her now, hands in the pockets of his jeans. The backs of his ears were bright red from the cold, a black stocking cap pulled down over his bald head. She pressed her white earmuffs harder to her head and tried to stay behind him so that his body blocked the piercing north wind tearing across the compound.

Sitting in a metal folding chair at the front desk was a thin black soldier whose identification tag read *Snowden*. He rose when Lucinda and her father walked through the doors. "Hello. Can I help you?"

Her father looked annoyed. He liked to be recognized and saluted, even out of uniform.

"I'm Major Collins," he said, "and this is my daughter Lucinda."

Snowden duly saluted. "Major Collins, sir. What can I do for you, sir?" he asked, peering at Lucinda.

"*May*," her father said, rocking back on his heels.

Jerk, Lucinda thought, and looked up to see Snowden reading her expression.

"Sir?"

"What *may* you do for me—that's what you meant to say."

"Yes, sir. What *may* I do for you?"

Snowden smiled at Lucinda and pulled a clipboard off the olive-drab cinderblock wall in front of him, preparing to look up whatever room assignment Major Collins asked for.

"Here to see Nately."

Snowden looked surprised.

"Oh, yes, sir. He's here. He's my roommate, matter of fact. Room 109. That's right down the east hall, sir. Let me run and get him."

"At ease. We'll go knock on the door."

Dread flashed across Snowden's face.

"Pardon me, sir?"

Major Collins, who had already started down the hall toward Nately's room, turned and looked at Snowden. Lucinda's presence in the barracks was strictly *verboten,* and she knew that her father intended to pull rank to get her in. Normally this would have made her feel ashamed and embarrassed, but the prospect of quadrupling her rock library all at once had made her willing to take advantage of her father's conviction that rules were for other people. Still, watching her father staring at Snowden, daring him to say they couldn't go to Nately's room—all the records in the world weren't worth the kind of scene this might become.

"Dad," she said, grabbing her father by the elbow, "I'm going to wait in the car. Just whatever Nately thinks would be good sounds good to me. Ask him for his favorites."

Snowden looked relieved and jumped in to endorse her plan.

"Thank you, Miss Collins, that's great—because I was

just saying, or fixing to, that we can't let you past this desk, you being a girl. I know it's not fair, but those are the rules, and we've got to follow them. My boss, Sergeant Gordon, he won't be happy if he finds out."

Lucinda's father shot her a look that told her to stay put.

"Glad to see you're upholding standards, Snowden. But this is a different situation than the one that the rule about women in the men's barracks is meant to prevent. Or does my daughter look like a cheap German whore to you?" he asked, gesturing to where Lucinda stood, growing mortified in her powder-blue parka and white earmuffs.

The dread was back in Snowden's face. He held out his hands. "No, sir, course not. That's not what I meant."

"I didn't think so. I'm glad we're in agreement. Come on, Lucinda," he said. He turned his back on Snowden and strode down the hall without looking back.

Lucinda touched Snowden's sleeve and whispered, "I'm so sorry. We'll be out of here fast, I promise."

"It's cool, just go on." He snatched his arm away from her and waved her off in the direction of her father's fast-moving form.

No one answered the first time Major Collins knocked on the door of room 109.

"He's supposed to be here," he said. "I told him we were coming today."

She couldn't tell if her father realized he'd made a scene just moments before. He knocked again, this time more loudly. Finally the door opened, and a tall, skinny boy with a quarter inch of bright red hair and pale, nearly invisible eyelashes stood looking down on Lucinda and her father. He ran a freckled hand over his scalp and straightened his posture, becoming even taller than he had been when he was leaning against the door. "Major Collins, hi. Come on in, come on in—what's your name?" he asked, extending a hand to Lucinda as he moved out of the way so she and her father could enter the small room.

"Lucinda," she said, grabbing his hand. "I don't mean to bother you. My dad said you didn't mind, but he's your boss, so I don't really see how you had much choice. But you can tell me if you're too busy to make these tapes for me, don't worry."

Her father palmed the top of her head.

"My daughter," he explained to Nately, "is a smart-ass."

Nately grinned.

"No problem," he said. "It's hard saving up your money for a new album, always having to pick one out of all the ones you'd like."

When Nately spoke, Lucinda could not keep her eyes off the bobbing of his Adam's apple. She wondered if it ever got cold. She hoped Nately owned a good scarf. As he spoke, he ran his fingers lovingly across the slick surface of his turntable/cassette player, which took up all the space available on his small metal end table.

"That's a nice-looking record player," she said.

"A Philips GP-414," he said, beaming. "Made in Holland. You can't get this model back in the States. It was almost worth joining up just to get my hands on this baby. I'll have to find a decent voltage converter for when I take it home."

He sat down on his bed, a metal cot covered with an Army-issue wool blanket pulled tight from corner to corner, and reached under it. One by one, out came four wooden crates full of records.

"Have a seat," Nately said, indicating Snowden's cot, opposite his. "Welcome to my castle." The crates filled the two feet of space between the cots, so that, once Lucinda and her father sat down on Nately's roommate's cot, they couldn't get up and walk around.

"I have a list here of what I'd like you to record for me, if you have these records," she said, drawing the list out of her pocket and handing it to Nately.

"That you in the middle, son?"

Lucinda's father was holding a picture he had taken from Nately's dresser. Lucinda leaned toward her father and looked. The picture showed a family of five standing in the driveway of a redbrick house—two pensive parents, one girl, and two boys, one of them with long red hair and a black leather jacket.

"That's what I really look like," Nately said, touching the top of his nearly bald head and pointing at the photograph. "That's the real me. One more year of this, and I'll be home."

"Maybe nobody told you, son, but this is a volunteer Army now. Back in Vietnam, we had no choice, but you didn't need to join up if you didn't want to."

Nately looked embarrassed.

"I got in trouble in my hometown, sir, Gainesville, Florida. The sheriff is my uncle, and he got me a deal. Army or jail. My family, they thought the Army would make me grow up. Sense of responsibility and all that, sir."

"Is it working?" her father asked.

"Oh, yes, sir. I'm all better."

Much to Lucinda's surprise, her father stood up and made to leave the room.

"You kids have fun," he said as he walked out.

She supposed he couldn't resist the chance to poke around the private quarters of some of his troops. He said he could always tell a soldier was smoking pot if incense burners were lying around, and he could tell a soldier was gay if no porn was on the walls. On Nately's wall was a risqué poster of Wendy O. Williams in bondage gear in front of her band, the Plasmatics, and another poster of a scantily clad blonde astride a Harley-Davidson motorcycle. Lucinda wondered if this was porn.

Nately unfolded Lucinda's list. He made disapproving sounds and a few approving ones as he read.

He raised his green eyes and took in Lucinda. "Okay, let me make a suggestion," he said. "You've got some good stuff on here—Beatles, of course, Hendrix, of course, Fleetwood Mac, all right. Blondie—that's cool. That's showing some promise. But then you've got some stuff that's just wrong. You don't really want the Eagles."

"I like that song 'Take It to the Limit,'" Lucinda said. It startled her that Nately would cast aspersions on her list.

"You don't really. You just don't know any better yet. And Journey? Foreigner? I wouldn't let those records in the same crate with my other records."

"Not even 'Don't Stop Believin''?"

"Okay, that's catchy. But it's like—you know how little kids want to eat candy for dinner? Brain candy; that's what this is."

"So I need some protein and veggies."

"You need something with real power, real energy, yeah. So here's what let's do: let me make a list that makes sense, that puts things in context for you. I promise you'll love it. You don't even have any Zeppelin on here, for chrissakes. No Dylan! And you need to know what's happening with punk. The classic stuff is great—it's essential—but it's 1985. Where's Black Flag, where's Elvis Costello, where's X, the Replacements, the Sex Pistols, Dead Kennedys, the Minutemen, R.E.M.? Where's U2?"

Lucinda felt ashamed. "I don't know," she said.

"Exactly." He pointed a finger at her excitedly and Lucinda saw something of the long-haired boy he had been six months earlier.

"Nately," her father said, reappearing in the doorway. "Did you say 'the Sex Pistols'?"

Nately looked abashed. "Yeah—sorry, sir. I wasn't thinking."

"That's a great name," Major Collins said. "What a name—sex and violence all rolled into one. Rock and roll—you can take a sluggish, demoralized bunch of guys and get them to kick ass if you let them get all jacked up on their music."

Lucinda wondered if she had just heard her father's philosophy on raising teenage daughters. Let them get all jacked up on their music. Then she remembered the rain in Berlin, back when she and her family had first arrived in Germany. They had been doing the tourist thing and had just hopped on a bus to take them to Checkpoint Charlie. Lucinda took a window seat and had watched from the steamed bus windows as a young woman with an orange Mohawk and dressed in a garbage bag with chains wrapped around her torso and legs attempted to board the bus. The chains hitched her stride, so she couldn't step up the bus steps, causing laughter on the bus as everyone watched her hop and hobble. "She wants attention, she's got it," her mother said. Her father had looked at the punker with the special contempt he reserved for unattractive women—what was the point of her? What was her life worth? Both her parents had laughed, and in their laughter, Lucinda detected real discomfort. Lucinda hadn't laughed—the public humiliation mortified her and she ached for the woman. Rain fell as she struggled to board the bus and orange hair dye ran down her face in serpentine rivulets, the proud spikes of her Mohawk melting like hot metal. What was that woman listening to? Lucinda had wondered.

"My dad dated Tina Turner," she told Nately.

"Hey, hey," Nately said, giving her dad a round of applause.

Major Collins looked embarrassed. "I wouldn't say dated. I never said dated."

"But you knew her, sir?"

"I was a busboy at a club she used to play in Dallas. I

talked to her. She let me come to breakfast with Ike and the band one night after a show."

"That's cool, Major Collins. She's smokin' hot."

"I thought you dated her," Lucinda said.

A few days later, Lucinda's father knocked on the door of her bedroom and handed her the dozen TDKs, no longer blank. She lined them up across her dresser, sliding her ballerina jewelry box to one end and leaning the tapes against the cassette player at the other end. On her bookshelf she had a leather-bound set of Great Classics of Literature, and now she had what seemed like the musical equivalent: the Velvet Underground and Nico, Leonard Cohen, Joni Mitchell, the Doors. The Band, the Allman Brothers, Janis Joplin. David Bowie, Tom Petty and the Heartbreakers, Roxy Music. Black Sabbath. Steely Dan. She needed a full week of afternoons after school just to hear everything once. Nately had started with the Beatles and the Rolling Stones and Bob Dylan, and worked forward from there, tracing three lines of development like a genealogist tracking a population from its original ancestors. The tapes were chronological and color-coded—blue ink for Beatles descendants, red for Stones descendants, and green for Dylan's children.

The window in Lucinda's room had a wide ledge that she covered in pillows and sat on, staring out the window at the tower rising above all the other buildings on the base. Its red-tiled roof and Bavarian shutters drew her eyes as she concentrated on the music.

Soon she began to have questions: How was the Velvet Underground related to today's punk rock? What were the boundaries between rock and country rock and blues, rock and jazz? Why did lyrics by the Police always refer to works of literature? When did Jefferson Airplane become Jefferson Starship, and why did they begin to suck immediately afterward?

She also began to doubt Nately's tripartite approach. It seemed too simple, and it left out other threads of rock that didn't seem to Lucinda, from her newcomer's perspective, to fit in under any of the three big umbrellas Nately had laid out. What about Elvis? Simon and Garfunkel? Sly and the Family Stone? Where were John Mayall's Bluesbreakers, considering all the other bands—Cream, Blind Faith, the Yardbirds—that included some of the same members?

She voiced her questions to Liz, who sometimes listened to the music with her, but Liz would shake her head. To her, the music was the least interesting part of Lucinda's new friendship. "I can't believe you got to go to the barracks," she said. "This guy, Nately. He's, like, a *man*."

Soon Lucinda realized she would have to go see Nately again. She had a new list of stuff she wanted him to tape, another long list of questions, and, ricocheting like a stray bullet, Liz's insinuating words, "He's, like, a *man*." One evening her dad knocked and came into her room. She was listening to Glen Campbell sing "Wichita Lineman."

"This song," her father said. "Now, that's a song." He stood listening, arms crossed, until the end of the song. "Reminds me of your mother."

"Why?" Lucinda asked.

"It was playing in that diner in Tucumcari when we met. It was popular then—we heard it every half hour when we were first together." Then he nodded and walked back out of the room.

A minute later her mother came in and sat on her bed. "Your dad says you have 'Wichita Lineman.'" Lucinda played it for her and then her mother, after listening with an absorbed, pained expression, rose and floated out of the room. Lucinda looked after her and wondered for the thousandth time about the hidden selves inside her parents. What was the song even about? What was a lineman, anyway? Lucinda added the questions to her growing list for Nately and determined to go see him.

Maneuvering freely in Graf was something of a challenge. She and Liz were always scheming to roam free, sneaking off base to wander the old town, but it took planning. Her parents warned her never to walk anywhere alone, especially when the fluctuating GI population was high. "You're a hunk of raw meat," her father told her, "dangling in front of a bunch of lions." Her mother's explanation was less picturesque—she just reminded Lucinda that the GIs were lonely. The message was clear, but the restrictions on her freedom chafed, and she resented the increasing amount of lying she had to do to get around her parents' fears. Fortunately, in the winter months, night fell at three in the afternoon, about the time Lucinda got home from school after the forty-five-minute bus ride from Vilseck. One dark Tuesday afternoon, having told her mother she would be downstairs studying with Liz, she lit out for Nately's barracks as soon as she stepped off the bus.

She reached the familiar gray exterior after a brisk ten-minute walk through biting cold and realized that she couldn't go through the front door. Whoever was on duty would turn her away immediately. So she circled the building until she found a side door that opened onto the east hall, near Nately's room. It was locked. She knocked.

A short, muscular Chicano guy in gym shorts and a gray Army T-shirt opened the door.

"What the fuck?" he said, drawing back in amazement. "We don't want no Girl Scout cookies, *chica,*" he said, and began to close the door.

"No, wait." Lucinda held out a hand to keep the door open. "I'm dropping something off for Nately. I'm Major Collins's daughter. Kind of an emergency. Quick errand."

She slipped through the small space under the soldier's arm, feeling him close the gap between himself and the door just fast enough to pinch the back of her coat. But as she propelled herself forward, the coat came with her, and the GI, who seemed to decide immediately against the idea of laying hands on her, let her go. She found herself standing in a sort of gym area plastered with posters of naked women, where half a dozen soldiers were working out on the gym equipment stationed around the room. The windows were steamed over, and the whole room reeked of sweat. AC/DC's "You Shook Me All Night Long" was cranking full blast. They all stared at her.

A huge, red-faced man in a Nike sweatsuit cupped his hands around his mouth and bellowed, "Jailbait on the compound! Jailbait!"

The GIs in the gym laughed, most of the doors down the

hallway were flung open, and the faces of several more GIs peered out, Nately's among them. A chant was beginning: "Jail-bait! Jail-bait! Jail-bait!"

The immensity of her miscalculation shocked her. What had she been thinking? She felt like the blood in her veins had suddenly begun running in the opposite direction, backing up against her heart like a tidal wave. She waved at Nately, becoming aware as she did so of her white mittens flying above her head like a surrendering flag. They were so little-girlish. Mittens, for chrissakes.

"Nately! Nately!"

He strode toward her, looking surprised and embarrassed.

"Lucinda Collins?"

"Hi. I just brought some more blank tapes and was wondering if you could tape some more music for me."

"Holy shit," he said, shaking his head. Around them the chant was giving way to whistles and a teasing refrain, "Nately's got a girlfriend."

"Fuck off!" Nately shouted. "Come here, Lucinda."

She followed him to his room, where he waved her in with a sharp crook of the hand. He closed the door and stared at her.

"I just wanted some more music," she said, "and I had some questions. I guess I didn't realize what a big deal it would be. I'm sorry."

Nately grinned at her. "I guess you come by it honestly," he said.

"What do you mean?"

"Your dad kind of does whatever the hell he wants, too, doesn't he?"

It was true: her coming to Nately's barracks the second time was just as brazen, if not more so, as the way her father had brought her the first time. She resolved to be circumspect forevermore, to paint a circle around herself and never step outside it. Rules are for other people—that was her dad, not her.

"You gotta get out of here," Nately said. "Seriously. But let me see your list, since you're here. What are your questions?"

He sat down on his bed and again slid his record crates out into the middle of the floor.

"The chorus to 'All Along the Watchtower,'" said Lucinda, "what's he saying?"

"I can't think with that other music down the hall. But you know, it's about these guys on the watchtower standing guard, watching out for bad news coming at them. People are inside the walls, women and children, working, keeping it together."

"Have you ever seen the watchtowers at the Czech border? Oh my God, they have guns up there and you can see these big guys pacing back and forth and smoking cigarettes. And there's a town actually named Hell."

He pulled a record from the middle of one of the crates and looked up. "For real?"

"Hell means *light* in German, though. But still, it sounds creepy."

"See, when I get some time off to travel, I don't think I'll be touring the border. Call me crazy, but I get enough of that crap in my job."

"You should really see the Iron Curtain, though. You should travel while you're here. I wonder if Hendrix ever saw it? He was in the Army, wasn't he?"

"Hendrix?" Nately looked at her. "No, no. Who wrote 'All Along the Watchtower'?"

Lucinda looked at him like he was crazy. "Hello? Hendrix?"

He shook his head and handed her the album he had been holding. "Bob Dylan."

"No way." She looked down: *John Wesley Harding.* She turned it over to look at the track list. "Dylan wrote that?"

"Sings it, too."

"He wrote everything!"

"Another Dylan song for the ages. Next question."

"That album *Zen Arcade* is something else. The band, though—"

"Hüsker Dü."

"Yeah—what does their name mean? It looks German, but it doesn't translate."

"You want to hear the extent of *my* German? *Ein Bier, bitte. Wo ist die Toileten?*"

"What if you want two beers?"

"Ah!" He opened his hands. "Then I'm screwed."

"*Zwei Biere, bitte,*" Lucinda said.

"*Zwei.* Okay. Anyway, Hüsker Dü is like Norwegian or Swedish or something. I don't know what it means."

Just then the door opened, and Snowden walked in. He was in uniform and stood in the doorway with his hands on his hips like a mother who has just caught her son with one leg out the window in the middle of the night.

"I know," he said, pointing his finger at Nately, "that I am not seeing what I think I'm seeing, and that all this ruckus I'm hearing up and down the hallway is just crazy talk. I know a little white girl is not in my room. I know that's not what I'm seeing, because that would be flat-out insane.

"And yet," he said, extending his arms wide to encompass Lucinda standing amid the crates of records, "a little jailbait-white-girl-officer-spawn is in my enlisted-black-man's room. And that is how I know that my life is over. What the hell are you thinking, Eddie?"

Snowden's reaction to her presence was a shock. She and Snowden had bonded on her first visit. Hadn't they shared a moment when her father corrected Snowden's grammar? *May* and *can*? She just wanted some new music.

"Yeah, yeah. I'm sorry, Jay. She's on her way." Nately stood up and nodded to Lucinda.

"I'll make your tapes," he said. "Come on, you need to go before Snowden here starts crying."

"Crying? Crying?" Snowden reeled back as if he had been shot. "Black people've been lynched for less back in that great country of ours. Now I'm serious, snowflake, you gotta go."

"How will you get the tapes to me?" Lucinda asked

Nately as Snowden stood outside in the hall, holding the door open impatiently.

"I'll meet you by the water tower Friday at five o'clock. Can you do that?"

"Along the watchtower, huh?"

"Exactly."

"Okay, yeah. Five o'clock. Thanks, Nately."

Snowden, in a parody of a white newscaster's voice, delivered his version of the nightly update aired by the Armed Forces Network: "And so the white people have arranged a delightful rendezvous for Friday afternoon, ladies and gentlemen. It's four o'clock in Central Europe. The news is next on AFN. Do you know where your children are?"

NINE

In North Carolina, she could have looked forward to field trips to the beach or to the mountains, and of course Germany had endless beautiful and interesting cities, lakes, opera houses, museums, castles—what about Neuschwanstein? She had tried to talk her teacher into a trip to Ludwig's castle.

But instead her ninth-grade field trip was to Dachau. While part of Lucinda already felt morally superior to her friends back in the States who never had and probably never would confront the remains of evil on such a scale, another part of her wished for a trip to the beach. At the moment, she would gladly have given up moral superiority for salty waves and a new bathing suit.

Laughter and cruelty usually held together the pecking order established daily on the forty-five-minute bus ride to the junior high through the training area between Grafenwoehr and Vilseck, but as the bus merged onto the autobahn, the usual suspects looked uncomfortable flexing their muscles. They were on their way to Dachau, and nobody knew how to act. They'd listened to grim lectures and watched unspeakable documentary footage in preparation for the trip, and quite a few classmates whose parents wouldn't sign the release forms were simply absent that day.

Derek, a stocky ninth grader who held the backseat bench like a medieval warlord, blasted his favorite song, Ozzy Osbourne's "Bark at the Moon," over and over again on his boom box as usual, but didn't raise his fists through the chorus like he usually did. Lucinda had gone to school with Derek in North Carolina, too—the Army was a surprisingly small world—but she never spoke to him and doubted he remembered her. He had been too busy getting picked on then, and now that he had grown and grown and grown, he was busy turning the tables. His two sidekicks were Isaac, a green-eyed black guy, and anemic-looking Phil, with posture like a praying mantis. They rested their backs against the windows on either side of Derek, Isaac with his girlfriend leaning against him wrapped in a green-and-white Vilseck Junior High letter jacket. Lucinda sat in the safe middle of the bus, a few seats in front of the backseat cabal and a few seats behind the untouchables in the front rows. At the very front, right behind the German bus driver, sat Ms. Adams, their young teacher, marking papers with a red pen and never looking up.

Although Lucinda didn't easily cop to liking metal, she was kind of partial to "Bark at the Moon." After the opening chords, resisting it was like trying not to fall downhill once you've been pushed. Nately had given a grudging nod to her request for some Ozzy Osbourne, so she listened at home, but on the bus, she kept her musical tastes to herself.

Today the song just seemed stupid.

Next to her Liz sat like a zombie. "You shouldn't be back at school already," Lucinda said quietly.

Liz raised her hands and let them drop. "I can't stand to be in the house."

Lucinda's mind kept returning to three days earlier, to their last normal moment, when Liz had been upstairs in Lucinda's room. They were sitting on Lucinda's bed with a math book open between them and "Strawberry Letter 23" on the boom box when they heard the shot downstairs. Lucinda's hands flew to her own face as if to hold it on. Liz's head jerked back like she had taken the bullet and then she tore off, propelled by a long, soaring cry that carried her down the hall and into the stairwell. But Faye was in motion, too. She bolted from the kitchen, oven mitts still on her hands, and tackled Liz on the top flight of stairs. Faye laid herself over Liz, holding her wrists with mittened hands and absorbing Liz's furious contortions. Lucinda's father, followed by Lucinda, dodged Faye and Liz and bounded downstairs and through the Fryes' apartment door, where Lucinda's dad, realizing that Lucinda was behind him, pushed her back through the door and slammed it on her. "No, Lucinda!" he shouted.

Long minutes passed and they free-fell into darkness. Jacob sat on the stairs pounding a soccer ball against the far wall again and again, like a second hand booming. Erin spread herself over her mother, cheek flat against Faye's back, holding on while Faye continued to struggle against Liz. Liz's cries filled the stairwell and everyone else living there came out of their apartments and stood around waiting, heads down. When the Fryes' apartment door finally opened and Amy Frye came out, Faye released Liz with a gasp, like someone dropping a heavy weight. Big-eyed little Blake clung to Amy's chest like something melted. Liz ran to her own mother. "He's alive," she said. Later, Lucinda's father came out and told them that Captain Frye's hands had shaken or something; he missed and took an ear off, shattered his right cheekbone, messed up one side of his head pretty badly. When the ambulance arrived, Lucinda looked down the stairs and saw them take Captain Frye out on a stretcher, the right side of his face covered in gauze.

Now the Fryes were packing to leave. In a week, they would be gone, heading stateside for discharge. But in the meantime, Liz was at school. Lucinda couldn't figure out why Liz had been allowed to come along on the field trip. She didn't know if Liz could deal with it; she didn't know if she could herself. Dachau. Death and more death.

The concentration camp was less than two hours away. Lucinda was shocked how close it was; a satellite of Munich. Midmorning, the bus drove into the half-full visitors' lot, and she thought of the municipal animal shelter outside Fayetteville, North Carolina, where she had gone with her father to rescue a cat that had vanished from the neighborhood. "So people don't smell the death," her father said, when she asked why the shelter was outside of town. Still, it wasn't far outside. The bus had passed residential neighborhoods minutes before it reached Dachau. Lucinda wondered if the Dachau docents and groundskeepers lived in those neatly kept houses.

There were sixty students in all, and they walked along a broad, tree-lined boulevard to the front entrance, crunching gravel beneath their feet. Before they reached the wrought-iron gate, Liz muttered, *"Arbeit macht frei,"* in a voice dry as matches.

Lucinda glanced at Liz, whose breath blew clouds of cold air as she breathed. Work makes us free. "You sound like my dad," she said, immediately regretting the reference to fathers. Lucinda thought Liz was bucking herself up, coming up with a solution to her own despair. Dedicate yourself to a task, idle hands are the devil's workshop; that sort of thing. *Arbeit macht frei.* But they drew closer to the entryway and Lucinda saw the slogan in iron letters across the top of the black gate. She stopped and touched Liz's sleeve. "Have you been here before?"

Liz shrugged. "Yeah."

"Why did you come today?"

Their fellow students shouldered by them as Ms. Adams stood at the head of the gate and counted them entering the grounds. "I don't know," Liz said. "Maybe it will help."

"Help? How? This isn't exactly Disneyland," Lucinda said.

Liz's eyes flashed. "Yeah, butthead, I know that. Compared to this, what happened to my dad was like a bad day

or something. A little mistake." Lucinda thought of Liz
three nights earlier, pinned by Faye to the stairs and screaming. A little mistake.

Liz pointed at the wide, dusty courtyard through the
gate. "You'll see," she said.

Then she fell silent again and they followed a tour guide
across the large, open campus into low, white-walled buildings, through the sleeping quarters and the photographic
history of the place, black-and-white photos under glass and
belongings, glasses, boots, buttons, books, the real things of
real people, almost too many of them to kill. At this one
small camp, hundreds of thousands.

Their deaths had been hard work for a lot of people. They
shot them straight into mass graves, hung them forty at a time
right in front of the burning ovens that would shortly inciner-
ate their bodies, gassed them in showers. Lucinda held up until
the gas chambers at Baracke X. Standing under the plate-size
showerheads, evenly spaced in the low ceiling, she looked
down and saw the drains. She imagined it—it was impossible
not to—the showers turning on, the people standing there,
naked and trapped, their mothers and fathers, sisters and
brothers, all dying, wanting to save each other and being
unable to save anyone. Lucinda was sandwiched among her
classmates, but she pushed through them, running out the
green steel door, the locker rooms, outside to the sharp air.

She raced up and down the side of the long building, concentrating on her breath. She looked to the armor-colored
sky and listened to birds gathered in the branches of surrounding spruce trees. Leaning against the redbrick wall,

she noticed steel chutes along the wall. She walked up to one and closed it.

"That's where they put the gas pellets." Liz had followed her outside and joined her at the wall. "My dad told me there used to be a fence around this so the prisoners couldn't see who shoveled in the poison. These chutes go straight into the gas chambers—did you see those holes along the walls inside?"

She thought of the still, straight profile of her Nazi ghost, who almost seemed to float beside her now. He was hers because she saw him, hers because she let her mind reach inside him and imagine what he saw. Now she wondered: Had he shoveled poison pellets into gas chambers? Or shoveled bodies into incinerators? Or shoveled dirt over freshly executed prisoners? Who did those jobs? She had imagined her Nazi ghost gazing out the window and thinking about a sylvan scene from his boyhood, but she revised her assumptions now, saw that he was haunting because he was haunted—by something he'd done, maybe many things, horrible things he couldn't abide and to which he had been unable or unwilling to say no.

"How's your dad?" she asked.

"Mom says he's okay," Liz said. "They've got him doped up. I get to see him tomorrow. His ear is goners."

"Like van Gogh," Lucinda said. "Van Gogh cut his off. He was a great artist."

"My dad's not a great artist."

"Maybe," Lucinda said. "Maybe he will be. He's still alive—he could be anything."

They stopped for lunch at a McDonald's in Munich and everybody spilled into the bright restaurant like shipwreck survivors reaching land. The air, the light, the food was warm and good and something else, too—American. Lucinda bought french fries and a Big Mac and a Coke and sat at a bright yellow plastic table with Liz. Her parents had taught her to disdain Americans who came to Europe and never experienced it; when the Collins family visited Munich a year earlier, they had marched right by the McDonald's where Lucinda now sat and gone to a bratwurst kiosk in the Marienplatz. But her parents weren't there and she wasn't going to tell them. The Big Mac was good; the fries were hot and tasted like home. Something deep inside her, it felt like her very life force, reached hysterically for the light, heat, and familiarity. What she really wanted was to bury her head in her mother's lap, but this would do, would more than do. Liz was right. Next to Dachau, Captain Frye trying to blow his brains out *was* a little mistake. Across the table, Liz's eyes were lit up with a kind of artificial brightness as she sucked on her Coke.

"After Wednesday," she said, "I'm never going to see any of you again."

"Any of us?" Lucinda felt offended. As if Liz were lumping her in with the Dereks and the Sheilas and the Justins sitting around them, about to pile back onto the bus.

"We'll keep in touch, won't we? You and me?"

Liz looked out the window. "We're moving in with my uncle Ted and aunt Dee in Philly. It's a pretty cool place."

"We'll keep in touch? Liz?"

She wanted reassurance, but Lucinda also knew she would feel relieved when Liz was gone, her apartment empty so a new family could move in, maybe one with a girl her age that she could trust not to go off the edge of the world. And Captain Frye—she couldn't even think about him, couldn't square that strong man who carried her up the stairs on the Fourth of July with the red, swollen face she had seen on the stretcher leaving his apartment three days ago. Damn him. Zero Defect Policy—she understood it now. You just had to save yourself.

Liz seemed to read her mind. "No. We won't keep in touch. You'll be glad when I'm gone."

Lucinda's breath caught in her throat. She started to deny it, but before she could speak, Liz stood up and headed through the dining room toward the bus.

Back on the bus and recharged from the trip to McDonald's, everyone seemed to realize that Dachau was behind them now and they could begin forgetting about it, as quickly and as completely as possible. Derek cranked up "Bark at the Moon," flashing devil horns with both hands. Ms. Adams, legs crossed in the front seat, pumped her foot to the beat. The geeks in the front seat slumped out of sight with their Rubik's Cubes and comic books. Relief was on the air like a smell.

But Lucinda saw Liz's eyes go dim as she returned to the real world, her suicide dad, imminent departure, and uncertain future. Lucinda slid her knees up the back of the seat in front of theirs and said, "I'm so sorry."

Liz looked at her. "Whatever." She leaned her head back and closed her eyes.

Lucinda studied her friend's still profile. After a while, she turned and watched the autobahn unfurl in the bus's windshield, counting the cars that zipped past the bus. The bus driver was taking it easy and most of the cars that passed them weren't going all that fast, either, probably all driving within ten miles per hour of the same speed. Yet there was no speed limit on the autobahn, so Lucinda kept watching, hoping to see at least one car let out the throttle and really go.

TEN

A week after the trip to Dachau, Lucinda stood with Nately, shivering in the rounded wooden doorway of the old German water tower. "I feel like we're spies," she said, "trading info that could end the whole Cold War." They were a stone's throw from the generals' quarters. A broad sidewalk passed between the structures, providing a shortcut through the wooded area between the residential neighborhood where Lucinda lived and the PX/commissary compound and library, where her mother was working at that very moment.

"Be careful," Nately said. He craned his head from side to side. "My bow tie is really a camera." His pale pink skin was red from the cold, his green eyes watering. "What's that from?"

"Oh." Lucinda squinted in concentration. "I know those words. Hang on." The melody began to come to her.

"'Counting the cars on the New Jersey Turnpike, they've all gone to look for America,'" she sang. "Simon and Garfunkel."

"Good call. It's a great song. Great album, *Bookends*."

"It's okay," Lucinda said.

Nately smiled at her. "I was about your age when I first heard it. I found it in my big brother's collection, listened to it because of the cover. Those two guys, and all that gray around them. They looked like they knew something they were afraid to tell you. I didn't much like it then, either. I didn't really understand it, what it's about."

"What's so hard to understand?" Lucinda asked, thinking she had caught a dig at her age.

Nately's eyes were still smiling at her. "You're just not far enough away."

"Away from what?" Nately was acting like a big brother. She didn't like it.

"Home."

"Home?" She looked up at him. "We're at the end of the world here, Nately. I have one good friend, one, and now she's leaving. Her dad tried to off himself, so *auf Wiedersehen, adios.* Don't tell me I'm too young to understand stupid Simon and Garfunkel."

Nately reached out with his freckled hand to touch her shoulder. Lucinda shook it off.

"Look what you've got here, Lucinda. You've got your mom, your dad, your little brother and sister. Me, I've got Simon and Garfunkel."

"Oh, cry me a river."

"I'm just saying the lyrics might mean a bit more to somebody who's away from everything he knows, like the guy in the song. And one of these days it'll mean more to you, too. That's all, dear Prudence."

"Prudence?"

"That's your new nickname," he said.

She loved it.

"I brought a few more blanks," she said. "And a list."

"You've got a bad habit, sister."

The next Friday, Lucinda waited at the water tower for Nately to show up with her new tapes. Her parents thought she was at ballet class, so she'd had no trouble getting away, and in any case she didn't have far to go—she could see her own quarters from where they stood. She knew she would have to stop bothering Nately, but she couldn't. She didn't even have time to listen to all the music she requested of him. She just kept asking so she could see him. She hadn't told her father that she was meeting Nately, and she knew, somehow, that Nately hadn't mentioned it, either. The secrecy around their meetings exhilarated her, a hidden door in the center of her life.

He was late, and she had almost decided that he had forgotten about her. Just as she was about to leave, feeling sadder than she should have for not being able to pick up her new music, he appeared over the top of a rise, trotting in a long black leather coat that she had never seen before and dark shades.

"You look like KGB," she said.

"I've been to Amsterdam," he said, as if this explained his new look. "Things are happening there, Prudence. The music scene there is wired. One more year and I'm out of the Army, and that's where I'm going. I'll start a band. I had a feeling about the place."

"One more year," Lucinda said.

A truck rattled by carrying troops who looked like they might as well have been prisoners. She would need at least four more years before she could think of moving to Amsterdam, or anywhere else, without her parents. In four years she could be anywhere. Nately would be a memory.

She had always envied people who were from somewhere, who had one constant place that tethered their memories. Her memories felt fabricated, because she could never return to their sources to verify them; other people, she imagined, had traces of their own lives everywhere around them, in their neighborhoods and towns. They were *from* someplace. Maybe she could be, too, when she finally got free of the Army. Would she become a Texan someday after she had breathed the ancestral air of Shiloh for a few years?

Nately was breathing hard from his run, his breath crystallizing on the air. Lucinda concentrated on him. She could tell that their meeting was for her one of those moments that shine out from the continuum of moments, a luminous freeze-frame that would later be all she would remember of the entire month, or maybe the entire year. He reached into his new coat pockets and withdrew the tapes she had asked for. *London Calling, Station to Station, Disraeli Gears, Exile on Main St., Darkness on the Edge of Town, Bella Donna.* All there.

"Do you spend all your paycheck on music?" she asked.

"Pretty much. Here, I got you something from Amsterdam." He pulled one more tape out of his pocket, a store-bought tape. *Unbehagen,* by the Nina Hagen Band.

"*Uneasiness,*" Lucinda translated. "Thanks, Nately. Wow. Thanks for thinking of me."

She stared down at the cassette in her gloved hand, Nina Hagen's black-winged eyes staring back at her, offering the promise of a new sound like a new room, but one she could carry with her, unalterable. Music sounded the same wherever you were.

"I'll bet you've got a new list for me, haven't you?" Nately asked.

"Depends. I don't know if you'll have all this," she said, handing him her list.

"*Shoot Out the Lights.* Good girl! I'm going to Amsterdam again next week, so I don't know if I can get to everything, but I'll try hard. Meet me here same time two weeks from today, and I'll give you what I've got."

She watched him trot off in his heavy coat.

"My KGB agent," she said.

ELEVEN

A few days later, Lucinda sat in the deep windowsill of her room, looking out at the water tower and listening to U2's *The Unforgettable Fire*. That morning, she had said good-bye to Liz, who stood on the landing outside of her apartment waiting for Lucinda to come down on her way to the bus stop. Lucinda knew she would be there. She carried a stack of cassettes bundled in ribbon, a going-away gift. Of all the music Lucinda had played for her, Liz had been struck by Stevie Nicks's scratchy voice and her whole gypsy queen persona, so Lucinda was giving her all she had, all the Fleetwood Mac and the solo stuff, too. "Here," she said, thrusting the bundle at Liz, who took them without looking at them.

"Thanks."

"My address is in the *Rumours* case."

"Okay." Both girls looked down. Lucinda gave her her

address to end with some hope. But they had both been through it before, the letter-writing thing. It never worked out, even in a normal situation.

"As soon as I get to Philly I'll send you a postcard."

"Okay."

"Lucinda?"

"Yeah?"

"Something's wrong with my dad's memory."

Lucinda crossed her arms. "What?"

"I don't know, but he doesn't know me or Blake. He keeps asking Mom when our parents are going to come get us." Liz's face crumpled and she put her head in her hands.

Lucinda threw her arms around her friend and said what she didn't believe: "He'll get better, Liz."

And that was it—Liz was gone, Captain Frye was gone, and Lucinda felt every emotion in screaming slow motion. The loss. The relief. She felt the guilt for feeling the relief. The only person who seemed to notice the rough time Lucinda had been having since Captain Frye's suicide attempt was her nine-year-old brother, Jacob.

She heard a knock at her bedroom door and reached to turn down the volume. "Hey, dude," she said, when he peeked around the door. "Come on in."

Her brother stepped into the room, pulling self-consciously at his rumpled sweater. "You could start a fire," he said, nodding at the red scarf she had draped over a lamp. He glanced down at the rows of cassettes lined up across the top of her dresser, all with Nately's tiny block lettering along their spines. "How many records is that?"

"I never counted them," Lucinda said, sliding from the windowsill onto her bed.

"How could you not count them?"

"I don't know, Jacob. You can count them if you want."

He looked at her like she'd just told him she could get him on a spaceship that very minute. "Okay." He began fingering through them, counting out loud.

"Do that later," she said, patting the space next to her on the bed. "Have a seat."

"Who's that?" he asked, pointing to a black-and-white poster on the wall of some guys with tall fountains of dark hair.

"Echo and the Bunnymen."

Jacob blew a long raspberry and flopped over in a fit of giggles. "Say that again."

"Echo and the Bunnymen."

Peals of laughter. Not since he was a toddler had she seen him laugh so hard. "It does sound silly," she admitted. As she laughed, something that was curled tight inside her loosened and let her breathe a little easier. "I think it's Greek mythology."

"You like them?"

"They're pretty good," Lucinda said. "Here, listen." She slid off the bed and found the tape for *Ocean Rain*. She played "Killing Moon" for her little brother, whose blue eyes widened, an absorbed half smile settling onto his face as he listened.

"They're not American, huh?"

Lucinda cocked her head and looked at him. "No. How can you tell?"

"Just can. Can't you?"

"Yeah. There's something about it, a mood or something we just don't use much. Like the name Nigel."

"It's spooky," he said, propping his head up with his arm. "But really pretty. It makes me want to do something brave."

"Like what?"

Her brother put a finger to his lip and gave her a devious look. Of course—he had a reason for visiting her. "Mom told us you know where there's a ghost."

"Ah," Lucinda said. "You want to see him?"

"She said he's a Nazi."

"He is, but he doesn't do anything but just stand there and look sad. He's not scary. Really, he's kind of boring." Lucinda had checked in on the ghost a few months before and had found him there, unchanged. Seeing him gave her a jolt every time, but it was hard not to conclude from watching him that whatever limbo layer of the afterlife he was caught in was a bit tedious.

"I don't want to see him if he's boring. Boring people are stupid."

"Jacob, he's a ghost. That's kind of interesting, isn't it?"

"Mom says he's not real."

"What do you think?"

He nodded. "Okay," he said. "Let's go."

They left the apartment and crossed the soccer field into an orange-tinted winter sunset to the elementary school, heading around the back of the building to the side door where the janitor's rusted-out DAF was parked. Lucinda tried the door. "Hurry up," she said, ushering him in.

"He lives at my school?"

"One of the classrooms used to be the morgue."

"Gross!"

"I know, right?" Lucinda said as they walked down the shadowy hallway past rows of gray lockers. If they were caught, she planned to tell the janitor Jacob had forgotten his spelling book.

"That's grosser than kissing."

"Kissing's not so bad." Kissing made her think of Syd, long-gone Syd, and his kiss-and-run the day before he left. And Nately. She wanted badly to kiss Nately, that was the truth. She wanted all kinds of things from him, not just the songs, but the things in the songs.

Jacob wrinkled his nose. "You sound like Dad."

"Dad talks to you about kissing?"

"Naah," he said. "Just when I saw him do it."

"I know, it's weird when they kiss, but that's what they're supposed to do. They're married."

"Not Mom," he said.

They were in front of the old morgue room. Lucinda stopped, her hand on the doorknob. "What?"

"Not Mom?"

"Who?"

"It was after Erin's swim meet," he said.

"Jacob." Lucinda spun around to face her brother. "Tell me what happened."

In universal playground code, Jacob turned, ran his hands frantically over his shoulders, canted his head, and made sucking sounds.

"Got it. That's what happened," Lucinda said. "But who was he kissing?"

He dropped his arms to his sides. "That girl that coaches Erin's swim team."

"And he knows you saw him?"

"I want to go see your ghost."

"Just a minute. What did he say?"

Jacob deepened his voice and said, "If you tell your mother, I might not be able to be your daddy anymore."

Lucinda's legs went weak, and she leaned against the classroom door. "Goddammit," she said, irradiated by help-lessness and fear. And anger. All they had was each other, her family. There was no home, there were no permanent friends. There was only the family. The people you ate bugs for when they showed up in your lunch.

"What do we do, Lucy?"

Jacob looked younger than he had a moment before. Lucinda put her arms around him, and they stood that way for a moment. She touched his hair.

"You won't tell her, will you?" he asked.

"I don't know."

"Lucinda, you can't!"

It didn't make any sense. Her mother was smart and beautiful. Men flirted with her all the time in parks, grocery stores, at the movies. Once a man had slid into their booth at a Dairy Queen in Tennessee and read to her a love poem he had spontaneously composed for her on the back of a napkin. Faye had just laughed and said, "I have three kids," as if that settled it.

"Mom doesn't deserve this," she said.

"He made me promise, and he said it's against the rules to break a promise."

"The rules," she said. "*His* rules. Not *the* rules." Bulletin boards in the dark hall were decorated for Presidents' Day and Valentine's Day. Lucinda had to fight the impulse to tear them all down and rip the colored cardboard into tiny pieces. She wanted to smash out windows, set the place on fire. She wanted to hurt somebody.

"This is the sixth graders' class," Jacob said, looking around. "The ghost lives here?"

"How long ago, Jacob?"

"Couple weeks."

"Come on."

They stepped inside and Lucinda pointed to the bricked-in window where the ghost usually stood. "Let your eyes go out of focus," she said.

"Do you see him?"

Jacob stood with his eyelids half closed staring at the spot in front of the window. Then he sucked in a sharp breath. "Yeah," he said. "Oh, Lucinda, I do."

"Really?" Lucinda couldn't believe it. Jacob saw the ghost? She wondered if he was making it up. "Really? Are you sure?"

"Yeah."

"Is he alone?"

"Yeah."

"Tell me what he looks like."

"Look at him yourself."

But Lucinda didn't want to.

Jacob spread his arms wide. "Lucinda," he said, his voice rising in wonder, "I bet there are ghosts all over the place."

She cupped her brother's shoulder, pulling him nearer. "I bet you're right."

TWELVE

Surrounded by books, Faye Collins looked safe. She had been working at the base library for over a year and had made the place her own, arranging the reception desk so that when she sat behind it, she was backed into a corner created by bookshelves. People could not approach without her seeing them first. She always arranged the furniture in their quarters that way, too, reminding Lucinda of a rabbit burrowed deep in its hole. It was a defensive posture that Lucinda figured had something to do with her being an orphan. A car wreck had killed her parents and broken three of her tiny ribs when she was two, and she had ended up at the orphanage in Broken Arrow, Oklahoma. Lucinda walked up to the library reception desk. Lucinda said, "Yes, I was wondering if you could check a title for me?"

Faye glanced up from the pages of an open book and gave her a tired smile. "Why aren't you at ballet?"

"I'm going," Lucinda said. She was lying. She had plans to meet Nately in a few minutes and had only stopped into the library to get out of the snowstorm. The library was in a small building hidden in the greenbelt where the water tower stood. If the building had a window on its east wall, Faye could have looked out and witnessed her daughter's coming rendezvous, but there was no window.

"Is it still snowing?" Faye asked.

"Yeah—even harder."

"Why don't you skip ballet today and go straight home? I don't like you out in this weather."

"I'll get home soon."

Faye closed the book in front of her. She was working her way through the novels of Iris Murdoch.

"What's that one?" Lucinda asked.

"*The Sea, the Sea.*"

"Any good?"

"Bewitching," Faye said.

"Well, that's good, then. Right?"

Faye laughed. "Is it? I don't know. There's a roast in the Crock-Pot, sweetie."

"I'll do the potatoes," Lucinda said. "See you in a little while."

"Hey," her mother said as Lucinda turned to go.

"Yeah?"

"Don't you want to check out a book?"

"Can't I just come by to see you?"

"Oh!" Her mother blushed. "You can come see me anytime."

When Lucinda left the library, the snow was falling even heavier than before and she could hardly make out the figure standing in front of the heavy wooden door of the Nazi water tower as she approached. She felt as if years had passed since she had seen Nately, and she reviewed all her insights about Nina Hagen and Richard and Linda Thompson as she walked. She didn't want to forget anything. She saw him pacing in front of the door and figured that he must have been freezing, so she began to run. As she drew closer, she realized that the figure was not Nately but Snowden. He had stopped pacing and now stood with his hands deep in his front pockets, staring at her. She stopped running and waved. Nately must have the flu or something. Yet it was good to see Snowden—his presence showed that he didn't hate her, in spite of her jailbait status.

"Snowden, hey! You order this weather?" She reached him and ducked under the narrow awning over the door.

"Hey, Prudence," he said. His face was tight.

"You know my nickname! What's the matter? What's got you out today doing Nately's dirty work for him?"

For a long minute he looked away over her head like he might sprint off in that direction. Finally, he said, "I can't do this."

"Do what?"

"Shit." He puffed out his cheeks.

"What?"

"Nately's dead, Lucinda. Got killed in a bar fight in Amsterdam last weekend. Wasn't his fight—he was trying to break it up and he stepped in front of somebody's knife."

Lucinda stared and stared at Snowden. She watched his exhaled breaths crystallize. She watched him blink. "Is he . . . where is he?"

"Shipped home already, to Gainesville. I can't believe it. I've already got a new roommate. Every morning I open my eyes and have to remind myself that Nately's not the one breathing across the room."

"No," she said. "Oh no. No, no, no." Tears froze on her cheeks.

"He had marked his calendar. I thought I ought to show up in case your dad hadn't told you what happened. Here," he said, handing her a plastic sack. It contained tapes she had given Nately to record with the last time she had seen him. Snowden patted her on the shoulder. "He put so much time into making those tapes for you. You were a bright spot for him."

Lucinda nodded.

He hesitated for a moment, then said, "You know, he never had any girlfriends."

Lucinda looked up at him. "Thank you, Snowden."

She walked home slowly, the cold seeping through her clothes and her boots. Her father hadn't said anything. Not a word. Of course, he didn't know that she and Nately had seen each other more than once. For a week, a whole week, Nately had not been in the world, and she hadn't known it. She reached into the bag and drew out a tape. Still blank. She reached in and pulled out two more, both blank. Then she pulled one out and saw Nately's handwriting. *Closer* by Joy Division.

She stopped and stared at his handwriting. Black ink, because she had convinced him that his color-coded tripartite system didn't work. She thought about his hands, the freckles on the backs of them, how they had written these words, and where they were now, his hands. She was colder than she had ever been, the cold going all the way to her core. She wondered why her heart didn't stop.

She picked up speed until she had covered the three additional blocks to her dad's office. At 5:10, the building was still bustling. She could see the light on in her father's second-floor office.

"Hello, little Collins!"

Three NCOs who worked across the hall from her father were coming down the stairs. They separated to let her pass. She climbed the stairs and pushed open the door to her father's office without knocking. He looked up from whatever it was he was reading, then stood up when he saw her.

"Lucinda! What brings you here? I thought you had ballet."

"Nately's dead?"

"Sure is. Poor bastard got himself killed. He was a good boy. That time he made all those tapes for you—that was nice of him, didn't you think?"

Lucinda nodded.

"That reminds me, sweetie, I keep forgetting to tell you. When I heard he died, I went over and got these for you."

He pointed behind where Lucinda was standing. In the far corner of the room, under the windows, sat Nately's crates of records, lined up against the wall.

Her father was standing beside her. She went down on her knees in front of the crates. In the first crate she saw the honey-colored photo on the front of *Shoot Out the Lights*, along with all the other albums she had most recently asked Nately to record. As she thumbed her way through the records, she realized that he had separated those he had already taped for her from all the others. He had been keeping track so he could tell, she supposed, how many he had yet to record for her, how close he was to running out of music.

"I didn't try for the turntable," her father said. He was standing next to where she knelt. "I thought his folks might want it."

"But you didn't think they'd want his *records*? What he *listened* to? What gave him his—" Outrage made her tongue-tied. How could she explain to this man what music means to people who really hear it? What it meant to Nately and to her?

"Sweetie, these would have been tossed. Or the other GIs would have divvied them up." He put his hand on her shoulder. "I thought you should have them."

Lucinda shrugged off his hand, stood up, and walked over to the window behind his desk. It was getting dark on the base, and she saw the lights come on at the top of the old stone watchtower, spotlights that bathed the nearby exercise yards in an amber glow all night long. She was surprised at how far away the lights seemed to be. She had walked a long way to get here.

"It's stealing, Dad. It's something you're not supposed to do. I guess it's one of those rules that just doesn't apply to you. Right?"

He looked a little confused. "Baby. I got these records for *you*."

Lucinda noticed she was holding a record from one of Nately's bins. She didn't remember pulling it out. Kate Bush, *Hounds of Love*.

"What do you do with her?" she asked. "That lifeguard?"

"What?"

"Is she better than us in some way?"

He moved behind his desk and sat down. He shuffled some papers. "You're not making sense."

Realization spread over his face. "That little son of a bitch," he mused aloud. "Lucinda, have you told your mother? You know what it would do to her if you told her?"

"What it would do to her? Sure, I think I do. And what about what it's doing to us? To Jacob and Erin and me?"

"I know, sweetie, but a man's children . . . a man always has his children."

"I hate you," Lucinda said.

He shook his head. "That's the thing, honey. You don't."

Lucinda walked out of the office and set off for home, fighting tears, slipping in the snow. She was still carrying the album, *Hounds of Love*. She had never heard it, had only read about it in a couple of music magazines. It was supposed to be terrific, but she wouldn't be able to play it when she reached home. She didn't have a turntable.

THIRTEEN

"You having the currywurst?" her father asked, closing his menu.

"Yeah, with fries," Lucinda said. "And a spätzie."

A month had passed since their confrontation in his office, but things were still weird between Lucinda and her dad. They tried not to be alone together. He had brought home Nately's crates of records one day while she was at school, and the next day, she came home to find a new turntable set up on her dresser. He never mentioned it and she wouldn't play it when he was home. She didn't want him to know she loved the records, would treasure them forever, that they both deepened and healed her grief over Nately, both deepened and healed her grief over him, her dad, and his infidelity. When he was home, she observed absolute silence and holed up in her room like a submarine in enemy waters.

But today there had been no avoiding him; he had shown

up at her school and checked her out of her algebra class, announcing he wanted to hit the slopes. She could tell he wanted to make her talk about something. All the way there he had told stories about work, and had waited until after they finished skiing to broach his subject. Now they were sitting in the lodge restaurant next to a wide picture window with a view of the slopes. Lucinda drank hot cocoa and worried. He was leaving them? Divorce? She didn't think so—he had gone out of his way to be sweet to her mother lately. They had orders to go back to the States—that would be his announcement—to who knows what state. It was about that time; they had been at Grafenwoehr more than two years. He ordered a beer, something she had never seen him do in the middle of the day. They had to be moving someplace awful.

While Lucinda drew her initials in the steamed window glass, her father reached into the breast pocket of the flannel shirt he wore beneath his ski jumper and handed her a brochure about mental illness. "I don't know anything about this kind of crap," he started.

Lucinda picked up the brochure. It advertised the Army's psychiatric services. She looked up at her father.

"What do you think?" he said. "About your mother? I don't know what to do, Lucinda."

"With Mom?"

"Do you think she needs to go away for a while?"

Lucinda looked again at the brochure. Against the blue background was the silhouette of a man with his head in his hands. She prided herself on being able to read her father pretty well, but he had ambushed her this time.

"Are you kidding me?" Lucinda said. "Mom's not crazy. She hates it here. She wants a normal life."

"I know," her father said, signaling the waitress for another beer. "But she's depressed. It's not normal. I can't hack all the self-pity."

"Self-pity?" Lucinda said, leaning forward. "Get a clue, Dad. She's picked up and moved for your career over and over without even thinking about herself."

"She cries a lot, and she looks sloppy. A team is only as strong as its weakest link, babe. She talks about dying."

Lucinda sat back and crossed her arms. She took her father in. Who was he? What was in his mind? For a month she had been carrying around the image of him kissing Erin's swim coach, worrying about the effect the secret was having on Jacob and Erin, in constant torment about whether or not to tell her mother. His confidence that she wouldn't tell on him made her feel filthy. "She doesn't need to *go away*. Unhappy isn't the same thing as crazy."

"I talked to your grandmother about this," he said, looking away from Lucinda, out the window at the skiers gliding in from the slopes. "She agrees with me. Says she always thought your mother was a loose cannon."

"Dad, Grandma Esmé has been divorced four times. I don't know why you ask her for advice about marriage. She doesn't think anyone's good enough for you, anyway. Like she's ever given Mom a fair shake."

"She always puts me first," he said, watching out the window.

"She's trying to sell Shiloh out from under you so she can buy a condo!"

"I trust my mother."

"Trust! Yeah, well, I trust mine. And she's not crazy. Look, if Mom needs anything, she needs a vacation. We're a day's drive from Paris. Maybe she and Marcie could take a week and just have fun."

Marcie Byers and her family lived in the Frye family's old quarters below the Collinses. She and Lucinda's mother had become friends despite having nothing in common—Marcie had three passions: cake decorating, gnomes, and Princess Diana, while Faye still bore traces of the hitchhiker and would-be hippie she had been when she met her husband in Tucumcari. Still, the two women made each other laugh.

Her father took a long swallow of beer and set the glass down, smiling at her.

"Lucinda, you're a genius," he said, the tension easing out of his voice. "A vacation might be all she needs." He leaned back and planted his elbows on the arms of his chair. "A vacation! I wasn't going to commit her; I just wasn't sure *what* to do."

"Let me borrow your black miniskirt," Lucinda's mother said, standing in front of her closet.

"What do you need a mini for?"

"You never know. Marcie and I might have a night on the town."

Lucinda sat on the bed watching her mother pack. She couldn't remember the last time her mother had looked so cheerful. "Oh, yeah. I can see Marcie in a nightclub."

"You've never been in a nightclub."

"True, but you know what I mean. I can just imagine her standing at a bar showing some hot man pictures of her kids."

"Pictures of her prize cakes, more like it. 'And this is a *Star Wars* one I did for Tom and Sasha's Hail and Farewell. The buttons on R2-D2's little head are cherries!'" They laughed.

"She is good, though," Lucinda said, feeling guilty.

"She is." Her mother nodded soberly. "She is very good. You know what she made for her husband's birthday last year? A penis—a buttercream penis with balls."

Lucinda covered her face, laughing. "Mom! Oh my God!"

Faye sat on the bed, shaking the mattress with her laughter. "He said, 'Honey? Do you think I'm a homosexual?' He told her it should've been a pair of woman's breasts." Faye took a deep breath. "She told him, 'I tried that, but I wasn't satisfied with the nipples. You'll eat this penis and you'll like it!'"

Lucinda felt her cheeks heating up. Her mother was looking at her, eyes bright with amusement. Seeing Lucinda's embarrassment, she reached across the bed and slapped Lucinda's knee. "Oh, Lucinda. Loosen up."

"Now I'm worried about you two in Paris!"

Faye waved a hand. "We'll probably be in our rooms by nine o'clock, anyway. I've never had a vacation without my family. What do I want at a French disco?" She stood and began tossing sweaters into the suitcase, open on the floor. She moved back and forth from the closet to the suitcase like a hummingbird zipping from flower to flower.

"Mom, you're supposed to have fun."

"I will, I will. Just walking through the Louvre without constantly corralling kids will be a huge treat. Do you need a prescription refill before I go?"

"I'm good," Lucinda said. "If you happen to get a chance, could you bring me some music?"

"Like what?"

"I don't know—I don't know anything about French rock. Surprise me."

"What will you all do while I'm gone? If I find out that he's taken you kids out of school to go skiing again, I'll wring his neck."

"We wouldn't do that."

"Like hell." Faye had bent down to arrange clothes in the suitcase. "Your father does whatever the hell he feels like."

This was the opening Lucinda had been waiting for. Here it was, presented to her like a gift. The perfect chance to tell her mother what she knew. She considered her words carefully. "Don't you think he'll miss you?"

Her mother picked a bra out of the suitcase and tried to shove the underwire back into the lining. "Your father wants me out of the way. He doesn't want to deal with me. Here, darling, take a vacation. See the sights. Do some shopping. Just come back smiling and forget you're sitting in a medieval hovel watching snow pile up and ironing my fatigues. The prick." She threw the bra back into the suitcase.

"Lucinda, don't ever get married. I'm serious. If somebody wants to come along for the ride, fine, but don't expect some man to put you first, because he won't. Especially not an Army man. And don't have kids, whatever you do." She tossed a hair dryer into her suitcase.

"Hey, thanks."

"You know I love you. That's why I'm saying this. Anybody that tries to muffle you, or shut you up—what kind of a sick bastard would that person be? What's he afraid of? He should be shot," she said, making a pistol out of her fingers and firing her weapon in the direction of the headboard. "Taken out and shot."

Her mother's rage killed Lucinda's resolve. No need to ruin her mother's vacation. Maybe he would miss her so badly he'd reform. Faye would come home, things would be better, and she need never know about his dark passage. There was no harm in hoping.

FOURTEEN

The first night her mother was away, Major Collins told Lucinda he was going to drive into the village and have a few drinks with some of his troops. After Erin and Jacob went to bed, Lucinda decided to have some drinks herself. She had tried alcohol a couple of times, once at a Hail and Farewell her parents had dragged her to because they were afraid she'd have a seizure if they left her at home, and once on a ski slope when a stranger handed her a paper cup of glühwein as if she'd ordered it. Tonight she got trashed on her parents' peppermint schnapps. By the end of the evening, the bottle was almost empty and Lucinda sprawled on the couch, her eyes closing over the television image of an American flag waving in the breeze above the words THE ARMED FORCES NETWORK HAS SIGNED OFF.

She woke when the grandfather clock in the entryway began chiming discordantly. The usual quarter-hour chimes never woke her; she was used to the sound, but this racket broke her drunken sleep and she lay terrified, watching as a dark figure crept into the hallway. Whoever it was had bumped into the clock—evidently a stranger to the layout of the apartment—and was carrying a flashlight. She watched as the figure opened the linen closet in the hall. From the couch she watched, trying to think of a plan and wondering where the hell her father was, as the figure bundled two heavy wool blankets under his arm and closed the closet. She heard the front door close and footfalls echoing down the stairwell.

Lucinda slipped along the hallway in her socks and tipped open the blinds of a window that looked down onto the parking lot in front of their building. She saw her father, unmistakable under the streetlight, slide back into his car, handing the blankets to someone sitting in the passenger seat. Something bright glinted in the streetlight on the person's lap. Something round with ears. She recognized it: she was looking at the big brass owl clasp of Leanne Murdoch's brown leather purse. For a minute, Lucinda was surprised it wasn't Erin's swim coach. That one she knew about. But it was Leanne Murdoch, wife of Dan Murdoch, mother of Tina Murdoch. Dan was a general contractor, a civilian. He wore a beard, Leanne wore Birkenstocks, and they lived in a two-story house that shared a backyard with Lucinda's apartment building. Their daughter, Tina, an angry, square-jawed girl who made a point of not learning how to distinguish rank from uniforms, went to school with Lucinda. They weren't really friends, but they had, on two recent occasions, shared a joint in the girls' restroom.

Lucinda wished Tina were with her to witness her mother reaching over and kissing Lucinda's father. Then Lucinda could have clocked Tina in her big jaw, then run downstairs to give her father and Leanne Murdoch a good thrashing. But Tina wasn't there, and Lucinda didn't move. She watched as they pulled away, and followed the headlights of the car for as far as she could see them. Then she went to bed.

The next day at school, Lucinda checked the girls' bathroom for Tina between every class. She found her during lunch, staring at herself in the bathroom mirror, dragging hair gel upward from her scalp and then teasing her bangs. Lucinda approached Tina and turned to talk to her through the mirror.

She ran a comb through her shoulder-length hair. "Hey."

"Hey," Tina said, rinsing hair gel off her fingers. She watched Lucinda while drying her hands, then pulled a joint out of the pocket of her ski jacket. No one else was in the bathroom. Tina opened a window, letting in a blast of sub-zero air for ventilation, and they stepped into the farthest stall from the door to the hall and lit up.

With her lungs full of pot, she watched Tina inhale and took the joint as Tina handed it back. She tried to think through the ramifications of telling Tina about what their parents were up to. But she couldn't think; she only felt rage rising up like something foreign about to take over her body. She felt like landing a punch square in Tina's nose, but she executed a split-second course correction, grabbing Tina by the chin and landing a kiss instead. Tina started to kiss her back, but Lucinda pushed her away.

"I'm not a lesbian," she said.

Tina shrugged. "I'm not, either."

"My father and your mother are having an affair. I saw them last night."

Tina sat down on the toilet and looked up at Lucinda. "My dad's away in Wildflecken this month. She went out last night and didn't get in until dawn."

"Yeah. She was with my dad. He came home and took two blankets out of the closet and left again. I recognized your mom in the car by her silly goddamned owl purse."

"Your father's an ass."

"Your mom's a total bitch. You have no idea what this could do to my mother. What about your dad? What are you going to do?"

"I don't know. Do you think they're in love?"

"Love, hell. I'm hoping it blows over before my mom finds out. I can't tell her; she'd lose her mind. But if they're in love—shit. There's just no way my dad could be in love with your mom."

"Fuck you!"

"Nothing against your mother," Lucinda said.

"Your dad could be court-martialed, you know."

"Come on."

"You know the code: an officer and a *gentleman*. That's serious business, not just some movie. He could go down."

"I'm not going to let that happen. I'm going to stop this," Lucinda said, flinging open the door to the stall.

That night, Lucinda's father was out again, no doubt with Leanne Murdoch. Lucinda put on her long underwear and pulled her jeans over them, preparing for at least thirty minutes in the elements. She doubled her gloves, pulled a ski mask over her face, and took a flashlight out of a kitchen drawer. She stopped in the basement of her building and grabbed a gas can next to the lawn mower. Then she crossed the narrow strip of field, dotted with communal playground equipment and picnic benches, which dipped between her family's apartment and the Murdochs' home. Her dad said the little field was a perfect miniature of the Fulda Gap, that lowland corridor from the upper Rhine Valley through the middle of Germany where so many thousands of NATO troops and weapons sat, permanently massed against Warsaw Pact invasion. It was a natural invasion route; Germans had ridden through it to fight the Romans and then Napoleon, just as Lucinda was going to use its miniature now, for smaller stakes, but bloody-minded and ready to fight, ready to hurt. Ready to defend her homeland.

Her dad had told her about listening to the AFN during a firefight one night in Vietnam and how everybody's blood-lust let up when the Beatles came on. "Made me want to lay down in a park and drink some goddamned tea," he said. Lucinda loved the Beatles, but she hadn't made the mistake of bringing them with her tonight. Instead she had popped a tape of the Who singing "Eminence Front" into her Walkman, a whole tape of just that song, so she wouldn't have to stop and rewind.

The Murdoch quarters looked much homier than the Collinses', white stucco with dark wood crossbeams, tiny, deep windows, and heavy, rounded wooden doors. Like most of the doorways on base, a stone eagle held an empty wreath in its talons, with a blank center where the swastika had been cemented over. Shining her flashlight over the house, Lucinda saw that Leanne Murdoch had covered this circle with a sign that had THE MURDOCHS painted in purple lettering over a faint orange peace sign. Lucinda noted the peace sign with grudging admiration, amazed they had been allowed to leave it up. She knew that Tina was in the house alone and considered abandoning her plan and inciting Tina to invade her parents' liquor cabinet, but instead she opened the gasoline can and poured gas over the hard-crusted snow in the front yard until she had spelled out the word SLUT in large letters. She stood and watched as the gasoline melted the snow down to the ground until the letters appeared, written in mud.

She walked home. The hard snow was slippery, and she had to step hard, breaking the crust of ice to keep from falling.

Her thoughts came between long pauses, like late-night trains flashing through a station. She thought of the Baader-Meinhof Gang's grim compensation for the passivity of their parents; she saw the tidy neighborhoods near Dachau and the poison chutes outside the gas chambers of Baracke X surrounded by high fences to protect the workers dropping in the poison. The Nazi ghost's mute vigil. Hiding and pretending. It was silence that let death take hold. Virginia Dare. Truth or Dare. Both, please. It would have to be both. Truth *and* Dare. Balls like the Liberty Bell—Captain Frye and his broken face. And Nately, standing up for some stranger in Amsterdam. It had killed him, but still. The pieces locked in place and her decision was made. When she got home she pulled the phone number to her mother's Paris hotel from under a magnet on the refrigerator door and dialed it.

"*S'il vous plaît, chambre* eighteen," she said to the Frenchman who answered the phone. "Eighteen—*dix-huit?*"

Her mother picked up on the second ring. "Hello?"

"Mom?"

"Lucinda, what is it?"

"You'd better come home."

FIFTEEN

To avoid her dad, Lucinda stayed in bed the next morning. She listened to him and Jacob and Erin shouting across the apartment as they got ready for school and for work. Erin flew into Lucinda's bedroom and said, "Up, sleepyhead," pushing Lucinda's shoulders.

"Go away."

"What's wrong?"

"Soul sickness," Lucinda said into her pillow.

"Oh. Okay." Erin bent down and pecked the back of Lucinda's head, then left, closing the door softly. Lucinda heard her sister yell to her dad, "Lucinda's soul is sick."

Clattering in the kitchen stopped. "Her soul?"

"That's what she said."

The clattering started up again. He didn't say anything. Some part of her wanted to pummel him with her fists; another part wanted to give him fair warning. Her mother would be arriving sometime that day, two days before her trip was due to end. Lucinda rolled over and slept until nine. Truancy seemed so trivial. Besides, she didn't want to see Tina on the bus.

When finally she was ready for school, she called a German cab, which drove her by the Murdoch home. The word *slut* was no longer visible on their lawn. Someone had taken a shovel and scraped snow back into the grooves created by the gasoline. She wondered if Tina was going to be angry. She would have understood perfectly had Tina felt the need to burn a derogatory term about her father into her lawn. She tried to come up with the right word for what her father was, but nothing came to her. There were a dozen words for the woman. Her father was—what? An adulterer. Their lawn wasn't big enough for that word.

Tina *was* angry. She was waiting by Lucinda's locker at the beginning of the lunch period. "How could you do that?" she asked, shoulders flat against Lucinda's locker. The set of her jaw made it look even squarer than usual, Lucinda noticed, recoiling from the memory of their having kissed.

"Gasoline. It cuts through everything," Lucinda said, shifting the books in her arms.

"*To me.* How could you do that *to me?*"

"Like we're so close, you and I. Anyway, I didn't do anything to you. I did it to your mother, and I promise you that what she has done to my family and me is much worse." Then she couldn't help asking, "Did she see it?"

Tina pushed herself off Lucinda's locker and lunged for her. She grabbed Lucinda's hair in one hand and landed a solid punch to Lucinda's eye with the other. Rage took Lucinda like a seizure. She knocked Tina to the ground and fell on top of her, landing clumsy blows on Tina's neck, face, and shoulders. She heard nothing, felt nothing, releasing herself completely into the service of her fury until Frau Brinkman, the hall monitor, pulled her off Tina.

She and Tina were both suspended. The principal, Herr Munsch, had been unable to find any of their parents but left messages for them and sent the girls home anyway. He just wanted them off school grounds. He called a cab that they would have to share and made them sit in the office together until it came. In the cab, the same one she had taken to school two hours earlier, Lucinda pressed as far against her side of the backseat as she could, flattening her nose against the window. The cold felt good to her burning, swollen eye. She could have looked at Tina through her good eye, but she made no effort to do so. When the car hit a bump, and her knee touched Tina's knee, they both drew back. She was still angry, but the rage was gone. Depression was settling in like fog on a mountaintop. She was afraid to think about what would happen when her mother got home.

When the cab stopped at Tina's house, Lucinda heard rather than saw her get out of the car.

A minute later, the cab stopped in front of her apartment building. As she waited for change from the cabdriver, she saw that the green Opel was in the parking lot, which was very strange. Her dad never came home during the day, but then again, what did she know? She was never home this early in the day herself.

As she walked by his car, she saw flat, broad footprints like monster tracks leading from the Opel's passenger side to the front door of her apartment building. Leanne Murdoch's ugly shoes. Her mother's blue Saab was also in the driveway. She was home, too. Already. Lucinda quickly walked toward the building, fear making it hard to breathe. From the yard she could hear her mother yelling three stories up. She couldn't tell what she was saying, but she didn't need to. Lucinda knew what must have happened.

She didn't want to go in. She walked to the middle of the lawn, threw herself down, and made a snow angel. Then she stood up carefully, so as not to mess up the angel's wings, and hopped left a few feet, fell backward, and made another one. She did this one more time, listening all the while to her mother's screams drifting down from above.

She imagined her mom killing the two lovers. *Won't you gimme three steps, gimme three steps, mister.* Most of the rock songs about murdering lovers were about men killing women, which Lucinda took as a good sign. In fact, she couldn't think of a single song about a woman killing a cheating man. Even as she climbed the stairwell two steps at a time, she knew her mother wouldn't kill anyone. Once, shaking her head over the Falkland Invasion, Faye had said, "Women know how to go to war without killing. We don't kill. You know why? Every person we look at, we see another woman's child."

Lucinda stepped through the apartment door and could hear it all. She could also hear her father now, voice lower, saying, "Now, Faye. Baby, I'm sorry. Calm down." Leanne, somewhere in the house, was silent. Lucinda slammed the front door as loudly as she could, called out, "I'm home!" and walked down the hall. The door of the master bedroom hung open, a huge hole kicked through the particleboard. Her mother was standing in front of the bed with a kitchen knife, and her father was in front of her, wearing only undershorts, stepping side to side like a boxer. Lucinda still didn't see Leanne, but she heard her finally, from behind the closed bathroom door, sobbing.

Her father saw her first. "Oh, hell. Oh, God. Look, baby, this is fine, everything is okay."

"This is okay?"

"Go away, honey. Go away for a little while."

Lucinda's mother spun around. "You see, Lucinda? They won't put you first. They'll—"

"Mom! Stop it." Lucinda stepped toward her mother and hugged her, pinning her arms to her sides and taking the knife out of her hand. Lucinda used all of her strength to hold her mother's body, as if it might fly apart if she loosened her grip. Her father walked over to the closet, pulled out a suitcase, and threw it open onto the bed. He started packing, not taking his eyes off his wife and daughter. The bathroom door opened and Leanne, her Birkenstocks and her owl purse clutched to her chest, darted past them, shooting Major Collins a dazed glance as she left the room. Then Lucinda heard the front door slam. She walked her mother to her side of the bed and tried to get her to lie down. But Faye fought to keep standing.

"I can't sleep on these sheets. No, no, no." Faye seemed to

speak without breathing. She was drenched in sweat, muscles quivering beneath Lucinda's hands like those of a horse ridden to its breaking point.

Nobody knew how to proceed. Lucinda's parents stared at each other, breathing hard. Finally, Lucinda's mother left the room. Lucinda followed her, afraid of what she might do, but she only walked into Erin's room and lay down on her narrow bed, pulling the quilt over herself. Lucinda marched back down the hall, passing the master bedroom without looking in at her father, and went into her own bedroom.

When Erin and Jacob came home, stomping snow from their boots and pulling them off inside the door, Lucinda dashed from her room and shushed them. She pulled them into her room and told them their parents had had a fight.

Jacob nodded knowingly. "The kissing," he said.

Erin, who knew all about the kissing, too, punched a pillow. "It's just dumb," she said.

"What happened to your eye?" Jacob asked.

Lucinda felt the swollen skin around her eye. She had forgotten. "I got in a fight," she said.

"With Mom?" Jacob asked, his brow lowering.

"What? No!"

"With Dad?"

"At school. With a girl at school."

Erin said, "I didn't know you could fight."

"You'd be surprised," Lucinda said.

They talked about divorce, whether their parents would get one or not and whether or not they wanted them to. They didn't. After a little while, they migrated to the living room and watched television. Lucinda made fried eggs and toast for dinner and they shared a half gallon of ice cream, huddling around the bucket with their spoons. They could hear the Byerses' TV downstairs, and occasional sounds in the stairwell, but in their apartment, nothing but a suffocating stillness. Once they heard the toilet flush in the master bedroom. Neither of her parents had left the apartment; neither of them came out for food.

Jacob and Erin went to bed at ten, Erin in Lucinda's bed. Lucinda tucked her in. "If we split up," Erin said, "can I go with you?"

Lucinda kissed her on the forehead. Erin looked like a miniature version of their mother, same auburn hair curled around her small face. "They're not splitting us up."

Around eleven o'clock, Lucinda took a bottle from the liquor cabinet and slid out the front door in her warmest ski clothes. It was snowing. She walked across the backyard, allowing herself to slide sometimes, as if she were on skis, to the Murdochs' quarters. The house was dark. She had never been in it, but she saw that a light was on in the ground-floor room and guessed it to be Tina's room. She made a snowball and threw it against the window, making and throwing three more before Tina finally came to the window.

"What the hell do you think you're doing?" Tina whispered loudly from behind the screen.

"Détente?" Lucinda said.

"What? Yeah, okay. Détente."

"Has the shit hit the fan at your house?"

"My dad doesn't know," Tina said. "But I confronted my mom. I had to—she came dragging in, all shook up, after I got home from school. I guess you know. I guess you found her."

"My mother found her."

"Holy shit. She didn't tell me that."

"Yeah. Do you want to come out? I've got licorice schnapps."

"I've got a joint. Meet you in the front yard." Tina emerged a few minutes later with the keys to her mother's car. They got in and turned it on, with the heat on full blast.

"Where do you want to go?" Lucinda asked.

"I thought we'd just sit here and get as fucked up as we can."

Tina unzipped her parka and took the joint and matches out of the inside pocket. She lit it and passed it to Lucinda, who took it and handed the bottle to her.

"Where'd you get this shit?" Lucinda asked.

"Derek Tanner. He says it comes from Czechoslovakia. You believe that?" She sucked on the end of the joint. "Sorry about your eye."

"That's okay. I wish I could find eyeliner this color purple. It's really gorgeous." Lucinda looked over at Tina and noticed for the first time a couple of nasty scratches down her cheek. She pointed. "Sorry for those. Do they hurt?"

"A little."

"Are you going to tell your dad?"

Tina, holding in a hit, shook her head.

"You're not?"

"No," Tina said, exhaling. "She promised it was over. She swears she'll never do it again. It's worse at your house than mine."

"I wonder what will happen tomorrow," Lucinda said, taking the joint. "I just can't imagine. I can't imagine that we'll wake up and there'll be another day." As she watched the spring snow hit the windshield, accumulating fast and eliminating the view outside the car, she felt like a character in a movie about nuclear war, one of the survivors who has to walk out into the desert after the war is over and rebuild the human race.

SIXTEEN

That summer, Lucinda sat in the passenger seat of a Humvee, afraid, hurtling toward Nürnberg on the A9. The windows were cracked, letting in a hot wind that dried the sweat in her hair. Outside, the symmetrical rows of Third Reich–era pine forests clicked by like the bristles of a giant hairbrush. The forest for the trees—a saying that means missing the big picture. Guilty, she thought. Guilty, guilty, guilty. How could she have been so stupid? She glanced at Private Rob Dalton in the driver's seat. He was out of the uniform he wore when she had met him on post. Its patches and pins told one story—private first class, 27th Field Artillery, U.S. Army. The black wife-beater T-shirt he now wore told another, and she could see the tattoos that spread from his wrists to his collarbones, a mélange of contradictory symbols—a swastika, peace sign, encircled *A* of the anarchy symbol, Celtic cross, sign of the Tao, Dead Kennedys logo,

Confederate flag, even the golden arches—M for McDonald's. Could he explain? She shouldn't have asked, but she just had, so he was trying.

"Nazi punk just feels right to me," he said. He was excited to be stationed in Germany for that very reason, and he was hoping to hook up with "the real thing" there. Rob reached into a bag of gummi bears.

"What real thing?" Lucinda asked.

"Nazis. Nazi punks. Ought to be some people I can call friend at the gig tonight. Always looking for new friends." He smiled at her. "Cohorts." He said the word slowly, as if he had just learned it, and looking at his smile, Lucinda realized he thought he had made a new one out of her. A cohort.

The inside of the Humvee smelled like axle grease and diesel fuel, a combination that evoked her father as strongly as if he had been sitting next to her still chuckling over her "date" as he had that afternoon at his office when she told him she was going to Nürnberg with Rob. "I thought you wouldn't date GIs," Major Collins had said, leaning on a file cabinet.

"Sometimes things just happen," she'd said, echoing his explanation to her of why he had cheated on her mother.

Now they were on their way to the Tiefes Loch, a punk club in Nürnberg's warehouse district, an hour west of Grafenwoehr. She was with Rob because a couple of weeks earlier he had made her a fake ID card and because he told her he had a car. But he didn't have a car. The Humvee belonged to the Army, and Lucinda was afraid to ask how he got it from the motor pool. The same way he made her an

ID card that said she was eighteen—illegally. She'd had her reservations about Rob from the beginning, but he seemed no more than an overeager dork with access to things she needed. She might have canceled but for her father's teasing, and now she felt like she was on a real live date. It wasn't a good feeling. As soon as they reached the autobahn, Rob had held out a handful of gummi bears and told her she could have all the red ones, apparently a romantic gesture. Then he called Abraham Lincoln the biggest thug in American history, and although a GI in the U.S. Army, he had referred several times to "the Yankee guvment" and challenged its legitimacy.

Lucinda tried to untangle what he was saying. She couldn't understand how Rob could think Nazism had anything to do with punk rock.

"What about freedom?" she asked.

"I'm all about freedom." He lifted his shirt, rounding his bulldoglike torso about the steering wheel to show her the word *freedom* stenciled between his shoulder blades. "Freedom to kick some ass!" He laughed and Lucinda cleaved to the passenger-side door. Outside, darkness was falling and she couldn't see the forest or the trees anymore, just the autobahn blacktop unrolling ahead of them and the taillights of cars swimming by and passing in front of the Humvee. Rob took offense at each car that passed. "If I had my El Camino, I'd show these krauts a thing or two," he said. He broke into song, "Flirtin' with Disaster."

"Molly Hatchet, huh? Not very punk, Private Dalton."

"Don't call me that name. That's my slave name."

"Your slave name." She looked at the Confederate flag on his right forearm. "What should I call you?"

"Toxic." He grinned at her. "I am Toxic."

When she'd met Toxic he was Private Dalton and she was wearing a Hüsker Dü T-shirt. The shirt instantly meant a lot to him—*Land Speed Record*—and he interpreted her presence on the slick padded swivel stool, where he would shoot her ID picture, as the message he had been waiting for. "What are the odds?" he kept saying. "What are the odds on that?" Lucinda's black-and-white T-shirt showed the album cover—a World War II photograph of six military caskets draped with American flags in an airplane cargo hold. Soldiers going home. Her dad had assured her that the shirt would land her in trouble, so Toxic's strong reaction to it hadn't surprised her as much as maybe it should have. She took his instant interest as a sign of esprit de corps among underground music fans. Besides, she could see that he was lonely. He wanted friends and offered to take her, anytime she wanted to go with him, to shows at the Tiefes Loch, where all the good bands played in Bavaria. Nately had gone there a lot, so Lucinda was dying to see the place firsthand.

Toxic said he went every weekend, but it was becoming clear now, as they headed into the city, that he had never been to the club. "Keep your eyes peeled for Maxplatz," he said, concentrating on the city's narrow streets. Nürnberg at night looked like a fairy tale, the medieval city walls and old churches lit up while the modern buildings faded to shadows. She traveled there to the American hospital every few months to have an EEG for her epilepsy, but never at night.

When they found the old brick warehouse, no one asked for her ID. Only for hard liquor, the doorman told her. Of course she knew beer drinking was legal now that she was sixteen, but she hadn't known she could get into a nightclub.

Sixteen. Her birthday had come the week after her mother, Erin, and Jacob left for the States. Her father had been on maneuvers, so she'd taken the fifty bucks he had given her for her birthday down to the record store and the liquor store and had thrown an impromptu party. Half a dozen people showed, including Tina, and they all sat around listening to "Alabama Song" on the Doors's first album and drinking the first beer Lucinda had ever bought. The more she drank, the more she said, "Stars fell!" whenever Jim Morrison sang, "Oh moon of Alabama." No one had asked what she meant. It was an old drinking song, after all, one that Bertolt Brecht wrote, a German who had been as anti-Nazi as they get.

Unlike Toxic. When she told him that the fake ID hadn't been necessary, he wasn't ready for her to forget her debt to him. "Took balls for me to make those IDs," he said, cupping his crotch. "Nobody thinks they can fuck with the Yankee guvment, but the system's decayed. I can do whatever the fuck I want."

"But maybe I should throw it away," she said. "You could get in real trouble for making it."

"They won't do shit—slap my wrist—that's all."

Low brick ceilings with arched doorways made the Tiefes Loch feel like a war bunker, and even the long room with the stage in front felt cramped—a slam dancer thrown too high into the air could have easily hit the ceiling, which was hard to see despite its closeness, obscured as it was by all the cigarette smoke. The band onstage was an American hardcore group. Stripped down and visceral, they were thrashing through a set as Lucinda and Toxic pushed through the crowd. The Sub Plots from Redondo Beach, California. They brought a whiff of home, and it was much different from the German punk scene, which was theatrically dour. She watched the band members lean into their set as if the music was a writhing animal they were killing on the floor of the stage, plaid shirts tied around their waists, barechested, short hair. The German punks looked overdressed in comparison, a sea of black and purple, Lycra, leather, fishnets and black lipstick, black eyeliner. Sartorially, Lucinda fit right in with the Germans, but she felt a rush of identification with the Sub Plots. *American—that's me.*

Soon she would be back in the States with her mother, Erin, and Jacob and she was nervous about it. She felt distant from the ahistorical mall life she saw in the movies, and she dreaded having to get used to a new life with divorced parents at the same time as she got used to America. But the Sub Plots were getting her excited about going back. Harddriving and straightforward, they made her jump, made her sweat, made her lose herself in the rhythmic rise and fall of the crowd. Toxic stuck close at first, a protective arm at her waist. She pushed him away again and again. The best way to get through the night was not to think about poor, confused Toxic. Curiosity got the better of her, though, and she shouted in his ear, "Who was Hitler?"

He looked down at her as if this was a very good question. "The guy with the mustache." He moved toward her. She moved away from him through the crowd, pressing toward the front. The strobe lights cut holes through her brain, through her mind, and for a moment she was afraid she was heading into a seizure—the first in months. She remembered the last one she'd had, coming out of it to find herself sprawled across the kitchen floor with her sister sitting next to her, back against the refrigerator, reading a magazine. She had looked up and said, "I didn't know what to do," when Lucinda opened her eyes.

"Hey," Toxic said, his blunt face taking on angles in the light of the strobes, "I've seen your old man."

She blinked at him. "Yeah?"

"You got some issues with him, don't you?"

She closed her eyes. The strobes were doling out too much information to this little man. "What makes you say that?"

"I don't much like him, either," said Toxic. "Major Collins. He's one of them motherfucking sheep who thinks he's a wolf."

"True enough," Lucinda said. And it was, but something in her objected to the pronouncement coming from Toxic. As they rocked with the movement of the crowd pressed around them, she slammed into a moment of clarity, a post-seizure feeling, a calm in the mind that sometimes followed the cataclysm. How odd to feel it now, without having to go through the seizure first. A freebie. In the clearing suddenly open before her, she saw her father, diffident since the divorce proceedings began, and she felt all her frustrations with him overtaken by a strange, almost giddy rush of gratitude. Compared to Toxic's incoherent cultural compost, her dad's attitudes seemed cozy, his self-absorption the devil that she knew. The devil that she didn't know smelled like gummi bears and was a thousand times scarier, his allegiances too contradictory for her to predict what he meant or what he'd do. Still, relating more to her father than to this little creep wasn't exactly solidarity with the patriarch. It was a question of degree.

"At least he's not a little Nazi," Lucinda said.

"A what?" asked Toxic, moving closer.

Lucinda craned her head to see the band.

Toxic nodded at her. "Guess I'll take him down a peg or two."

"What? How?"

"I got you, don't I?"

The music was beyond loud and she wasn't sure if she had heard him correctly. He wasn't looking at her, but was straining to see the band above the heads of the crowd. They were at the back of the room, but the centrifugal force of the mosh pit still threatened to suck them in. "My dad doesn't care what I do," she shouted, hoping to defuse any plan he may have to use her—to what end she couldn't imagine and was afraid to try. "He doesn't care about me."

But it looked like Toxic had already forgotten her, having tossed himself into the middle of the mosh pit. Lucinda watched as he was sucked under like a ship in a hurricane, reappearing every few seconds as the waves of bodies parted. She worked to push her way to the front of the stage. The slam dancers in the pit were all guys and the women in the club were lining the walls, out of the fray. She was no fanatic, but she had come to see the show and she was going to see it. Making it to the front by skirting the mosh pit, she planted her hands on the stage, which was elevated to the height of her rib cage. She had the bass player's legs planted on either side of her hands, and when she looked up she saw right up his shorts, everything, the whole package. The force of the crowd surged, pushing at her again and again, the weight of a hundred people grinding her ribs against the edge of the stage. She felt like her spine was touching her sternum, every centimeter of breath squeezed from her body, and it became clear why none of the other women were up front. Panic flooded her; she imagined dying there and wondered if her father would grieve, if her mother would come back to Germany to get her body, where on the planet they would bury her. She could see herself lying on the club's dirty floor after being fatally trampled, gasping out her last breaths as someone asked her where her remains should be put, and saying the same thing that ex-slave jockey who died at Shiloh said: "Right here." Because it was as good a place as any. Because she belonged here as much as anywhere.

In the nanosecond between songs the bass player reached down and pulled her out of the pit, pushing her to the side of the stage with a hand on the small of her back. "Get out of here," he said. She stood onstage for a few seconds getting her balance, shielding her eyes against the spotlights, then she ducked backstage, finding herself in a ten-foot margin between the stage and the wall, behind a black curtain and in front of an open cooler full of beers. Every breath she took ached. She lifted her shirt, felt her ribs, but couldn't tell if anything was broken. Helping herself to a beer, she peeked out of the curtain and watched the show.

After a few minutes the lead singer started yelling at the crowd, telling them to calm down. There was a fight in the pit—not its usual swirling violence, but a fight that killed the rhythm and brought the moshing to a stop around a small group. Then she heard Toxic yelling, *"Sieg Heil! Sieg Heil!"* The crowd responded with a low rumble and a rip and she saw Toxic lifted high into the air. The crowd spewed him out like flesh pushing out a splinter, and he was carried across the top of the crowd into the waiting arms of two security guards. Toxic hollered the whole time.

The bouncers had him by the shoulders, holding him down against the side of the stage where Lucinda stood. *"You* are a Nazi?" one of them asked in English. Large and long-haired, he looked like he should be wearing skins. Toxic's small eyes darted over the man's face, trying to divine the right answer, as if the man might clasp him to his bosom if he said yes. Lucinda had a bird's-eye view of the conversation, watching from above, from behind the curtain. Toxic looked small and pitiable, and she realized, as she watched him search for the right answer, that he was more ignorant even than she had thought. She could have told him that most punks weren't Nazis. Or more importantly, that most Germans were not amused by any reminder of this part of their past. They were sensitive about it. Lucinda remembered a few years earlier at Halloween when her little brother had come out of the bathroom, ready to walk in a parade through old town Grafenwöhr done up like Hitler. Faye had stopped him. "It's not a joke," she said, holding his jaw firmly in one hand and wiping the penciled-in mustache from his upper lip. "We're two hours from Dachau. You want to get beat up?" Here in Nürnberg, where the Nazi party officials were famously tried, the same question echoed through Lucinda's head.

Toxic answered wrong. "Hell yeah," he said. "Fuckin' A."

The band was just finishing another song and the lead singer, a wiry blond with long surfer bangs, came over in time to catch the guard's and Toxic's exchange. "You're American?" he said.

Before Toxic answered, the lead singer shouted something at the band, then swung back to the mike and said, "Just so there's no confusion about how we feel about this fascist bullshit in the States, we wanna do this next song for our American friend here. The Dead Kennedys said it best." They launched into "Nazi Punks Fuck Off!" and the mosh pit convulsed like a giant mouth. Lucinda watched as Toxic stood still between the bouncers, bemused, glancing at the Dead Kennedys tattoo on his left forearm like it had betrayed him. The lead singer ran across the stage and stood above Toxic, pointing at him when he got to the lyric "In a real Fourth Reich, you'll be the first to go!"

The crowd echoed the line—"first to go, first to go"—directing fists, spit, beer, and lit cigarettes at Toxic. He looked at the floor, letting the top of his head take the brunt of the barrage. He was at the edge of the mosh pit and then, like that, he was in it. Lucinda couldn't tell if he jumped in or was pulled, but suddenly he wasn't there anymore. She came out from behind the stage and stood over the edge searching, but the room was full of shadows and the pit was circling fast.

SEVENTEEN

Shouldering through the bar, looking for Toxic, Lucinda was dreading the ride home. A neo-Nazi. It was sickening. A lot of people behaved as if death was just an idea.

She looked around. So many tortured hairdos against the black palette of the clothing. Every system had its uniform, and here was the punk uniform all around her, as regimented as a roomful of GIs in battle-dress uniform, and proof that what may have started as pure emotion had hardened into just another codified set of rules for representing abstractions.

The music was real, though. She imagined Nately smiling over the noise, his Adam's apple sticking out above the crowd, his fuzz of red hair bleached in the spotlights. Lucinda saw him smiling as he listened to the music and found something at its center, something outside language, tumbling into violence, as the song went off the rails and the lead singer of the Sub Plots screamed like a dying bird. The white-hot center—Nately was there. From the outskirts of the crowd, Lucinda swam toward it, and the purple-and-black crowd faded out of her consciousness for as long as the band played. She gave herself over to the music, her body lifting off the floor, rising and falling with the motion of the tightly packed crowd. But then she saw Toxic. Off to her right, the men's restroom door swung open and she caught sight of rows of men urinating with their backs to her, framed by the club's surrounding darkness. By the sinks she saw Toxic's face, pale between the shoulders of men who surrounded him, all in motion. She saw one punch connect before the door swung shut.

She sprang forward, shouting, *"Entschuldigung, entschuldigung,* excuse me," into people's ears as she tried to get through the crowd. Toxic was an asshole, but what was she if she stood by, hiding in the crowd, and let him be beaten up? "Goddammit," she said, pulling clear of the crowd.

As she crossed the bar, a hand grabbed her arm. She turned and looked up into the angular face of a guy wearing black cross earrings, a wedge of shiny black hair falling over one eye. His gap-toothed smile was ecstatic, intimate, and familiar as he pulled her out of the line of traffic to the edge of the bar. "I can't believe it," he said. "I saw you onstage a few minutes ago. It's really you."

His smile. She saw it through glass, through a car window. She remembered ignoring him with all her might for two months because she didn't want to hurt when he left, and then, when he was gone, hurting anyway. God, the Army was a small world. "Syd?"

He laughed and hugged her. "Lucinda!"

"What are you doing here?" she yelled above the noise of the band.

"We're back, what can I say? Cycled back around to Nürnberg."

He had grown; his voice had deepened. The silky black hair was cut asymmetrically and he had facial hair, muscles, earrings. She stared at his new face under the flashing club lights while time inside her caught up with real time. "How long have you been here?"

"A couple months."

"Oh. And you didn't even try—?" Lucinda worked to keep the disappointment out of her voice. She had no right, after all, after how she had treated him.

"Hey, now. I thought you were long gone. Three years— that's a long time for you to still be here."

"It's the longest I've ever lived anyplace," she said. She had been taken so off guard by Syd that she forgot her mission to save Toxic, but it came to her as she glanced over and saw him stumble out of the door of the men's toilet. He was in bad shape. He saw Lucinda and staggered toward her.

"Let's go," he said. Blood was running down his face and one eye was swollen shut.

"Are you okay?" Lucinda said.

"What? I'm good."

"This is an old friend," she said, indicating Syd. Lucinda could imagine Toxic in another mood giving her and Syd a hard time, but he barely glanced at Syd before stumbling off toward the bar.

"Say it isn't so," Syd said, shaking his head. "Tell me you're not with him."

"He's not my date. Just my ride."

"You leave me standing in a parking lot like a little chump but you let that freak show drive you off base, all the way to Nürnberg." He shook his head, smiling at her.

Lucinda felt her face burning with embarrassment. "Come on, I just wanted to see this place. I've heard so much about it."

Syd placed his hand over his heart. "You killed me, you know. You tell your dad you love me after we've known each other for an hour and then you dump me cold, cold as anything. Your dad told me to keep trying, but when I leave, do you write? No! Even after you let me kiss you!"

"Let you? You grabbed me."

He looked surprised. "That's not what I remember."

"Look, I didn't have your address."

"I left it for you in my room—your room—in the a/c vent."

She looked to the ceiling, for some version of events she recognized among the track lighting. "Like I'd find that!"

"It was sticking out. I folded it like a little tent." He made a pulling gesture with his fingers.

Toxic slumped across the bar, ordering a drink. Syd looked him over with distaste. "My dad's always griping about the volunteer Army," he said. "Looking at that piece of work I can see why."

"He made me a fake ID."

"Really? He knows how to laminate?"

"Come on."

"Seriously, would you hand that guy a loaded gun?"

"I guess he is a low-water mark," she said. "My dad gets on his high horse, too, about the new Army, but I don't buy it. He's just trying to feel better about staying in after Vietnam."

"Mine, too, really."

"Our dads should relax," she said.

"They should be darn proud."

"At least they've shown their kids the world."

"Well, Germany, at least," he replied.

"Saudi. And North Carolina."

"And certain shabbier parts of Texas. That's a world all by itself."

"A little Oklahoma, a little California." Lucinda laughed, and so did Syd.

"Syd, Syd, Syd," she said. If she had just met him for the first time that night, she'd have thought he was gorgeous and been a little intimidated by his supreme self-confidence. But she had a place in his memories. She had even hurt him, a little, maybe. They had history.

"I'm leaving in less than a week."

"Oh, Christ. You're kidding?" He smacked his forehead. "Fuck. Fuck! Where?"

"Fort Sill."

"Dammit. My dad's not field artillery—we'll never go there. What about college?"

"I have no idea."

"I see myself at Cal State."

"Cal State. Not Crimson Tide?"

He pulled on one of his earrings, looking lost in thought. "We've been living at Fort Irwin for the last two years. I like California. A week, huh?"

"Three days."

"We could hang out tonight. I could give you a ride home just as well as Doctor Love over there."

She considered this. Sydney Greenstreet Eliot. She remembered sitting thigh to thigh in the passenger seat of her dad's Opel. Now they wouldn't both fit. "My dad will freak out if I'm not there in the morning." She glanced at Toxic, who was taking a pull on his beer. "You have a car, huh?"

"An old Beemer. We're living on the economy next door to this cool German guy who rebuilds old cars."

"Could it make it to Graf?"

He leaned down and gave her a swift kiss. "In a flash."

They made a plan for him to come the following night. "And you know where I live," Lucinda said.

"That's right." He laughed. "I guess I do."

EIGHTEEN

Cars flashed by as Lucinda held the Humvee to its lane and tried to keep it going above sixty miles per hour instead of half that speed, where she felt in control of the vehicle. She had never driven on the autobahn before, never really driven anywhere but the dirt roads of the training area between Grafenwoehr and Vilseck. She had learned to drive a stick there, the deep ruts made by M-1 tanks keeping her in their path like a train on a track. She had no license. In the passenger seat, Toxic passed in and out of consciousness. He was a bloody mess, nose broken, one eye swollen shut, ears bleeding. It looked like someone had tried to cut the swastika tattoo off his chest—flesh was opened and bleeding from a line cut horizontally across the symbol.

When the band finished and Syd had gone, she found Toxic at the bar knocking back a row of shots and pouring one over his open wound, pounding the bar and gritting his teeth as the alcohol hit his flesh. When he saw her next to him, he asked if she had liked the show.

"Great band," she said.

"They sucked." He made no reference to his fight and seemed to hope she hadn't seen anything.

She took her eyes away from the road long enough to look at his face lolling against the headrest in a streak of light from the headlights in the other lane.

"Hey," he said.

"Yeah?"

"You think you're smarter than me?"

Lucinda watched the road. She was determined not to engage him, not to fight. He looked docile now, but she had seen him yelling, flailing, fighting, and she didn't want to see it again.

"I know a lot of things about a lot of things," he said.

If she looked at his wounds, she felt sorry for him, but she didn't want to feel sorry for him. He hadn't crumpled and apologized the way she thought he would when he found out nobody else in the club was a Nazi. She would rather have thought he was amoral and clueless, trying on Nazism like boots—but whatever it was he thought he stood for, he was sticking to it.

"You know," she said, "most of the Germans who fought in World War Two weren't that into Hitler. They were just soldiers who thought they were being patriotic."

He looked at her hard. "You know that for a fact, do you?"

"I saw one once. He was just about your age."

"My age? Like hell. They're all old now. Shit, the war ended in . . ." Out of the corner of her eye she saw him scrunch up his face in concentration. It didn't help.

"Shit," he said after a while, "they must all be in their forties, at least."

"Forget it."

But Toxic clearly thought he had hold of something that was going to win him back some of the swagger beaten out of him in the bar. "Whoo-whoo," he said, "Little Miss Smarty Britches. This so-called Nazi was feeding you a line of shit, and you just ate it up. Haw haw."

Lucinda felt blood rising to her face. This little prick was getting her angry. "The war ended in 1945," she said. "Now, how long ago was that?"

"I'm saying you never met a twenty-two-year-old Nazi." His voice had taken on a coldness that she hadn't heard before. Her anger vanished like smoke in a high wind.

"You're right," she said. "I've never met a twenty-two-year-old Nazi."

Toxic leaned his battered face close to hers. "So tell me, Little Miss Smarty Britches, were you just fucking lying to me about that Nazi, or what?"

Oh, shit. She was worried now in a way she hadn't been before. How to calm him? She thought for a moment, decided the truth might work, like the way she'd heard music sometimes works to placate a dangerous animal.

"He was a ghost."

Toxic squinted at her with his one good eye. "A ghost?"

"I say *was*, but he might still be there, for all I know.

Probably is. In the grade school on post—it used to be a Nazi hospital."

Toxic was silent for a moment, and Lucinda held her breath, wondering what his take on the afterlife would be.

"A hospital? That's nasty," he said.

"The nastiest thing is that the old morgue is a classroom. That's where the ghost is. I used to see him there, standing in that room looking out a window, but the window's bricked in. There is no window."

To Lucinda's great relief, Toxic moved away from her, sat up straight in his seat. The truth seemed to be working.

"Maybe he's a crazy guy," Toxic said.

"No, no. He's a ghost. Nobody but me—and my brother—can see him. My dad tried, but he couldn't see it."

"A ghost?" Toxic whistled. "You're just trying to trip me out." But the scales had fallen off his voice.

"I guess I wouldn't believe me, either. I don't go around telling that story, but all this Nazi business tonight reminded me." The ghost story represented her only other moment of sympathy with a Nazi. She hoped she had found some common ground, enough to get home on.

Toxic, it turned out, was cool with ghosts. "You think he's still there?"

"I'm pretty sure. He's been there every time I looked."

"Why you think he's haunting the place? No rest for the wicked?"

"Maybe—but then, why aren't there millions of ghosts?"

"He wants something."

"I wouldn't expect you to believe in ghosts."

"I believe in everything," he said in an exhausted voice, as if the effort of so much believing had cost him.

She looked again at the tattoos running the length of his arms. "That's right, you do, don't you?"

They got back to the base about four o'clock in the morning. She parked the Humvee near the motor pool, in an empty parking lot, and woke up Toxic. She wasn't sure how he got the vehicle, probably out the back gate, but she planned to let him put it back without her assistance. Her apartment was just a ten-minute walk and she thought she could slip in without waking her dad if she got there soon.

Toxic startled awake. "We here?" he asked, looking around. In one sweeping motion, he grabbed her, coming forward and pinning her against the driver's seat. He was incredibly strong, and Lucinda couldn't move him at all, his stocky torso pressed against her like a wall, while he grabbed at the buttons of her jeans. But the pants didn't yield easily, the denim too tough to rend. "Cut it out," she yelled, and his efforts got more frantic. "You idiot! Get off me!" She was fighting with all her strength, the low-grade fear she had felt all night in his presence ramping up into a rage with adrenaline behind it, something with force. The booze and hot candy stench of his breath filled her nostrils. His expression was vacant, as if he were still asleep, but his body was wide-awake, struggling to hold her. She couldn't quite believe he was serious, although each second removed her doubts as she confronted his superior strength.

While he wrestled with her jeans, she worked her left leg up and hit the horn on the steering wheel, pressing it as hard as she could. The sound of the horn shattered the air, and Toxic froze. "Dammit!" he said, pulling away from her. He looked surprised and betrayed. As soon as he lifted off her she pushed the door lever and slid out the driver's side like spilling liquid. On the pavement, she picked herself up and ran without looking back. She heard him behind her, yelling that he was sorry, that he'd make it up to her.

NINETEEN

It was still early—not yet six—when the phone rang in the living room. From under the covers, her clothes still reeking of booze and cigarettes, she heard her father walk down the hall in his bare feet and pick up the receiver. She had never heard the phone ring this early. It must be her brother or sister calling from Oklahoma. Maybe it was her mother, although Lucinda doubted it. Faye was observing a sort of scorched-earth policy regarding the end of her marriage. Lucinda's part in bringing her home from Paris somehow made things hard between mother and daughter. Faye had thanked Lucinda for telling her the truth, but she was sad and distant and had encouraged Lucinda to stay in Grafenwoehr with her dad until he transferred to Fort Sill in the fall.

That morning she wished for her mother's calm bedside manner, the way her normally nervous energy smoothed out when something heavy was going down—she could be great in a crisis when she saw a way to help. If her mother were there, Lucinda probably wouldn't tell her what Toxic had done, but it would have helped seeing her face.

She listened to her father's voice, thinking she would get up and talk on the phone, too. But she could hear that it wasn't family. His voice had the hard, impersonal edge it got when he was talking to someone he worked with. There was some sort of crisis.

Before her father was off the phone, another sound rumbled through the apartment. Lucinda watched the long, jagged crack in her ceiling, caused by the constant vibrations of artillery fire, begin to shake and slide. Bits of plaster drifted down onto the bedsheets. That sound—she had heard it all her life, but never this close to her bedroom. It was a tank. Lucinda threw off her blankets and ran to the living-room window. Sure enough, an M-1 was rolling down the street in front of their apartment building. It cut right as she watched, rolling over a curb and crushing a yield sign as it made its way across the soccer field.

"What's going on?" Lucinda asked.

"Some kid," her father said. "They don't know who it is yet. Probably drunk or messed up on drugs. I gotta get down there."

Lucinda watched the long cannon of the tank swing from side to side like a roving eye searching for something. "What will they do to him?" The tank flattened a soccer goal and kept straight on toward the far side of the field. A quarter mile away stood the elementary school, the old Nazi hospital.

Her father paused. "If he doesn't hurt anyone he may make it out alive."

"Alive?" Lucinda said. It was Toxic. She knew it. It was Toxic, come to get her ghost. She remembered his cries of remorse as she ran from the Humvee earlier that morning. His promise to make it up to her. She still felt his body pressed against her, smelled his gummi bear breath, and she wasn't sure what she felt. She had lain awake since sneaking back into the house, seething, waiting for her father to get up and leave so she could shower the filth of Toxic, of the whole night, from her skin. She even stood outside her father's bedroom door for some long minutes after she got home, working up the nerve to knock and tell him what had happened. But the longer she stood there, the more unsure she was of her father's response. Besides, she had handled the situation herself. Fought Toxic off, gotten away. She didn't need further assistance, especially not from her dad. Now the idea that Toxic may be in grave trouble struck her oddly.

Her father pulled his eyes from the window and scanned her up and down, arms crossed over his chest. "Why are you dressed like that?"

"Woke up early," she said, placing a hand self-consciously over the pearl buttons of her sheer black blouse. "This is new."

He turned back to the window. "That equipment costs more than that boy will make his entire working life," he said. "It's worth more than he is." He disappeared into his room and two minutes later came out dressed in fatigues.

She watched him leave, then took off for the school on foot a few minutes behind him.

It took her less than ten minutes to get there. MP cars had formed a semicircle behind the tank, which was crashing slowly through an outer wall of the school building, empty for summer. Lucinda watched as the ornamental swastika high on the wall, mortared in after the war, reappeared, its mortar shaken loose a few seconds before the wall itself crumbled. The MP lights flashed in the gray morning light, synchronized with the rise and fall of the car sirens like the light show at the concert the night before. Her father and a knot of other personnel stood behind the police line watching the tank while MPs in black helmets lined up like a firing squad, M-16s pointed at the tank. The tank had knocked out the walls on the east end of the building, leaving classrooms open like rooms in a dollhouse. Small desks crumpled under the tank, which was quickly decorated with swirling papers. The rear wall was next, and the tank breached it in one giant push, rolling through the hole it created, which Lucinda noticed was at the bricked-in window where her ghost had stood when she saw him years ago. The long cannon swung from side to side, clearing the space before it. Then the tank stopped, its engine switched off. Toxic had accomplished his mission. Lucinda's ghost should finally be at rest. The police sirens still blared, but without the rough noise of the tank, silence filtered through the rhythmic wails like water rising around a sinking vessel.

Nothing happened. The tank sat still. It made her think of a toad in a shoe box, trying to camouflage itself in the wrong environment, the M-1's olive-drab body framed by the white plaster and concrete of the building it had just destroyed. She heard her name being called and thought for a moment that it was Toxic calling her somehow from within the tank, but then she saw her father watching her. He left his group and strode over angrily.

"What are you doing here?"

She shrugged. "Best show in town this morning."

"How did you know where to come?"

"Like it's hard to follow a runaway tank." She looked up at him and saw that he was only half listening to her. Suddenly she wanted to break through the distance between them worse than anything in the world. She wanted to tell him about Private Rob Dalton, his idiot nickname and his idiot tattoos; she wanted the joke to be funny and the night to have stopped before Toxic laid hands on her.

"Whoever this is," her father said, "he could come out shooting. Get the hell out of here, Lucinda."

"Did you notice what he wrecked?" she asked. "Remember, Dad?"

"Remember what?"

"The ghost? I got you to try to see it once, remember?"

He put his hands on his hips and looked at the rubble for a minute. "I remember," he said. "You think I don't notice anything," he said, shooting her a look. "But I do."

"Me, too," she said. "I'm a noticer."

"Yeah, so I learned." She wondered what he meant by that, but she didn't ask. Could it be he knew that she had discovered his affair with Leanne Murdoch and had called her mother home from Paris? Were they enemies? His behavior toward her hadn't changed at all since the marriage broke up—Lucinda thought maybe he did know about the part she had played and understood. Maybe he felt like he deserved it, but she wasn't sure. Or his mildness could have been simple indifference.

Then his gaze locked in on her, suspicion dawning. "You don't have anything to do with this mess, do you?"

"No!" she said, hands up in a gesture of innocence. "How could I?"

Her father raised his chin, peering over her head at the tank. "I wonder what the hell he thinks he's doing?"

The top hatch of the tank opened a crack and Toxic's black wife-beater T-shirt flew out like a drunken crow, caught on the jagged remnant of a wall, and flapped in the morning breeze. They heard the voice of an MP speaking through a megaphone to assure him that he was safe. Then the hatch opened all the way and Toxic emerged, naked to his waist, with his hands high above his head. From where Lucinda was standing, the tattoos that covered his arms and chest formed an indistinct pattern.

"What the hell?" her father said. "Looks like that GI lost a fight with a Magic Marker."

"I'm sure he thinks it means something."

"But it doesn't," her dad said. "Stand for something or fall for anything, right? That's a boy who falls for anything. You may be sure of it, my dear."

Lucinda was sure of it, and hated that her father was right. She looked at the space where her ghost had stood. It was all wide open now, the playground behind the school showing through, with the first rays of morning sun glinting off the chains of the swing set.

TWENTY

"I don't know how you got that poor dickhead to steal a tank, but you damned sure did." Her father sat on the floor of their apartment rolling packing tape over a box of knickknacks.

It was a strange sight—her father packing. For most moves, he had gone ahead of them with nothing but a suitcase of his own clothes, while her mother had packed the house they were leaving, and unpacked in the new one.

"I keep telling you, I had no idea he was going to steal a tank. This isn't my fault." Lucinda sat next to him, stuffing packing material around the mantel clock, an heirloom from Shiloh. It was a simple and not very attractive timepiece, with dozens of pin-size wormholes across the face, but they had carried it all over the world. Their ancestors had been lugging it around for a long time—a hundred years before Shiloh, someone had supposedly carried it from

Scotland, across the Atlantic to the United States. Now it would again make the crossing.

"He said your name."

"I can't help that, Dad. I went to a concert with him, that's all."

"Sure is funny that he tore down that old school."

"Maybe he's anti-education."

"Huh," her father said. "I'll say, but that's not why he did it."

"Why does anybody do anything?"

He cut the tape, took a black permanent marker, and wrote FAYE'S LIVING ROOM CRAP across the top. "Why do fools fall in love? That's the question of the day."

"Oh no. It is not. You don't get to talk about that with me, Dad."

"And you, my dear, need a job. As soon as we get back to the States, I want you employed. I think you have too much time on your hands to sit around judging your old man."

"Not that I care, but what will they do to Private Dalton?"

"Court-martial him. He'll probably do some time at Leavenworth, then a dishonorable discharge."

The doorbell rang and Lucinda leaped to her feet. Her father beat her to the door. "Yes?" he said.

"Hello, Major Collins! Remember me?"

"Dad, it's Syd," Lucinda said, sliding under his arm to stand in the doorway.

"Syd?" Her father's face was blank.

"I used to live here," Syd said, grinning. "*Right* here." He had taken out his earrings and was wearing khaki shorts and a plain black T-shirt. His hair fell over one eye and he flipped it away every few seconds. "Major Eliot's son."

"Oh." Her father looked him up and down. "Crimson Tide?"

"That's me."

Major Collins cracked a smile. "You've grown. What are you doing here?"

Lucinda explained that Syd was stationed at Nürnberg and invited him in, apologizing for the absence of furniture. "We're moving," she said, as if she had not already told him.

Syd strolled into the living room and stopped with his hands in his pockets. "Wow, this is it, all right." He stepped into the kitchen, where he opened the refrigerator door like it was his own. "Grab me a beer, Syd," her father said. He was sitting on the floor in the living room, unfolding a new box and punching it into shape. "Get one for yourself, if you want."

Lucinda narrowed her eyes at him. "He's my age."

"He's a guy," her father said.

"Excuse me, but what the hell?"

Her father sighed. "Have one, then. I guess you're legal over here. Just remember that all that changes in the U.S."

Syd brought out three bottles. He scanned the kitchen, opening a small drawer from which he pulled a bottle opener. "That's where we kept ours, too," he said.

Major Collins accepted the beer Syd extended. "I remember you now. You two were in love, isn't that right?" He looked from Lucinda to Syd.

Sitting against the wall where the TV used to be, Lucinda gave a breathless laugh. "We were thirteen," she said.

"We were, though," Syd said. "In love." He slid down the wall next to her, grinning. It looked like he was having a great time.

Eventually the talk turned to the events of that morning. "You know anything about this tank fiasco, Syd?"

"I heard about the runaway tank," he said. "That was all over the news this morning."

"Yeah, well, Lucinda was with the guy who did it. I'm just trying to figure out what part she played, which is why she can't go anywhere tonight, Syd. If that's what you two had planned."

"She knew the guy?" Syd pursed his lips. "Lucinda, you know that guy?"

She rested a hand on Syd's arm. "The neo-Nazi," she whispered.

"Private Dalton is a neo-Nazi?"

"That guy?" Syd laughed. "Oh, man—did I call it, or did I call it? I told her, sir. You could see that guy was bad news from across a room."

Lucinda put her head between her knees.

"Sit up, Lucinda. You better tell me about this neo-Nazi business."

From between her knees, she said, "Nothing, Dad, it's nothing."

"He got his butt kicked at the club last night for saying 'Sieg Heil.'"

Her father cleared his throat. "Club? What club?"

Syd covered his mistake immediately. "The DYA, sir. I guess it's a reach to call the Dependents Youth hangout a club, but we like to pretend it is. It's got a pool table, and we're all real proud of that."

Lucinda looked up. Her father was giving Syd a look of such paternal satisfaction she wanted to throw up. He had actually bought it.

Syd continued: "He has a swastika tattooed on his arm. He was crazy, sir. I wanted Lucinda to let me drive her home, but she felt sorry for the guy, I guess."

Her father held up a hand. "Wait, wait, wait. A swastika tattoo? Where?"

Lucinda and Syd both held out their arms and pointed.

"Kids, there's no way the Army would let him get by with that. Not a swastika. It must have been a fake."

"A fake?" Lucinda said.

"A temporary. Drawn on. You know," he said, holding up the Magic Marker he'd been using to mark the boxes.

"Oh, man." Syd shook his head. "Think of all the ways that's pathetic."

"That kid is history," her father said. He turned to Syd. "So how's your old man?"

"He's okay. Thinks the USSR is on its last legs. Thinks we'll have McDonald's in Prague before long."

"Not in my lifetime," Major Collins said. "Although I'd love to see it happen." He pressed his hands into his thighs and stood, stretching his back from side to side. "Kids, I'm turning in. Gonna watch the tube. Single life's not all it's cracked up to be."

Syd stood and shook her father's hand. "Great seeing you again, sir."

"You," he said, pointing his beer at Lucinda, "are not going anywhere. However, you"—he pointed at Syd—"are welcome to stay awhile."

Lucinda watched her father's back disappear down the hall.

They stood up and started toward her bedroom, the mother-in-law room on the opposite end of the house from the other bedrooms. "So—alcohol?" she said.

He nodded, gone quiet. They rummaged in the kitchen for more beer and grabbed two bottles from the fridge, which Syd held on to while Lucinda untaped a box on the counter marked BOOZE in her father's upright lettering. She pulled out an opaque white bottle. "Here's coconut, do you like coconut?"

Syd made a face. "I think you're supposed to mix that with something."

"But they never use this," she said. "They won't notice if I take it." Lucinda grabbed the bottle and they returned with their stash to her room, where they spent the next few hours stretched out on top of her sleeping bag, drinking, talking, listening to music, like people floating down a lazy river who know a waterfall is up ahead and are slowly bracing themselves for the rush.

He talked about his years in the States, warned her about the vicious provincialism of townies in the high schools. "They'll have gone to school together since kindergarten," he said. "You're, like, outside their little bubble. They'll figure they have a free pass to run you and shun you since their parents don't know your parents."

"Sounds like the voice of experience."

"Let's just say I'm glad to be back in the ol' D-of-D school system. Here I'm not an outsider."

The summer sun finally set and the room changed to shadow. She wanted to light a candle but couldn't find one, so they sat in the moonlight coming through the window.

Syd knocked back a swig of the coconut liqueur, made a face, and said, "So, are you ready to apologize?"

She laughed. "What for?"

Syd flipped on the light and stepped over to the air conditioner vent by the east wall. It had been behind her dresser all these years, but now it was easy to reach. He wriggled the vent cover from side to side until it lifted out, then he reached in and came up with a tented piece of lined notebook paper. He held it up. "For this."

"Are you kidding me?" She took the paper and unfolded it, glancing up at him. "I can't believe this."

The note said, "I know you still love me, Godzilla. Don't lie. Write me. Love, Tokyo."

He sat down and put his arm around her waist, reading the note over her shoulder. "What a romantic kid I was."

Lucinda laughed. "But wait—how does Tokyo feel about Godzilla?"

"Oh, well. I thought it was obvious. Wasn't it?"

"I don't know. There's also the fact that you never wrote me."

"So let me make it up to you?"

There was no mistaking what he meant. She wanted him to act normal and she wished she could edit out the awkward line like fast-forwarding a song; she had a buzz but still it all seemed horribly embarrassing. He was leaning in.

She took a deep breath and met his shining gaze. No way out but through. "Do you have a rubber?" she asked.

He pulled back. "Why, Miss Collins, this is so sudden!"

"Don't talk or I'll chicken out," she said.

He pulled his wallet from his back pocket and patted it. "I do. You want this, huh?"

She nodded. "This seems like the right time. You're the right guy. And it's one less thing to worry about when I get back to the States."

He raised himself on one elbow and leaned over her. "Your dad won't come in, will he?"

"No way. As long as I don't scream."

"Well, don't scream."

"I'll try not to. Have you done this before?"

"Almost. But no."

"Toxic tried last night."

Syd sat up. "Are you okay?"

"Yeah, I got away. I hit the car horn with my foot and the noise scared him."

"Jesus, Lucinda. I'm going to kill him. I'm going after the motherfucker." He said it with such a lack of conviction that Lucinda almost laughed.

She rushed to let him off the hook. "You don't need to do that."

Syd lay back down. "Okay."

"He's in jail."

"Oh, that's right." They began kissing. Lucinda tried to relax. It seemed like it should have been more romantic. She tried to get into the dreamy, soft-focus mood she used to get into when she imagined Nately kissing her. The thought reminded her of the box of tapes next to her boom box sitting on the floor a few feet away.

"Hang on a sec," she said, pulling away from him. "We need a sound track." She scooted across the floor and started shuffling through the cassettes.

"It doesn't matter, Lucinda."

"Of course it does. What about side two from *Blood on the Tracks*, 'Pale Blue Eyes,' 'Crimson and Clover'? Have you ever heard 'Moonlight Mile'?"

"You're thinking vintage? Why not 'The Ghost in You'?" he said. "And 'More Than This'?"

"You're right. Roxy Music," she said. "I should've made a compilation. Now I'll have to keep changing the tape."

He laughed. As she hit play on a Velvet Underground tape, she felt him grab the belt loop on the back of her jeans and pull her across the floor toward him. "I don't think you understand how this is going to go. You will not be stopping to change the tape," he said. "I'll lose my goddamned mind. Don't even think about it."

She reached up and laid her hands on either side of his face. "So it's the Velvet Underground all the way?"

"All the way."

She thought of Tucumcari and how things had worked out for her parents. Was she starting something with Syd that would end in tears years later? She could be about to waste a whole lot of time. It hurt more than she imagined. Syd vacillated between solicitous inquiries about her comfort and eye-clenched, single-minded concentration. The arc of the whole event was determined by his thrusting, and it finished when he finished. It reminded her of the way a rock song was structured. Intro, refrain, refrain, drum solo, big finish! She felt like she should have been doing something more, but the pain was too much to let her do anything but hold herself in place. "We did it?" she asked when he collapsed on top of her.

"What do you think?"

She was silent for a few minutes while he continued to breathe against her collarbone. Wanting to leave it on a more encouraging note, she whispered, "You're pretty good at that."

"I practice a lot when I'm alone." They laughed.

"That's from a movie, though, right? Where have I heard that line?"

But he was asleep. She, on the other hand, was energized. It was just midnight; she wanted to sneak out and walk around the base with Syd; she wanted to rip open the boxes in the hallway full of Nately's records and tell Syd about each and every one. She thought about stealing something better from the BOOZE box. She slid out from under Syd, easing him onto his back. She got dressed, took a beer from the fridge, grabbed her Walkman, and sat in the sill of the open window watching the moon drift over the water tower.

Syd stayed until the morning blew faint sounds of

reveille through the open window of Lucinda's room. They both sat up in the sleeping bag. "My dad will be up soon," she said.

He stood up and stretched. "Fort Sill, huh?" he said as he pulled his T-shirt over his head.

She looked up at his skinny pale torso, bruises matching her own from where their awkward, exposed hip bones had borne in on each other's flesh. She had to look away. She had tried from the beginning to shut Syd out and nothing she did mattered. Fate and the Army—maybe they were one and the same—had brought him back around and would take him away again presently. A stern voice inside barked orders: break camp, don't look back, and everything else in her was hurting and resentful. People are supposed to be attached, she told herself. This is a universally acknowledged moment for sentiment. You shouldn't have to say good-bye and good luck right after you lose your virginity. But she did, she and Syd did, and that was that. "Are you going to give me your address?"

"I'll do better than that," he said. "This time I'm going to hand it to you."

She laughed. "Will I hear from you?"

"Sure you will."

"It would be nice to think so," she said.

PART THREE

Lawton, Oklahoma, USA
1988

TWENTY-ONE

Lucinda looked up from wiping a stack of dirty trays and saw through the restaurant window a new red BMW glide into the Wendy's parking lot, a streak of light and color across the early evening twilight. There weren't a lot of Beemers that color in Lawton, Oklahoma, but any doubt she might have had as to the car's ownership was removed by the real estate signs magnetized to its sides displaying her mother's name, FAYE COLLINS, and brightly colored head shot.

Here we go. Lucinda watched her mother fly across the parking lot to the front door, her long auburn hair streaming. She was on her way to the Christmas party at Benson Siegel, the real estate company where she'd been working for the last year and a half; Lucinda recognized the blue silk pantsuit her mother had bought for the occasion. And she was wearing the coat, a white fur of some exotic provenance that made her stick out like a polar bear dropped onto the red dirt plains. Jacob and Erin had named it the Divorce Coat.

As she yanked open the door to the restaurant, Lucinda saw that her mother's face wore the terrible expression she had seen too often since the day Faye came home and caught her husband cheating. It was a look that would scare anyone else, but it made Lucinda want to hold her mother like a child—rage that was really fear, fury that was really bewilderment. Lucinda set down the stack of plastic trays and wiped her hands on the front of her uniform. When Faye spotted her, Lucinda was ready, leveling a stare at her across the nearly empty dining room.

"You!" her mother said, pointing at Lucinda. She streaked among the tables like a comet in her fur coat. "You must think I'm stupid as a dead dog."

"Mom," Lucinda said. "Take it easy."

"Oh," Faye said, looking around in mock surprise. "Am I embarrassing you? Is this inappropriate? I suppose I don't have the right to be angry when my underage daughter steals my car and has a drug orgy in it."

"There was no drug orgy," Lucinda said. "What's a drug orgy?" She felt her heart racing. All day, she had felt contrite. Driving her mother's expensive new car to Oklahoma City had been a crazy thing to do, no question. She had been ready to apologize, but all her remorse evaporated when her mother stormed in.

Her mother caught sight of Don Malloy, a rent-a-cop whose security beat included Wendy's, and turned to him. "I want you to arrest that girl," she said, pointing at Lucinda.

Don blinked good-naturedly at her, then at Lucinda, who had decided over the last week that Don sort of liked her. "Arrest her why?"

From behind the counter, Lucinda's boss, Yolanda, said, "What's going on? Ain't this your mama?"

Next to her at the front register stood Frida, a recently paroled hippie who watched from behind huge glasses that magnified her eyes and left her looking permanently startled.

Lucinda picked up the stack of trays and held them like a shield. "I didn't steal her car."

"Ma'am," Don said, "I noticed you drove up in that pretty red BMW," he said, pointing out the window at the car. "Is that the car you're talking about?"

Her mother raised her chin at Don, ready to be taken seriously. "That's it, yes."

"It appears to be in your possession."

"She stole it last night. She took it God knows where and did God knows what with it. Then she snuck it back and actually thought I wouldn't notice."

"I just borrowed it," Lucinda said.

"Borrowed it?" her mother said. "That involves asking. Asking the owner, who is me."

From behind the counter Yolanda said, "Mrs. Collins, you can take it out of Lucinda's hide after a while—she'll be home in a few hours."

"No," Lucinda's mother said, stabbing a finger at Lucinda, "she won't. You won't. You hear me? Don't come home. You don't have a home. Not anymore. Not with me."

"That suits me fine!" Lucinda shot back. "I'm sick and tired of being treated like every goddamned thing I do is high treason."

It had been going this way between Lucinda and her mother for a while now. Lucinda couldn't help but think that if she had known how their lives would go, she would never have called her mother home from Paris that night in Graf, never have told her mother anything. Truth, that's what she had been thinking about. Truth, like it was some simple absolute. She had known she might damage relations with her father, might change her family, but she had imagined closeness with her mother after telling her about her dad's cheating. That hadn't happened. Instead, she had lost her mother, too. Faye was an orphan who had made her first and only real home in her first love, her husband. She had meant to nest there forever, in the bosom of her family, but Lucinda had forced her hand, blown her out, and now Faye was scrambling like a prairie dog cut off from its hole, desperate for cover and dangerous to approach. Faye Collins spun around and hit the door, the soft fur of her coat rippling like a gale of snow, and Lucinda felt a quickening in the pit of her stomach.

"Sweet Baby Jesus!" said Yolanda. "Lucinda, what did you do last night?"

Lucinda watched her mother's little red car disappear into the dusk. "Nothing."

She had sneaked out of her house about midnight and driven a couple of friends ninety miles up I-44 to visit a punk club in Oklahoma City. It wasn't her first clandestine operation since landing in Lawton, the town attached to Fort Sill, but it had turned out to be the first that wasn't worth it. She'd been carded at the door and never made it into the club. Her fellow renegades, Kyle, the asshole cloves smoker, and Stephanie, the one alert person in her history class at school, had griped all the way home, making her feel more than ever like the foreign nerd trying too hard to fit in.

"I know what you done, young lady," said Don, moving back to his customary chair beside the counter. "You found the straw that broke the camel's back."

"Boy," said Frida, her giant eyes blinking at the parking lot. "That's some coat your mama's got."

All through the busy night, as Lucinda took orders at the drive-through window, she tried to come up with a plan. Shelter for the night—that was the first order of business. She thought of Kyle and Stephanie, but they weren't the kind of friends she wanted to explain things to. Her sometimes-boyfriend, Bobby, was skiing in Estes Park with his parents, and her friend Emma was in San Antonio with her dad and his new family for Christmas. There was no more light in the sky and Lucinda could feel the temperature dropping each time she opened the drive-through window. As closing time approached, Lucinda had no choice but to use the pay phone by the restrooms and call her father. He was back in Germany, having been stateside just long enough to get the whole family stuck at Fort Sill, Oklahoma, and to get an American divorce. When she finally got to call, it was ten o'clock her time—she would be waking her father up with a collect call. After she heard her father's sleepy voice say he would accept the charges, she shouted, "Dad?"

"Lucinda?"

"I'm sorry to wake you up!"

"How's school?"

She leaned against the wall, coiling the metal phone cord around her wrist. "Mom kicked me out of the house."

"Goddamn! Why?"

"I borrowed her car and she found out."

"Her new BMW? Did you wreck it?" he asked.

"The car is fine. I don't have any place to go, Dad."

"What about that guy you were dating? Or that black-haired girl you run with—what's her name?"

"They're both out of town." She paused, giving her father a chance to ride in to the rescue. He almost always disappointed her in such moments, but then, there had never been anything quite like this. Silence stretched out between them. Lucinda sighed. "I was hoping you could give me your credit-card number so I can stay in a hotel."

"Hmm," her father said. "Who else do you know around there?"

"Dad."

"Well, look, honey. I think you've stumbled into one of those character-building moments. If I give you my credit-card number, then you've got a safe place to stay."

"Yeah," Lucinda said. "That's the idea." She couldn't believe it. He was going into his what-doesn't-kill-you mode.

"On the other hand, if I don't give you my credit-card number, then you'll have a learning experience that will make you stronger. You're not the weak type, Lucinda. If you were, I'd take care of you, but I'm kind of curious to see what you make of this."

Lucinda felt heat flood her face. "What doesn't kill me makes me stronger? Is that it? You know, Dad," she said, trying not to cry, "that little slogan of yours only has to misfire once, and bingo, you'll only have two kids left to use it on."

Her father's voice sounded earnest as he tried to placate her. "You know that saying about how the meek will inherit the earth? That's bullshit. You have to be a warrior, Lucinda."

"It's not bullshit," Lucinda said, crying now. "They'll inherit the earth because they get help when they need help. All the strong people like me will be dead. With lots of character!" She slammed down the phone. So much for Dad.

Lucinda returned to closing the restaurant down, lingering over her duties. Sitting in the tiny office with the others waiting on her, she lost count three times balancing the drive-through drawer. Finally, Yolanda had checked the restaurant and locked the drawers in the safe. Frida hit the lights and they all met in their coats by the back door, rushing out as Yolanda set the alarm and slammed the door behind them.

"Good night, ladies," Yolanda said, jogging to her Cutlass, parked in back by the Dumpsters. "Good luck with your mama, Lucinda. Kiss her ass—that a fix everything."

Frida stood on the curb trying to light a cigarette in the wind. Lucinda stepped up next to her and blocked the wind so that the lighter flame stilled and the cigarette took fire, the flame mirrored in the thick lenses of Frida's glasses.

"Thanks," Frida said. "You work tomorrow?" Lucinda nodded. A yellow Buick Skylark with a ripped black top pulled into the parking lot and stopped next to them. The backseat, Lucinda noticed, was piled high with stuff. "My old man," Frida said. "You going to be okay?"

"I'm fine," Lucinda said. After the Buick drove off, she walked to the main road and headed against the late-night traffic as it streamed past. She turned the collar of her vintage swing coat up against the wind. Her fingerless knit gloves, which were dreadfully cool, were unfortunately cold, and her coat had no pockets.

Most of the strip was closed, the Wendy's sign and most of the other fast-food signs dark. Up the road, she saw a 7-Eleven sign still on. She walked toward it, making it her goal. But what would she do when she got there? There was no one to call. The night was getting colder. She passed a vacant lot, a patch of uneven ground with tufts of weedy grass covering much of it. A wicker chair lay on its side a few feet from the curb, one of its arms worried to tatters as if it had been attacked by a large dog. Black plastic trash bags lay scattered about and silver-labeled beer bottles punctuated the scene like Christmas ornaments. She didn't know why scenes like this startled her, but they did. She had forgotten, living in Germany, about anything but America the beautiful. But there was this, too. Pretty vacant, like the Sex Pistols song. Pretty tacky. Pretty trashed. It was something to do with all the space out here in the West, which Lucinda still couldn't get used to. Vast, vacant space, tons of it, too much to attend to every lot and roadside, the way they did in Europe where they had been living within finite borders for centuries.

As she approached the 7-Eleven she imagined the night stretching into the day after, onward forever without a stopping point. She felt like she had been riding her whole life in a pressurized cabin that had now been blown open, leaving her in free fall, sucked into the vastness. The years seemed to stretch in front of her from that point forward, without walls, without ceiling, without the enclosure of family. Shelter, she thought, comes first. She scanned the 7-Eleven. The Dumpsters behind it were shielded by a fence. She could get behind that fence and sleep there.

For now, she decided to take shelter in the 7-Eleven, and as she stood in front of the microwave, heating a burrito, she felt a tap on her shoulder. Turning, she saw Frida's strangely magnified eyes staring at her. "You want to spend the night?" Frida seemed embarrassed, like she was afraid Lucinda would turn her down, but Lucinda wanted to hug her.

"Oh, I guess," she said, beaming. "You bet!"

And she climbed into the passenger seat of the yellow Buick Skylark, next to Frida, nodding hello to the hammered profile of Frida's boyfriend, small eyes lit by a cigarette he held in his mouth. "This is Jimbo," Frida said, gesturing to the little man.

As dwellings went, it was the worst Lucinda had ever seen, an efficiency apartment in what had been a roadside motel— window unit, shag carpet the color of dirt. There was a

smell that recalled the temporary attic quarters in Grafenwoehr. Mouse droppings, maybe mold. The counter of the
tiny kitchen area was covered with macramé holders full of
climbing houseplants that had not had time to climb anything, tangled clumps of long vines spread across the counter like dirty hair. A few cereal boxes and cans of soup peeked
out from under the vines. The living-room wall was decorated with a Led Zeppelin poster of the *Houses of the Holy*
album cover, naked cherubs clambering over rocks, and a
big American Airlines poster of Neuschwanstein Castle.

Jimbo closed the door behind them. He was sun-dried
and skinny, with oatmeal-colored hair he wore long in back,
wearing a high school letter jacket far too big and too young
for him. Frida and Jimbo evidently slept on a big blow-up
mattress in one corner, the kind you'd take to the beach,
and Frida motioned for Lucinda to make herself at home on
a swaybacked couch upholstered with purple cabbage flowers. "You'd be amazed at what people throw away. I got this
thing out on the curb on large-trash pickup day."

"Nice," Lucinda said, glancing sideways at the couch.

Jimbo opened three beers and handed them out. "We're
not all moved in yet. This is a brand-new arrangement," he
said, dropping onto the mattress. "I'm kind of a free bird,
Lucinda, like the song, but this girl's going to domesticate
me, I'm afraid." He threw Frida a playful glance and she
blushed. These people, Lucinda realized, were crazy in love.

From the couch she looked at the Neuschwanstein poster.
"I've been there," she said, pointing at the castle.

"Have you?" Frida asked, joining Jimbo on the mattress. "Me, too. I like looking at it. Do you remember the grotto?" she asked.

Lucinda laughed. "Crazy, right? Wasn't it right off his bedroom?"

"With a solid gold boat," Frida said. She fired up a joint. "You'd love it, Jimbo. You think Jimmy Page is living large. Or Michael Jackson—that ain't nothing on this guy, the king who built it. You must be an Army brat," Frida said.

"You, too," Lucinda said. "Unless you jet-set around Europe when you're not working at Wendy's."

Frida sat up straight, grinning. "The jet's out back," she said. "Just a little one, you know. Keeping it simple. Not like your mama. Bet you wish you had that coat of hers on tonight. You could stroll around the North Pole in that thing. What kind of fur was that?"

"I can't remember," Lucinda said. "Not mink, but something like it."

"She looked great in it!" Frida said. "That's the way to go to the company Christmas party."

The three of them sat talking for a time. Frida told them about how her father died in Vietnam. He'd been cut across one wrist by shrapnel during a firefight. It hadn't seemed like a major wound, so he had ignored it and worked on saving guys around him who looked a lot worse. Nobody noticed how much blood he was losing, but he bled out and died. "One tiny hole," Frida said, shaking her head. "You poke one tiny hole in a human being and that's it." Lucinda thought about Captain Frye. Her father had passed along the news a few months earlier that Frye had slashed his wrists and died in a bathtub somewhere in Pennsylvania. He was alone— the Fryes had divorced somewhere along the way. No news about Liz.

"He should've stopped after Korea," Frida continued, "but he just didn't. He was a trumpet player down at Bliss when the Korean War started. Didn't have nothing to do all day but toot his horn a few times. One day they put him on a plane, took his trumpet, and issued him an M-16. He never went back to the trumpet." She looked like she might stop, but kept on. "We were stationed in Germany before Vietnam. I was a kid—that castle's about all I remember. You miss Germany, don't you, sweetie?"

"How can you tell?"

Frida smiled at her. "I don't know. You got a kind of fish-out-of-water look."

"Yeah," Lucinda said. She had been stateside now for a while and yet was still spinning with culture shock amid the strip malls, the fast-food restaurants, and the megachurches. Lawton was an Army town and plenty of people there had lived in Germany at some point, but nobody else she knew seemed to miss it. Lucinda told them about her mom's fast rise in local real estate, and about the Benson Siegel Christmas party in full swing a mile down the road. And she talked too long about the twins, the pot going to her head.

Lucinda felt a surge of affection for her ruddy-faced coworker. Frida had been working at Wendy's for two weeks, and everybody knew she was fresh out of prison.

Her coworkers made fun of her and were afraid of her, yet it had been Frida and no one else who had offered Lucinda a place to stay.

Jimbo got up and brought back a few more beers. Frida sat cross-legged on the sticky-looking carpet next to the record player, sliding an LP onto the spindle. She took another hit off the joint while her cigarette smoldered in an ashtray on the floor. There was silence; then, from a long distance, came a rapidly repeating set of notes on a guitar.

"*The Joshua Tree*," Lucinda said.

Frida raised the joint in the air, "Best music since the sixties."

"I ain't a fan," Jimbo said. "I suspect it's faggot music."

"Swear to God, Jimbo. Sometimes I realize you're in emotional kindergarten."

"Emotional kindergarten?" Jimbo said. "That makes me feel like I got a long way to go with you. Makes me kinda tired, honey." He winked at Lucinda, smiled, and stood up. "I'm going for smokes and I'll be back in a bit. Can I get you ladies anything?"

"Doritos," Frida said as he shrugged on his jacket. "And milk so this girl can have some cereal in the morning."

"Thanks," Lucinda said.

"Stay as long as you want, sweetie," she said.

As the door closed behind Jimbo, Frida leaned back and closed her eyes. "See, Lucinda, you're like me. We could be sisters, you know? Our paths are the same. Neuschwanstein to Wendy's to this little room here tonight."

Lucinda looked at Frida—at her big, awful eyeglasses

and ruddy, dry skin, her frizzy hair and her rawboned knuckles. Underneath it all, Frida was kind and funny. But it was clear terrible things had happened to her along the way. She resisted the comparison.

"You're more like my mom's age, I think," she said.

Frida opened her eyes. "Yeah, but I bet your mom had you young, didn't she? Had to have. She's young yet. I bet she married your daddy right out of high school and found herself a wartime Army wife and knocked up before she even knew what a checkbook was. Am I right?"

Lucinda shrugged. "Pretty much."

"You see? I've got a daughter born when I was about the age you are now," she said. "And now she's your age, finishing up with high school. She lives in Albuquerque with her daddy. I didn't raise her. Couldn't have—I had too much running to do."

Frida reached over and patted Lucinda on the hand. "I'll be your mama for now," she said. "Helps me more than it does you."

They sat in silence for a few minutes, listening to the record until it started skipping, playing the same spot over and over again, "still, still, still," but Frida's last hit off the joint had put her past noticing, her head fallen to her chest and her big glasses hanging from her ears. Lucinda got up and turned off the record player and the lights. She rolled her ruby coat into a ball and stuffed it under her head, stretching out on the lumpy couch. After a while, she heard the front door open and Jimbo come in, but she kept her eyes closed while he rustled around and bedded down on the air mattress, leaving Frida slouched against the wall next to the record player.

The next day, while Lucinda was working the lunch shift at Wendy's, she got a phone call. Yolanda handed the phone receiver out of the office and Lucinda stretched the cord until she was standing in dry storage surrounded by cartons of to-go cups. "Lucinda?" It was Erin. "Something weird has happened to Mom."

"No shit," Lucinda said.

"No, I mean like crime."

"What?"

"You know her fur coat?"

"Of course."

"Somebody stole it. She thinks it was you."

"Oh, man," Lucinda said. "Where was it stolen from?"

"Did you do it?"

"What? No, Erin. No way. I'm not a big fan of it, but I wouldn't steal it."

"There's a ransom."

"Ransom?"

"Yeah. A note on the windshield of her car at Benson Siegel said if she takes five hundred dollars to the Putt-Putt golf course and leaves it in a bag in the windmill, she'll get her coat back."

Lucinda laughed. "That's pretty funny," she said. "When is she supposed to do this?"

"Tonight at midnight."

"I get off at four, Erin. I'm going to come over and try to make up with Mom." She had decided to eat humble pie. It was embarrassing, the whole mess, and Frida had been prodding her about it all through the afternoon shift.

Erin said, "Oh, good! But I don't know if she'll let you—she's really mad. She thinks you stole that coat. Here, Jacob wants to talk to you."

Lucinda heard her brother heave a sigh as he took the phone. "Hey dude," she said.

"Why do you have to be bad?"

"I didn't steal her coat, Jacob."

"What about her car?"

"I just borrowed it."

"You made Mom cry again. Dad's gone and now you're gone. Me and Erin are going to California."

"You're twelve years old."

"We're going."

"What's in California?"

"They got BMX parks there," he said.

"Do me a favor and wait, okay? Just for a little while."

When she got to the house, the garage was open and her mother's car was there. After a deep breath, she walked in through the garage door, straight into the kitchen. Her mother, with her back to the wall, sat at the kitchen table walled in by a stacks of papers and a calculator. She clutched the edge of the table when Lucinda walked in. "You!" she said. "Get the hell out of here right now, or I'm calling the police!"

Lucinda had hoped for calm, but she saw right away that

she had underestimated her mother's state of mind. "Mom, I just want to come home. I'm sorry about your car—I'll never borrow it without asking again."

"Oh, don't even try it." Her mother didn't look at her, jabbing at buttons on the calculator with the eraser end of a pencil.

"I didn't steal your coat, if that's what you're thinking."

Her head snapped up. "Then how did you know it was stolen?"

"I talked to Erin and Jacob. Mom, I did not steal your coat. How could you think that?"

"You want to destroy me," she said. "Everything I've built out of the ashes your father left us with. I fight to build us up, and you just want to destroy. First the car, now the coat."

"I want to destroy you?" She remembered her father, at the end of the marriage, comparing his wife's reactions during their last big fight to a friendly-fire disaster he had seen in Vietnam, when a soldier was so terrified and shell-shocked he had fired at his own before he realized what he had done. "Your mother," he said. "Sometimes she thinks we're the enemy."

"Get out," her mother said. "Out, out, out!"

Lucinda turned and saw her brother and sister hovering together in the hallway. As she went past, Erin shoved her backpack at Lucinda, saying, "Clothes and stuff!" Lucinda grabbed it and kept going.

Lucinda swung the satchel over her shoulder and took off running across the front yard. Friendly fire, just friendly fire. She had heard her mother's tongue-lashings all her life, but when she was little they had been aimed at outsiders: doctors or teachers neglecting Lucinda or the twins, or Army clerks in charge of shuffling dependents into corners. In the divorce Lucinda had sided with her mother and blamed everything on her dad for cheating, but as she ran down the sidewalk into the bitter wind, she realized her dad had suffered, too. People died from friendly fire.

"No! Lucinda, don't go! Don't go!"

Lucinda looked back and saw Erin running behind her, pigtails flying, tears streaming, and behind Erin came Jacob—and behind him, Faye, who continued to yell for Lucinda to get out. Three houses up the street, she turned and caught her little sister in a hug. Erin's familiar shampoo-and-applesauce smell blindsided Lucinda. Pulling her sister into a tight hug, she wondered if they would ever sleep under the same roof again. "It'll be okay," she said. "Everything will be okay. She's not mad at you."

She looked around and saw their next-door neighbors standing on their front porch, and the people across the street next to their car, watching. Faye Collins had stopped running and stood at the edge of their lawn, breathing hard and trying to look calm, one hand tight on Jacob's shoulder. Lucinda gave Erin one more squeeze and took off running. It was dusk already, a hot-pink sky glowing over the dead yellow grasses of suburban lawns. She made the two miles back to Frida's in twenty minutes, freezing in her vintage jacket.

Frida and Jimbo were high again and they were listening to Gram Parsons. As Frida alternated her joint with her cigarettes, Lucinda told her and Jimbo about the situation with her mom's stolen coat.

"Sounds like somebody at that party got wasted and stole it by accident," Frida said. "I been guilty of stupid stuff like that plenty. One time I woke up out in the middle of a field in a brand-new yellow Corvette with Dolly Parton playing on the cassette. Nothing but Dolly Parton tapes in that car. I didn't hurt it, thank God. I still don't know where I got it from."

"Drunk stealing," Jimbo said. "That shit's embarrassing. That's how I got this sweet jacket, though," he said, raising his shoulders and extending his arms to show off the letter jacket. Patches on the sleeves showed recent victories by its original owner: *Oklahoma All State Wrestling 86–88*.

"Okay, but if one of her coworkers got drunk and took her coat, wouldn't she just apologize and give it back?"

Jimbo shrugged. "Too proud, maybe."

"But the ransom note was on the car last night when my mom left the party, not this morning."

"Hey, it was just a theory," Jimbo said.

"I don't think my mom should go alone to get the coat. I mean, whoever stole it could kill her."

"Nobody's going to kill your mama," Jimbo said. "Somebody just saw an opportunity to make a little cash, that's all."

"I still think I need to be there to protect her. I wouldn't want her to know I was there—just hide out and make sure she's okay. We could all go," Lucinda said, smiling at them both. "Have an adventure!"

Jimbo shrugged. "I appreciate your enthusiasm. But I'm

plumb adventured out." He hugged Frida. "How about you, darling? You want to roust a coat thief or stay here and keep warm with your old man?"

Frida kissed him on the cheek. "Lucinda," she said, "I know it's tough, but you should let your mom handle this."

Lucinda couldn't forget about it, though. A couple hours later, around ten o'clock, when they had run out of beer again, she was getting more and more worried.

Jimbo dozed off and Frida whispered, "Come get some air," lifting Jimbo's arm from around her. "Beer run."

Jimbo's Buick Skylark was parked under a streetlight in front of the apartment. As Lucinda stood on the passenger side waiting for Frida to unlock the door, she looked in the backseat of the car. It was full of all kinds of junk—handyman tools and paint cans, cassette-tape cases and shotgun shells. And, peeking out from under a toolbox, a bright puff of white fur. She sucked in her breath.

"How long have you been with Jimbo?" Lucinda asked.

"Couple of weeks. He knew Dale, my ex, but I didn't meet him until I got out of jail."

"What did you go to jail for, if you don't mind my asking?"

"Oh, I don't mind. It was that yellow Corvette I told you about. Grand theft auto, even though all I did was drive it into a field and sleep in it. You try telling people what happens when you get your drink on and you'd think nobody else ever touched a drop. No understanding. Except Jimbo. He knows how it is."

"You love him?"

Frida smiled as she turned the car onto the road. "Oh, yes. He's the one."

When they pulled into the 7-Eleven where Frida and Jimbo had rescued Lucinda the night before, Lucinda waited until Frida had gone inside toward the beer cooler. Then she reached into the backseat of the car and lifted the heavy steel toolbox, pulling out the coat. She sat there looking at it for a second, a big ball of soft light in her hands. Inside the store, Frida swung a twelve-pack onto the counter in front of the cashier. Frida could have been in on it, but Lucinda didn't think so. So she jumped out of the car with the coat and ran, heading into the vacant lot behind the 7-Eleven, and from there, through an apartment complex and on to a network of residential streets.

For the second night in a row, she walked, exhilarated and terrified, without destination. She kept walking, with no idea where she was going or when she would stop, like a piece of shrapnel hurling through space after an explosion, for what felt like a long time until she noticed where her feet were carrying her. Home. She was at the entrance to her subdivision. She jogged the last two blocks.

Her mother hadn't changed the locks overnight, so she used her house key to let herself in and tiptoed down the tiled foyer, sliding off the fur coat to hang it in the hall closet. A light was on in the living room. Lucinda opened the closet door and, while she was reaching for a hanger, heard her mother's footsteps behind her.

"I can't believe it." Faye stood at the entrance to the living room with her hands on either side of the doorway. It was nearly midnight, but she was fully dressed, with shoes on and her auburn hair pulled back in a ponytail looking like she was on her way out.

Lucinda turned and held the coat out like a peace offering. "Hi," she said. It was settling over her how hopelessly guilty she looked. "I got this back for you."

"Oh, you got it back! Sure, sure. Of course you did—you're a detective! Give me that." Her mother snatched the coat from Lucinda's hands and balled it up with both hands.

"I didn't steal it, Mom."

"Just save it." Her voice was high and hoarse, and she bit off each word, hard and separate as stones. It was the voice she had used when she caught her husband cheating—Lucinda could hear it tumbling like a landslide down the stairwell in Grafenwoehr. "I cannot, will not listen to you lying to me like that. Why would you steal from me? I'm your mother!"

"Mom, I got it back from the people who stole it. I swear to God, I swear on anything you want—I didn't steal it. Why would I? I wouldn't."

"How in hell do you expect me to believe you found out who stole it and got it back, Lucinda? How? Come on."

"I guess I don't."

They stared at each other, and Lucinda suddenly felt too tired to fight the weight of her mother's disappointment.

"Tell me who stole it, then."

She could see that her mother wanted to believe her and the realization made her want to tell her everything. But she thought about Frida, just out of jail and in love.

"What will you do if I tell you?"

"I'll call the cops, of course."

She shook her head. "Then I can't tell you."

"Of course not! Because you stole it." Her mother's voice sounded pleading now.

"I wish you could just believe me," Lucinda said. "How could you raise me and not know that I'm telling you the truth? I know it's hard to believe, but I can't tell you who did it and I do have good reasons."

Her mother leaned against the wall and ran her hands over her face. "Go to bed. We'll talk in the morning."

"Thank you, Mom." Lucinda reached out to hug her mother, but Faye pushed her away.

"Just go," she said. "This isn't over."

Lucinda went to her room and threw herself on her bed. She couldn't think, didn't brush her teeth or wash her face, but before she went to sleep, she picked up the lone souvenir left from all her years in Germany, the Neuschwanstein snow globe, and shook it, watching it until the snow subsided around the tiny castle. She dreamed about a room of the castle she hadn't seen on the tour, where there were crates of records. They were Nately's records, she realized in the dream, and when she looked at Ludwig, he looked like Nately: Nately in white tights and a cape and with all the long red hair he had had in the family photo he had kept next to the turntable in his barrack. He was also Syd, some-how, in that weird way of dreams. They sat on a blow-up mattress like Frida's and listened to *Houses of the Holy*.

In the morning, Lucinda awoke to the sound of a light

knock on her door. Her mother came in carrying the coat. She sat at the foot of Lucinda's bed and watched while Lucinda sat up, trying hard to gauge her mother's mood before she committed to wakefulness.

"I believe you," Faye said.

"Oh, God," Lucinda said. "You do?"

Faye lifted the coat to her nose, then she tossed it to Lucinda. "Take a whiff."

Lucinda did as she was told and smelled the inside of Jimbo's Buick, a smell dominated by cigarette smoke, but with undertones of old fast food and beer and the greasy, metallic smells of tools and car parts. She looked at her mother.

"I know you don't smoke. Your father saw to that."

Lucinda nodded.

"So who are you protecting? Some man. Why? You'd better tell me, Lucinda."

"Mom, I just can't."

"Did he threaten you?" Her mother grabbed her leg through the blanket. The grim fury that had been for days directed at Lucinda was again directed outward, to someone else, to Jimbo. Lucinda felt giddy. "Did he hurt you? Lucinda, what did he do to you and who the hell is this son of a bitch?"

"It's not like that, Mom, I swear. He didn't touch me."

"I'll change your mystery man from a rooster to a hen in one stroke, I swear to God. You just watch."

"Mom, listen to me. Don't you know I wouldn't let somebody hurt me like that? He did not lay a hand on me."

Her mother leaned back, becoming curious. "Then what?"

"He has a girlfriend, and she's really sweet. She's my friend. She let me stay with her when . . ."

Faye finished her sentence: "When I didn't."

"Well, yeah. I mean . . ."

"Okay, then. I won't tell the cops about her. Just him. How's that?"

"But he lives with her. And she's on parole. Just got out of jail."

"Where do you meet such people?" Faye stood up. "Get dressed. Come on."

"Where are we going?"

"I said get dressed."

Lucinda swung herself out of bed and pulled on a pair of jeans and a sweater while her mother sat back down on the bed, watching her. Finally Faye said, "You're going to take me to them."

"Mom—"

"Shut up. I'm not going to call the police. But I want this episode put to rest. I want to know for certain that you didn't lie to me."

After securing promises from Erin and Jacob not to leave the house until her return, Faye started the BMW and followed Lucinda's terse directions to Frida's apartment. Lucinda was afraid her mother would keep pumping her for the thief's identity, but Faye said nothing. "Turn here,"

Lucinda said as they drew near the entrance to the old motel. "These are apartments."

Faye did as Lucinda asked, directing the BMW up a bumpy drive into the circular gravel lot that stopped at the apartment doors. "Which one?" Faye steered the car slowly around the parking lot. In a distant and more festive past, each apartment door had been painted a different bright color and prickly-pear cactuses had been planted to the left of each door. Frida's door was turquoise and the cactus next to it had been impaled by dozens of cigarette butts, its lobes resembling blackened lungs. Lucinda was relieved to see that Jimbo's yellow Buick was not parked in front.

"The turquoise one," she said, and jumped out of the car ahead of her mother. She ran to the door and saw as she approached that it was ajar. She pushed it open. The place was empty—Frida's blow-up mattress, clothes, records, and tangled houseplants were all gone. The nasty old couch was still there against one wall, and across the room, on the other wall, was the poster. As she stood looking at it, her mother popped her head in the door and peered incredulously around.

"Good God," she said, stepping inside. "I guess they won't be needing a Realtor." She looked the place up and down until her eyes rested on the poster. "Neuschwanstein," she said. She narrowed her eyes and looked from the poster to Lucinda. "You're sure," she said, pointing at her daughter, "you didn't meet some guy who told you he'd take you back to Europe or something?"

"Mom!"

"Hey," she said, flashing an open hand. "I'm just asking. That sounds like the line your dad gave me. Or something like it. Sounded all right to me."

"Well, that part was true, right? You saw Europe."

Faye took the point grudgingly. "I did, yes. I saw Europe."

"My friend used to live in Germany, too."

"Your friend?"

"The woman who lived here. She was stationed over there when she was a kid."

"I see. Well, she's not stationed anywhere anymore. She's just drifting. I wonder where she went? You know?"

"Could be anywhere," Lucinda said. "It's a big country."

TWENTY-TWO

They drove past the entrance to the driveway three times before Erin spotted a rusty mailbox lying in the ditch and noticed gravel among the weeds. "Could this be it?" Lucinda said.

Her father shifted in the passenger seat. "I don't think so. I don't recognize anything."

"It has to be," Jacob said, "according to the address on that little gas station we just passed."

Lucinda turned the car and cautiously nudged it over tall weeds between parallel rows of overhanging trees. "These trees sure look like they're supposed to be lining a drive, don't they?"

"Yeah, they do at that," her dad said.

"I don't see anything," Erin said, and then, "Wait, yes, I do. What is that?"

A wooden structure that seemed to float a few feet off

the ground peeked through the weeds ahead, along with the sparkle of sunlight reflected off water.

"The pier," Lucinda said.

"The pier? It is!" Major Collins sat up and pressed his hands to the dashboard. He turned and looked at the three of them, beaming. "I'll be damned! I wouldn't have recognized the place."

Another few seconds and the shroud of the driveway opened onto a weed-choked clearing where they saw the peeling and faded house, two-story and four-gabled, with a covered veranda that had caved in at one corner. The windows and doors were covered with plywood boards, and a tin "No Trespassing" sign was nailed to one of the paintless porch columns.

"It's not how I pictured it," she said.

"What a dump," Erin said.

As Lucinda pulled the car to a stop, their father unfastened his seat belt and sprang from the car without a word. They watched him wade into the weeds toward the house. No one said anything. Lucinda fought the urge to cry like an exhausted child. Of course Shiloh would be a ruin. Of course it would. What had she expected, Tara? Yes. She had expected Tara, a gracious old girl in a state of genteel neglect. She had imagined doing a little sweeping and dusting—what a joke.

"I thought it would be bigger," Jacob said.

"Hey," Erin said. "Check out Dad."

Their father, in jeans and a plaid shirt, had trudged through the waist-high flora to a dead tree that towered over the house like a reaching hand. It had been hit by light-ning, to judge by the black scar that split it down the middle. Just then, their father dropped down into the weeds.

Jacob was draping a camera strap around his neck. "What's he doing?"

They saw his back rise and fall. "Digging?" Erin said.

"With his hands?"

They piled out of the car and headed through the weeds to their father. "Dad?" Erin called. "Hey!"

Lucinda followed the twins, fighting with every step she took through the intractable weeds to keep herself from col-lapsing to the ground and screaming, "No! No! No!" This was not how it was supposed to be.

Her father had stopped digging and was watching them approach. When they reached him, panting, he held up a dirty green-glass bottle, three inches high, with a lid that was so rusted it had separated into water-thin layers, like croissant dough. "Nothing left," he said. "Just a little dust in the bottom of the glass."

"Oh, man," Jacob said. "Is that the time capsule?"

Her father nodded, his face pulled into a tight grin. "I expected it," he said, but Lucinda didn't believe him. All their lives, he had been telling them about the time capsule. He had told them again just hours earlier, on the road south from Oklahoma, how when he was twelve years old he had all the relatives sign a piece of paper that he rolled up and buried to save for posterity. "Your great-aunt Beulah signed it," he had said. "Her hands were so shaky that I had to hold mine over hers just so she could grip the pen."

"We know, Dad," Erin said, in a small voice.

"Her father built this house. Your great-great-grand-father. He used the pension money he got from fighting in the Civil War. Beulah could remember—"

"The Wright Brothers' first flight," Erin said, finishing her father's thought.

The major smiled at his children, gave a little shrug. Lucinda knew enough about him to know that he tracked these connections, one person to another, one generation to another, linking their family story to the greater historical narrative, with a kind of awe, finding in them some kind of evidence. Of what she was never sure. Something about himself, his place, his worth.

"I'm sorry," Lucinda said.

"Oh, well. It was just one piece of paper." Her father lifted his arms to take in the view. "This is a whole world. Let's go inside."

He led them to the front stairs and stomped hard to show them it was safe. His foot went through the second step with a brittle crunch. "Whoa," he said, yanking his work boot out through the splintered hole. "Be careful, okay? Move slow."

"Maybe we should stay out here," Erin said from the lawn.

"You don't weigh much," he said. "Should be fine."

They made it onto the veranda, stepping gingerly and staying away from the east end, where the roof had caved in, collapsing wood and greenish shingles to the floor. A pair of stout black rocking-chair runners protruded from under the collapsed area. "Like the witch's feet," Jacob said. "When the house landed on her." Major Collins gave his son a blank look.

"From *The Wizard of Oz*," Lucinda said.

It took them fifteen minutes to pry the rotted plywood panel from the front door and get in, with her father jogging back and forth from the front porch, around back to the smokehouse, a crude outbuilding where he remembered there being a store of old tools. Finally, he came back with a crowbar and pulled the bowed plywood away, revealing a dark wood door underneath with a beveled-glass window in its center.

"There it is," her father said as he yanked the last nail from the door frame. "I helped my granddad install that door."

He turned the handle and headed into the dark house. Lucinda had to remind herself this was where she had wanted to be for years. She had wanted to come here the minute they returned from Germany, the fantasy of Shiloh brighter than the reality of her new school and new home, but her father had turned around and gone back overseas almost immediately. Finally, he was stateside, and a pilgrimage to Shiloh had suddenly risen to the top of his agenda. She could little afford the time to go with him; she was missing class at the University of Oklahoma to make this trip, and she felt a bit like a spy activated by a code word in one of those Cold War movies that were a thing of the past now. Her father's voice on the phone had said, "Shiloh." And she went.

Lucinda thought it was probably her mother's marriage that had sent her father looking for something solid at Shiloh. That and the fall of the Berlin Wall. The two events— Faye's fancy wedding to a western-landscape painter and the dismantling of the Iron Curtain—had knocked her father's legs out from under him. He was retreating to Shiloh to regroup and replan. They were only there for an initial weekend recon mission, but she could feel her father's alertness, his tension. He had never been receptive like that, but she could feel his need today, the hole in him howling to be filled. She had the same hole. She also had his bony knees, blue eyes, and tremendous powers of concentration, but this hole was their most striking similarity.

Dust stood in the air. As much as her father had talked about Shiloh through the years, he had said very little about its interior, and Lucinda now saw that the interior had been of little interest to anyone in a long time. They stepped carefully over brittle-looking planks. The bottom floor was composed of three side-by-side rooms with fireplaces at the outer walls on either end. A stairway disappeared into the wall of the middle room. It looked like crown molding had been pulled from the doorways and walls, and signs of a squatter were all over downstairs. Empty cans of food were lying around, musty bedding was piled in the middle of the floor, and the whole place smelled smoky, like someone had built a fire in one of the dirty old fireplaces and found out the chimney was clogged. With all the windows boarded up, the place was stiflingly hot. "Look," Erin said, pointing with her sandaled toe to a pyramid of unopened cans.

"I'll be damned," her father said. "The son of a bitch is still here."

"Does this place have electricity?" Jacob asked.

Major Collins rubbed his chin. "Good question. It shouldn't, but maybe this character's jury-rigged something." He picked his way across the mess of bedding and switched on a lamp set atop a low-slung coffee table, tossing yellow light against the shadows of the room. "I guess that answers the question." He put his hands on his hips and swung around, running his eyes over the place. "The fool better hope I don't find him." He started picking up and discarding bits of junk strewn across the coffee table.

"Electricity is really amazing," Jacob said. "It flows where it's channeled. It probably wasn't too hard for whoever's sleeping here to tap into a power line."

Erin stood close to the stairway, arms wrapped around herself. "Dad, is this safe?"

Major Collins looked up, having one of those moments when he suddenly remembers that he has responsibilities as a father. "I would say no. Why don't you kids go back to the car?"

"I'd like to see upstairs," Lucinda said.

"Take a hike, Lucinda."

Erin didn't have to be told twice. She turned, her ponytail catching the air like a whip, and was out the door. Lucinda followed her, leaving Jacob to bring up the rear. Erin made her way through a few feet of tall weeds to the pier. She ran down its short length, out over the pond. The Bloody Pond, that's what her father told her it was called, after a pond on the Shiloh battlefield where their great-great-grandfather had lost a close friend. "Erin!"

Erin stopped at the end of the pier and sat down, dangling her bare legs over the water. Lucinda trod cautiously over the pier and eased herself down next to her sister. "Hey," she said.

"I want to go home," Erin said.

"I'm as surprised as you are," Lucinda said. "It's a shock."

"Somebody's been living here like a rat."

"I wasn't talking about that." Lucinda looked out over the stagnant water. "Why shouldn't somebody make use of the place? Probably some poor soul needing shelter."

"Then what were you talking about?"

With the edge of her hand, Lucinda swept dirt into the water. "Shiloh. The whole idea. I didn't realize how much I had idealized the place."

"I want Mom," Erin said. "Do you think she and Lord Cuckoo-Face miss us?"

"Sure they do."

Erin sniffled. "We can't stay here, Lucinda. I want my room, I want my clothes and my stuff and my phone. I want Mom."

"We just got here, Erin. Hang in there."

"God, you sound just like Dad."

It was true. And she couldn't stop herself from saying what she said next: "It's fine, Erin, really. Everything's going to be okay." It was one of her father's stock phrases and it sounded as phony in her mouth as it did in his.

Erin punched her shoulder. "It is not! It is not!"

"Lucinda?" Jacob had come up behind them, his foot-steps vibrating the loose wood of the pier. His voice was quiet, measured.

"Yeah?"

"Did your Nazi ghost ever stink?"

She twisted around to look at him. "Stink?"

"Like he really needed a bath?"

"He didn't smell like anything."

"Look!" Erin scrambled to her feet. "You two are crazy! That's not a ghost!" She was pointing at the house.

Lucinda followed the direction of Erin's gesture and saw a man standing at the corner of the house watching them. He had a dark beard and wore denim overalls and a dirty yellow ball cap. He leaned on a shotgun, his hand flat across the end of the barrel.

"Come on!" Erin said. She sprinted down the pier, through the surrounding weeds, and straight to the car, where she dove inside and started laying on the horn.

"Hold it, hold it!" The man had stepped forward and was calling to them. "Is there something I can do for you folks?"

"Who are you?" Lucinda called back from the end of the pier.

"I'm Wallace Shore. Now let me ask again, what can I do for you before you get off my land?"

"Your land?" Lucinda said. "This isn't your land, Wallace Shore. It's ours."

It was twenty or thirty feet from the end of the pier to the corner of the veranda where the man stood. Lucinda saw the man pull off his cap and scratch his head with the same hand.

"Your land?" he called back to her. "Well, that means you're . . . are you Jack Collins's kids?"

Lucinda's father appeared behind the man on the veranda.

"Dad!" shouted Lucinda. She began running down the pier. The two men were talking, but she couldn't hear what they were saying. By the time she reached the foot of the veranda, out of breath, they were shaking hands.

"Lucinda," said her father, "this is Wallace Shore."

The man looked at her and nodded. "Howdy, Lucinda. Your father and I are second cousins. Guess that makes us third cousins."

"Dad?"

Her father cleared his throat. "Yeah, we're cousins. Used to play together right in this yard. You know that story I've told you about getting caught with the girlie magazines?"

"Oh," Lucinda said. "That guy?" Jacob had joined them and stood next to Lucinda, peering up at Wallace like he hadn't decided whether he was real or not. Her dad looked over Wallace Shore, too. His face seemed to pass through a confusion of emotions: wariness, sadness, even jocularity, like he might slap Wallace on the back and give him a hug.

Finally, Wallace said, "I just stay here sometimes, Jack. Not all the time. I figured you weren't using it. And I figured you kind of owed me, you know."

"No, I don't know."

"Course you do."

"You know it's not my fault the old folks left this land to my mom, Wallace."

"Well, now, I do know that, Jack, I sure do. But you know, it's like you owe me in a cosmic way."

Her father shook his head as if this cryptic comment was just so Wallace. "Speak English."

Wallace seemed accustomed to such requests. "You been off living your life. Globe-trotting and getting paid. I fought in Vietnam, too, and what've I got? Not a damned thing." His face had grown serious and his voice measured, as if careful enunciation would make his argument clearer.

"I don't see how that's my dad's fault," Lucinda said.

Wallace craned around to look at her. "It's not fair, is all."

"I see," her dad said. "That's what you mean by cosmic."

Wallace nodded in a slow, exaggerated way. "That's what I mean, brother."

Lucinda loosened her hold on Jacob's hand as she saw her father cross his arms and give Wallace Shore a long appraising stare. She could see the humor playing at the corner of her dad's eyes. She took a deep breath. Jacob's grip, too, seemed to register the de-escalation.

"Looks to me," her father said, beginning to walk a bit from one side of Wallace to the other, "like you've been getting your cosmic payback selling this house off one piece at a time. How much have you made on our great-grandfather's woodwork, Wallace? It was handmade, you know. He sat right here on this porch and carved that crown molding, stained it himself. How much?"

Wallace looked down. "Not much, Jack."

"Well, Wallace, is there anything else I or my family can do for you? These are my kids—would you like one of them? They're real handy."

"I didn't think you'd ever come back here," Wallace said, a wheedling tone in his voice. "I figured you wouldn't miss it, didn't care."

"I'm going to renovate the place," her father said. "If the foundation's solid, I'm going to make this place a showpiece."

Lucinda listened incredulously. This was the first she had heard of any such plan and she wasn't sure if her father was telling the truth or just trying to make sure Wallace didn't come back once they ran him off. "Central heat and air, wall-to-wall carpet, going to rewire the electricity and plumbing. Might put a hot tub in, too."

"I see," Wallace said. Then he grinned. "Hey, you remember that time we caught that big old snapping turtle?"

Her father let out a sharp laugh. "Show my kids your finger."

Wallace gave a rueful smile and held up his left hand so they could see that his index finger was blunt and squared off on top, missing its tip.

Her dad turned to the car and waved for Erin to join them. "Are you hungry, Wallace?"

Wallace nodded.

"Is that diner on your hat any good?"

"Probably," Wallace said. He took the hat off and read the logo on the front, pulling his fingers through his long greasy hair. *Maizie's BBQ*, it said. Lucinda remembered passing the place just outside Nacogdoches. It wasn't far. "I never ate there."

Her father dug his wallet from the back pocket of his jeans and handed Wallace a few bills. "Go get us some chicken, won't you? With biscuits and jalapeños. Beer, too. You got a car?"

Wallace gestured toward an impenetrable-looking clump of blackberry brambles. He stuffed the bills into his shirt pocket and set off, turning around after a few steps. "You used to like coleslaw."

"Yeah, some of that, too. Oh, and some Cokes for the kids."

They watched Wallace hustle through the tall weeds and disappear into the bushes. A minute later a rusted yellow Camaro nosed out like a lizard and disappeared down the long driveway.

When the Camaro was out of sight, Erin jumped from the car and streaked toward their dad. "Oh my God, Dad! Who was that guy?"

He looked after the car and ran a hand over his face, pushing his fingers against his eyelids as if to wake himself up. "He's family," he said. "Haven't seen him since I was sixteen or so."

"Did you know he went to Vietnam?" Lucinda asked, feeling for a solid-seeming patch of porch and sitting down.

Her father leaned against a pillar and kneaded his forehead. "I guess I did. He's a couple years older than me and didn't go to college, so the draft got him early. I was still in high school when he went over. To tell you the truth, I always assumed he was dead."

"Why?" Jacob asked.

"I don't know," their father said. "He just never seemed lucky."

"Well, you were right about that," Erin said.

"I hope he hurries," Jacob said. "I'm sure hungry."

After a few minutes, Lucinda got up and announced that she was going to explore the graveyard. She could see it to the east of the house through the trees. A white-frame church stood in front of it, right off the rural route they'd come in on. "I'll be back when the food shows up," she said.

Her father squinted at her. "What are you after over there?"

"The grave of the jockey. I just want to see it."

Major Collins swung himself to a sitting position, "Come on, then," he said. "Let's all go. You won't find it by yourself. I'm not even sure I'll be able to."

They made their way through weeds, slapping mosquitoes off their arms and stopping to pull nettles from their pants more than once. But they found the jockey's grave right away. "Our people are over there," her father said, gesturing toward a row of modest white-marble tombstones. "And here he is. Your jockey, Lucinda."

Lucinda bent down to a small, flat stone, almost covered over with Bermuda grass and bright yellow with lichen. She yanked away the grass and ran her hand over the surface until she could feel the lettering. She took a quarter from her pocket and scraped it in the grooves until she could read what it said: 1866, and REST IN PEACE. GOOD RIDER, TRAVELED FAR.

She had felt dizzy for a while, but hadn't paid any attention to the feeling. But suddenly it was there, the aura of a coming seizure. She sat down hard and managed to say, "I'm going," before she was gone.

When she opened her eyes she didn't know how long she'd been out, but a pink-tinted sunset flamed overhead, suggesting it had been a while. She smelled chicken and raised her head to see her brother taking a bite out of a chicken leg. He and Erin and their dad were sitting around her like she was a table, eating. Wallace stood a few feet off, drinking a beer.

"Right here," she said.

Her father bent over her. "What?"

"That's what the jockey said, right? When they asked him where he wanted to be buried. He said, 'Right here.'"

"So the story goes."

"Well, not me," she said, struggling to sit up. "Not here, not now."

"We're all so relieved," Erin said.

"Hand me a piece of chicken," Lucinda said. "I'm starving."

TWENTY-THREE

Lucinda and Syd had agreed to meet in the parking lot of the Gypsy Tea Room, in Deep Ellum. Ordinarily she'd have been excited that she was finally going to see X in concert, but instead she wondered if she'd be able to concentrate on the show. She was going to see Syd. He had been back in the States for a while, going to college in Alabama—Crimson Tide after all—and although they had never been much good at writing, they had kept up enough of a correspondence not to lose touch altogether. Now, suddenly, he wrote to say he'd meet her in Dallas if she could get there. Of course she could. Here she was.

She sat in her car with the windows rolled down to the warm night, watching people come down the sidewalk and line up at the club. Wallace Shore had convinced her she needed to listen to Townes Van Zandt, so she was doing so,

"Highway Kind" turned low and seeping from her speakers like smoke. Wallace Shore claimed to have been Van Zandt's roadie and tireless drinking buddy, but Lucinda was learning, after a few visits to Shiloh, that Wallace was a bit of a tall-tale teller. She still couldn't get over her dad asking Wallace to stay on at the old farmhouse and get a full-scale renovation going. Her grandma Esmé still wouldn't set foot in the place, but her dad said he was hoping she'd move in once it was all slick and modern. Lucinda turned down "Highway Kind." Van Zandt knew about some kind of traveling, but not her kind. Sounded like he was traveling on purpose to get some character, not because he had to. Van Zandt had traveling shoes. Lucinda had traveling feet. She could tell Wallace she'd given it a listen, though, and someday maybe she'd try Van Zandt again.

For a few seconds she'd been aware of a GI in her peripheral vision, just the haircut registering its severe, familiar shape on her psyche. He was far from the nearest base, this soldier. She hadn't looked at him until she realized he was approaching her car.

"Lucinda!"

She turned. He had undergone a further metamorphosis almost as dramatic as his change from thirteen-year-old to sixteen-year-old. Syd had thickened and broadened. No longer a pale wispy boy, he had the kind of biceps often termed "guns." She remembered gripping his arms the night they had sex. They hadn't been that big then, had they? She didn't think so, but she would have to try them again to be sure.

The hair, though. Syd's silky black hair was gone. She remembered how self-conscious Nately had been about his GI buzz, alienated from his "real" self and pointing to a photo to show her who he really was. It was that kind of haircut. She prayed she was wrong. "You didn't."

He grinned and planted both hands on the window ledge. "What, no hello?"

She pushed open the door. "Hello." She wrapped her arms around him and he picked her up, crushed her to his sweat-soaked T-shirt.

"Look at you," he said. "All womanly. Damn."

"Tell me you've become a skinhead."

"Like your old buddy Toxic? No way."

"You enlisted, then?" She couldn't believe it.

"Well, yeah. We're at war, Lucinda."

"But why? You didn't even finish college, so you're, what? A private?" She had the nasty feeling that the Syd in her mind and the real Syd had grown apart. The real Syd had been walking around out in the real world and had gotten some ideas she wouldn't have imagined, had become someone askew from the dream-Syd who was still drinking coconut schnapps in the moonlight and trying to figure out how to put on a condom.

The real Syd nodded. "The timing's not perfect, I admit, but it's as good as I'm likely to get."

"What the hell do you mean?"

"This is my war, Lucinda. I'm nineteen. Sure, I'd rather wait till I'm done with school so I can go to OCS, but it's happening now."

"Are you kidding? Why do you have to go at all?"

He held up a hand and started counting. "My dad had Vietnam, his dad had Korea and World War Two, his dad had World War One—want me to keep going? You never went into our apartment in Graf, but you should have seen our hallway. Pictures of the soldiers in our family going all the way back. They're still in my parents' house in Montgomery. I've been looking at those all my life, Lucinda. The expectation was just there, on the wall. I always knew the next picture would be mine."

"Boy," she said. "I didn't know you were susceptible to that particular bug."

He threw his arms open. "Neither did I! It was like I just woke up with it."

"I guess your parents are thrilled."

"No, you know they surprised me—they're really upset."

"That's because they know war."

"My dad said he'd hoped I'd be the one to break the chain of war sufferers—that's what he said." Syd shook his head. "I sure didn't see that coming, but anyway, I'm in the Army now."

"Shit, Syd."

"It'll be an experience."

"You could get killed."

"Ah, I won't," he said, flashing his gap-toothed smile. "And you know what they say; what doesn't kill you . . ."

She held up a hand. "I know what they say."

She stepped out of the circle of his arms and tried to

think. Sydney Greenstreet Eliot was now Private Eliot. Their relationship had been completing circles since they met, coming back around again and again, but she felt they were caught in a larger turning now, inexorable and impersonal. "What was the first thing you ever said to me?" she said, hands on her hips, looking up at his naked, sweating scalp. Inside, pressure built and she tried to keep talking as if it would defuse her sadness and anger.

"I don't know. Something about Godzilla."

"You called my dad a privRAT."

"That wasn't me."

"Whatever. Why was that a joke?"

"I don't know. We were kids."

She poked him in the chest as hard as she could. "You're a privRAT."

"Ouch," he said, grabbing her finger and pushing it away. "I know it, Lucinda, and I'm proud of it. Come on. I thought you of all people would understand." His brow drew down and he looked baffled. Disappointed. He had a dream-Lucinda, she realized, and she was not that girl. She wanted to be, though, and the longing made her furious.

A pickup truck pulled up next to Lucinda's car and people piled out, slamming doors and laughing.

She flattened both hands against his chest and pushed. "PrivRAT. Cannon fodder."

He staggered backward and shook his head. "Why the hell are you so upset?"

She reached out and grabbed the dog tags hanging from

a chain around his neck. "They make you wear these things so they can ID your body, you know." Her voice shook. "Most jobs that's not a consideration."

"Damn, you don't have to take everything to an extreme, Lucinda. This is going to be a short war. This shit is going to be swift and painless and then I'll have combat experience I can hang on the wall at my parents' house. And these dog tags, I'll give 'em to you when I get back. How would that be?"

She glared at him, realized she would now have to escalate the fight or retreat. She took a deep breath. "I'm sorry."

"That's okay."

"I just, damn, I thought you were free."

"That's why we fight, darling."

"But can't you see you're caught in this war machine? It just keeps on turning, feeding itself on families like ours." She reached an arm tentatively around him, slid next to him. "If anything happens to you, I'll kill you."

He laughed. "So I take it you're not joining up?"

"I've been in the Army my whole damn life. I'm retired."

"You antiwar?"

"I don't know," she said. She didn't want to think about dog tags or Saddam Hussein. Dream-Lucinda was still in there, wanting to get to a dark room where she could be her simplest, best self. She wrapped both hands around one of his biceps and gave it a squeeze. "I just know right now I'm real pro-guns."

She looked up and saw him blush like the day they met, flipping the heater vent open and closed with that same satisfied smile on his face. "So, what's the plan? You really want to see this show?" He nodded his head in the direction of the Gypsy Tea Room.

There was a breeze kicking up as the sun went down, and the crowded sidewalks of Deep Ellum stretched away under streetlights. "It's such a nice night," Lucinda said. "Let's do something else."

They wound up walking to an elegant little restaurant serving Yucatán cuisine, and afterward renting a room in a Days Inn out on the LBJ Expressway. Lucinda needed to be back in Norman by noon the next day—there was to be a quiz in her European history class at OU, and then she had the five-to-two shift at the all-night diner on I-35 where she waitressed. And Syd had to be on his way to California. He only had a week of freedom before he was scheduled to report to Fort Bliss, in El Paso, for basic. They said good-bye over breakfast at an IHOP, promising to write regularly. Outside the window by their booth, the Dallas sky went straight up for a thousand colorless miles.

"Send me tapes?" Syd asked her. "Some X, maybe, so I can hear what we missed at the concert last night?"

"Do you regret missing it?" she asked him.

He smiled. "Nope."

She smiled back, but the request had a sad echo. When she was a baby, her mother had sent tapes to Lucinda's father in Vietnam. They weren't music tapes, but reel-to-reels of Faye's reflections about her daily life, narratives of what she'd been reading, what she'd cooked for dinner recently or seen on TV, what baby Lucinda had been up to. She told her husband about her feelings for him, using a voice that Lucinda knew her mother never used with anyone else.

Only a couple of the tapes had survived all the relocations, all the family battles, and Lucinda had them. She was on them, her baby voice, burbling, laughing, and, finally, saying a couple of words. Mama. Daddy.

Looking up from the menu, she said, "You don't want the OJ."

"I don't?"

"They've got one of those machines—see it? Last week, I opened one of those to clean it at the diner where I work. Roaches."

He made a face. "Inside the OJ machine?"

"Inside, lining the walls like bricks. Getting fat on nonstop OJ. Probably live forever, all the vitamin C."

"Did you have to clean it?"

"Yep."

His face twisted in anger. "So, let me get this straight." He rested his elbows on the table and held up his hands like scales. "You're working all night in a diner and going to school full-time. How much money has the good major given you for your education?"

"Oh, well, nothing."

"Literally nothing?" He looked at her as if she were crazy. "How about your mom? She's making decent money in real estate, right?"

"She feeds me, lets me do laundry. She even types my papers sometimes. We've just never talked about money.

She probably thinks he's paying. I don't know how he thinks I'm getting by."

"And you were just telling me about this big renovation he's doing of that old house. Doesn't that piss you off?"

"Well, he's hung up about that place. He likes to think of himself as landed gentry or something."

"What about you? I don't know how you can even talk to the man. Think how far down you are in his pecking order. Old useless house, girlfriends, new car, and whatever else. Basically, you're lower than even his lowest priority. Because even toilet paper costs more money than he's got for you."

"Are you trying to ruin our morning? I can't think about this stuff, Syd. What can I do?"

He settled against the red vinyl booth and stretched out his legs, staring at her. "Rat fink. Your dad's always been a rat fink, Lucinda."

Lucinda took a deep breath. There was no one like Syd. He felt like a human created just for her, but she knew it wasn't true. There were plenty of other people who knew him in their own ways, women who had spent much more time with him than she had. "Do you have a girlfriend?"

He looked out the window at the cars roaring by on LBJ. "Sure, I guess."

"I thought so."

"Come on, I haven't seen you in five years!"

"I know, I know. I'm not mad, just a little jealous."

"What about you? Somebody special?"

"Yeah." She had been dating a guy named Neal for about half a year. He lived across the hall from her. She thought a lot of him, but at the moment she couldn't conjure his face.

"So what's this?" he said, moving his hand back and forth between them.

She leaned back against the red seat and crossed her arms. "I figure we have a grandfather clause."

He laughed. "Is that the rule?"

"That's my rule."

"Your rule, huh? You sound like your dad now."

"Don't ever say that," Lucinda said, suddenly serious.

"Hey, I'm not complaining," he said. "As the sole beneficiary of this rule, I like your style."

"Does that mean breakfast is on you?"

"You bet," he said, slapping a hand down on top of the check. "I got this."

Standing in the parking lot of the IHOP, Lucinda watched this new rebuilt Syd climb into his battered Nissan pickup and head out to the interstate. She might have let herself feel hurt that he hadn't elected to spend more of his last week as a civilian with her, but as he drove away she knew their time together was enough. As much as she cared for Syd, loved him, really, she just didn't know if she had what it took to chain her heart to the Army one more time, not even for him, not even for a single day.

Syd seemed to understand that, and so didn't press her about the future. They didn't talk about what might happen after he'd served his time in the Gulf. They didn't talk about her plans for life after college. Let it happen as it will, she told herself. There: she had made her own saying, one to stand up against all those others from her father. She looked up at the Texas sky, shading her eyes against the sun. Let it happen as it will.

TWENTY-FOUR

Major Collins grew a watermelon plant in the Kuwaiti desert, the seeds planted in camel dung and watered with the soapy residue of his soldiers' showers. Lucinda had spent the last six months reading the details of the watermelon plant's development as her father's letters came in, landing dusty in her college mailbox, that Middle East APO on the envelope like the waxy signet of an exiled king. He told of saving some seeds from the last fresh fruit he had eaten for weeks, and then came the proud announcement—"I have a sprout!"—like a real child had been born, a fruit of his loins, and as the plant grew—"It's flowering!" Then: "I have a watermelon. All the troops come by and check on it now." Lucinda found herself almost resenting the damned watermelon plant, all that attention, all that anxiety for its survival, her father crouched over its tender leaves, shading it from the Persian Gulf sun.

Lucinda was half expecting to see the plant tucked under her dad's arm when he finally showed up in the hangar where she, her brother, and sister had been waiting for two hours. "How can you listen to that crap?" Lucinda said to her sister. Erin sat with her Walkman in her lap, swaying back and forth and occasionally singing a line from a Tesla song out loud, while Jacob, sitting next to her, hunched over a comic book.

He waved his comic at Lucinda. "Are you going to yell at me, too?" he asked. The hangar was dim and nearly silent, though full of people like themselves, sitting on cold metal bleachers, waiting to welcome home their soldiers. There was free coffee, at least, in giant metal percolators that stood on a card table at the base of the bleachers. Lucinda let the steam from her Styrofoam cup warm her face. It was five a.m., and this Quonset hangar would heat up fast when the sun rose, but Lucinda hoped the three of them wouldn't still be sitting there, waiting on their dad, waiting to cheer and smile and ask him questions about the desert, about the push into Kuwait. She was just too tired to fake any enthusiasm.

She hadn't slept in twenty-four hours. The day before, after a full day of classes and a six-hour waitressing shift at Liberty Diner, she was up at midnight finishing a paper on the siege of Thermopylae for a course in ancient military history when the phone rang in her tiny apartment in Norman.

It was her father announcing that he was in Maine and that his plane would land at Fort Sill at four-thirty that morning. "I hope you can meet me," he said. "Go round up the twins and come on down."

Erin stood up. "Want some more coffee?" she asked Lucinda.

"Sure. Are you getting some?"

Erin stretched her arms over her head and arched her back. "Yep."

"You're only fifteen and you like coffee?"

"Oh, I don't like it," Erin said. "But I'd lick caffeine off your shoe right now."

Lucinda had picked up Jacob and Erin from their mother's home in Oklahoma City at two a.m., surprised that her mother would let her siblings ride out of town in Lucinda's shuddering old Taurus, on a school night, just to say "welcome home" to her ex-husband.

"Maybe now he'll retire," Faye had said, standing with Lucinda at her front door as the twins shuffled sleepily out to the car in the early morning darkness. "Going to war at his age. Jesus." She shuddered inside her terry cloth robe. The sharp contours of her face, without makeup, caught the light. Her new husband, Carver, stood behind her in a burgundy silk smoking jacket and matching slippers, like a leading man in an old movie. Lucinda had never seen a man dress like Carver—it was a startling contrast to her father's habit of walking around barefoot in sweatpants.

"Oh, let's give him a break, Faye," Carver said.

Faye waved hocus-pocus fingers at Lucinda. "You see how they stick together, hon? Wouldn't you think this guy would be the last man on the planet to defend your asshole father?"

"I'm just sorry for the man," Carver said. "I know what he's lost."

"What did that man ever lose, Carve? Tell me that?"

He squeezed her shoulder. "You, Faye. He lost you."

Faye reached up and patted his hand. "You're so full of it." Carver grinned at Lucinda and kissed his wife on the top of her head.

"Anyway," Faye had said, "he was a Cold Warrior. And the Cold War's over."

In the drafty hangar, Jacob banged the heels of his high-top sneakers against the bleachers. "Tell me what he said again."

"He said he's retiring as soon as he gets home. He wants us to be here for his last hurrah."

"Then what?" Jacob said. "What's he going to do once he's not in the Army?"

"Guess."

"You really think he'll live at Shiloh?"

"If not, it's sure been a waste of a whole lot of money he didn't have. Grandma Esmé's got a new boyfriend in San Antonio," Lucinda said. "He's crazy if he thinks she'd pick up and move to the middle of nowhere."

Jacob looked across the dimly lit expanse. "Yeah, but what will he do? He's only forty-four."

It was a good question. Lucinda had no idea. What was her father good at? Growing watermelons? Killing Viet Cong? Codifying rules to live by. What had he been doing behind his desk all those years? The word *tactical* came to mind. Some sort of analysis?

"He won't be teaching you to paint," Erin said, stepping slowly up the steps of the bleachers with two Styrofoam cups full of coffee. "Like Carver is."

She said Carver's name insinuatingly and Jacob looked embarrassed, as if she were teasing him about a girl he had sworn not to like. Carver was teaching Jacob how to mix paints, use perspective, balance a composition, skills no one suspected their father of possessing.

"I don't even like painting," Jacob said. But Lucinda suspected what Erin had told her was true: that Jacob was impressed with the new man in his mother's life, and unsure whether that fact constituted a betrayal of his dad.

Erin yawned, looking ready for sleep in purple sweatpants with her junior high's logo on one hip and a long striped scarf layered over sweaters. "It's five thirty. What if we missed him and he's wandering around some other hangar looking for us?"

"Look around, yo-yo," Jacob said. "This is the right place." Many of the people stacked in bleachers along the north and south walls of the enormous Quonset hangar held handmade signs welcoming home their loved ones—HI DAD! SGT JAMES OVER HERE!—and more than a few said the name of the returning battery—Foxtrot 25th Field Artillery. On the east wall, a stage was set up with an American flag and a podium, a sash draped across the wall behind it: WELCOME HOME 25TH FIELD ARTILLERY REGIMENT!

"But are we positive he's in Foxtrot battery?" Erin asked. "Not one of those others—Charlie or Bravo or whatever?"

Jacob flicked her on the ear.

"Stop it, dweeb," she snapped.

"You never wrote him, did you?" her brother asked. "All that's in his APO." He wagged his index finger an inch from her nose. "You don't know what an APO is, either, do you?"

"Cut it out!"

Lucinda reached up and yanked her brother's hand away from her sister's face. Puberty. Had she been this bad? They drove her nuts. "Shut up, both of you, or I swear to God I'll leave you here when I drive home."

"Oh, like that's a threat," Jacob said. "I'll just stay here on the base with Dad."

"Like Dad would have you," Erin said.

"He'd have me, all right."

"No," Lucinda said, "he wouldn't. Not either of you. Now shut up."

They were silent for a time.

"I wrote him a little," Jacob said. "I just didn't know what to talk about. Band practice and stuff."

"It doesn't matter," Erin said quietly. "He'd have me."

Lucinda sighed. Unlike her little sister, she had written the major. She had found herself his chief point of contact, the person he regaled with details about his fragile watermelon plant. He told her it traveled through the desert like the battalion mascot in an empty ammunition box her father held in his lap all the way up Highway 80 toward Basra. He talked about the heat and boredom, the inadequacy of his current diet, the near impossibility of enjoying the local female population in a Muslim country. "You can't get near them," he complained. "They're hidden underneath those damned veils." About the war, he was less forthcoming. "Saw a severed head on the side of the road." "Had a scare with the gas masks." She could never tell the context for these details, so she imagined him observing without participating, bobbing along inside a bulletproof bubble, and she had responded by telling him about her college classes, her job, her friends. For the first few weeks she had written dutifully, even enthusiastically. He had given her power of attorney over all his financial affairs, and the pride she felt in this trust had rebuilt a connection with her father that she hadn't felt since the divorce.

But then his first bank statement came, and she learned about the money he was spending on Shiloh. Contractors, supplies, a salary for Wallace Shore—it was a massive, expensive undertaking. Shiloh, that pipe dream. Shiloh was getting the royal treatment. And there was another thing. Her father had established college funds for Jacob and Erin. When she opened the statements and saw what they were for, she had sat, almost catatonic, staring at the wall in front of her for so long she wondered if she had had a mild seizure. She kept thinking of Syd's outrage on her behalf in Dallas that morning six months ago. His had been a normal reaction; now she realized it was her reaction, too.

It wasn't that she hadn't herself been a little excited at the thought of Shiloh being revitalized. It wasn't that she begrudged Erin and Jacob help with college. They deserved it. But so did she. In all her life since the divorce, she had never been offered any financial help at all from her father. Not when her mother had kicked her out of the house. Not when she bashed her head in having a seizure at a restaurant where she worked and had to be hospitalized. Not to help with clothes, food, shelter, transportation, insurance, school supplies, tuition, doctor bills, or debts of any kind. Never. Despite years of promising to send her to the best college she could get into, when the time came to deliver, the only resource he had ever offered her was a slogan. "Baby," he would say, "whatever doesn't kill you makes you stronger."

She didn't ask anymore. Instead she worked three jobs, took out student loans, and told herself that at least this way she was truly free.

But the money situation made it hard for Lucinda to answer her father's letters. He began to complain that his watermelon grew faster than she wrote, and asked her to pick up the pace. But she found herself tearing up more letters than she sent. The ones she tore up griped about what it was like to survive on tips, how her sociology professor had twice brought her groceries, how during her freshman year she had lived a month in an abandoned house waiting for her financial aid to come through, keeping all her clothes and the crates of Nately's records in her car. She had even briefly, but seriously, considered selling Nately's records. She had written and torn up a letter describing the night a man tried to break into the abandoned house, the crunch of leaves as he prowled around, his face pressed to the glass of an uncurtained window in the room where she slept.

Flattened against a wall, with no access to a phone, her Neuschwanstein snow globe clutched to hurl at the intruder, she had thought of her father's slogan—if this didn't kill her, she'd be strong as hell in the morning.

After hearing his voice on the phone last night announcing he was coming home, Lucinda had realized just how sick she was of holding back. It was time to have it out with Dad. As she drove Erin and Jacob to Fort Sill that morning, she had composed a speech, and she promised herself that before she dropped him off at his apartment that day and started the drive home, she'd tell him exactly how she felt. Her speech was the real reason why she'd come, why she had given up a night's sleep and dragged her sister and brother ninety miles down the highway to give her father a ten-minute ride from the airfield to his apartment. Now, sitting in the hangar, she went back over the speech, cleaning it like a weapon, loading it carefully.

"Either of you know about trust funds?" she asked.

"What?" asked Erin.

"Either of you thinking about college?"

A loud squeal echoed off the hangar's metal walls, the sound of a massive gear engaging. "Look!" Erin rose to her feet along with everyone else in the bleachers. The west wall of the hangar was rising like a giant garage door. As it slowly lifted, they could see that outside the sun had come up and was shining on a stretch of blacktop the length of a football field at the end of which was another hangar identical to the one where they were sitting. Its door was open, and Lucinda, squinting against the sun, made out a row of troops standing in the hangar bay.

"That's them!" Jacob said. Noise erupted in the bleachers, a roar of stomping, cheering, and applause as the line of troops marched out of the distant hangar and into the sun. Behind the first row came row after row, emerging from under the shadow of the hangar, ten, fifteen, twenty rows of personnel in desert battle-dress uniform.

The stomping and clamoring in the bleachers intensified as people spotted their loved ones and went crazy. A general appeared on the American-flag-bedecked platform, waiting for the column of troops to cross the blacktop. Finally the entire battery was inside, filling the floor from back to front and from one bleacher to the other, like poured sand.

As the general began speaking, Lucinda and the twins scoured the rows of people below them, looking for their father. It was hard to see; the soldiers all wore their hats pulled low over their eyes, so that all Lucinda could really make out was a patch of profile for each person.

It amazed her that these exhausted people should be held at attention for long minutes while their families jumped up and down all around them, but the general was drawing a line under the soldiers' mission, stamping it officially over. "And so," he said, "as of right now, oh-five-fifty a.m. on February twenty-first, 1991, the fighting men and women of Foxtrot Battery, 25th Field Artillery Regiment of Fort Sill, Oklahoma, are officially dismissed."

The column of soldiers in formation broke apart, hats flew into the air, and the bleachers emptied as civilians flooded the floor. The orderly rows of soldiers dissolved into small clusters as family members found each other. Jacob and Erin raced from the bleachers the moment the troops were dismissed, but Lucinda hung back for a few seconds in hopes of spotting her father from above now that most of the troops had shed their hats. His bald head should have made him easy to spot.

As she watched the soldiers mill around below her, she was shocked with a cocktail of sensory input that slammed into her with a feeling she'd never had before. But she knew what it was: homesickness.

Acute, wrenching homesickness.

The echoes of all those voices reverberating in the metal building, the greenish fluorescent lights with their quiver and buzz, the smells of diesel and axle grease and shoe polish, metal and dust and the sweat of many bodies, unearthed a buried memory.

She remembered standing as a toddler with her mother in matching red dresses in someplace like this, watching some scene like this. Looking for her father and confused by all the men dressed just like him, she had wrapped herself around the green, jungle-camouflaged knees of a man she thought was him, only to see her father's face close to hers as he crouched, smiling, and held out his hands to her. Confused, she had looked up the legs and torso of the man she held on to and had seen a strange face smiling down at her from a great height. She had let go and run to her father. Had that been when he got back from Vietnam?

She sat down on the bleachers and put her head in her hands, closing out the noise and light around her. That memory. This feeling. She was home. All her life she had thought of the Army as what kept her from having a home. Come to find out it *was* home. She dug her palms into her eyes for a long minute, just trying to adjust.

After another minute, she stood up and scanned the crowd for her father, but still didn't see him. She had lost Erin and Jacob, too, down in the thronging mass of people. Descending the bleachers, she jumped to the floor and shouldered her way through the crowd, scrutinizing each face that passed her.

Space began clearing within a few minutes as the hangar emptied out. Now Lucinda could see stretches of empty concrete between groupings. Up near the hangar doors, Lucinda spotted the purple of Erin's sweatpants, and then the angular figures of her brother and sister, backs to her, heads upturned to their dad, whose head and shoulders rose above them.

He was changed. He was thinner, shoulders narrower, face and head dark as a nut, with the skin around his eyes still pale. The top of his head was peeling and he looked battered. He looked like someone who could someday die. She had never seen it before, his mortality, and it made her feel the danger of his having been at war for these months like a retroactive punch in the gut. While he was gone, she hadn't worried about him, hadn't seriously considered that he might be in harm's way—on the television that she watched at work, the war looked like a video game. She had worried more for Syd than for her father. Her fleeting sense of his mortality faded fast as she watched him nodding and laughing with the twins, boots on the ground. He couldn't die. He was her dad. The bright permanence of him, the elusive quality of his presence, reached her from across the room.

He spotted her, raised a hand into the air. "Lucinda!"

His voice echoed through the hangar as she closed the distance between them. Her father reached for her and Lucinda let herself be crushed against his chest.

"You forgot your sunblock," she said, straightening her arms to look at him. His skin was even darker up close, covered in a fine mask of new wrinkles like cracks in dark glass. "You look like a TV Indian now."

"The sun in the desert," he said, grinning down at her. "Unreal. No getting away from it."

"I can't get over you in desert BDUs," she said. "My whole life you were in those jungle BDUs. Deep greens. You look so different." Nothing had shown her the abrupt shift into a new era like the change in uniforms. The Army looked like a foreign force to her.

"I don't think I look good in all this khaki," he said. "Not my color."

They made their way out of the hangar and into the crisp, bright day. The blacktop between the two hangars was crowded with people. In one corner, the soldiers' baggage was being unloaded from the back of a truck, and all around giant coolers full of ice and Budweiser cans were being flung open and plundered. Her father pulled out a beer as they passed one cooler, then doubled back and grabbed three more, underhanding one to each kid.

"All right!" Jacob said, grinning up at his father. He shook the ice water from the can and popped it open like he drank beer all the time.

Erin held the beer with her fingertips, sniffing the foam that poured from the opening in the top. "Beer," she said.

"Here's to retirement," Major Collins said, lifting his can. "And whatever comes next."

They all raised their beers, and Erin sang out, "Hooray, Dad!"

As they stood around drinking their beers, a few GIs came up and shook Major Collins's hand. "Been a privilege, sir!" "Good luck in the real world!" "Now you're not the only one with combat experience, boss!" Major Collins introduced Lucinda to the last man, a tall lieutenant.

"Galloway, this is my eldest daughter, Lucinda. She's a sophomore at OU this semester."

"Nice to meet you," he said, taking her hand. "What's your major up there?"

"History," Lucinda said. "Welcome home."

"I hear we're living at the end of history. No more after the Cold War. What do you think?"

Lucinda nodded. "So says Fukuyama." She had just written a paper on this very topic. Galloway had nice eyes, big brown ones. Too bad he was Army. If she were going to go that route, she'd choose Syd, who would be shipping back to Alabama sometime soon. "It's a cool theory," she said. "But just because we're the only superpower now doesn't mean everybody likes us."

"You sound like a soldier," he said. "I tend to agree."

When Lieutenant Galloway had gone, her father said, "You could do worse, Lucinda. I can give him your phone number."

Lucinda thought about it. "He's career, right?"

"Yep."

"Forget it."

TWENTY-FIVE

"Here's the plan," her dad said, twisting around to talk from the passenger seat. The twins rested in the back, their father's heavy duffel was stowed in the trunk, and Lucinda drove down Sheridan Road through the heart of Fort Sill on their way to her father's spartan apartment just outside the gate in Lawton. "First I've got someplace I promised myself I'd go. Then we drive into Lawton and have a huge breakfast."

"Can't we eat first?" Jacob asked. "I'm starving."

"Yeah, me, too," said Erin.

"Sorry, gang. First things first. I'm on a mission." He turned to Lucinda. "You know the road behind the officers' club?"

"I haven't been on post in a while," she said. "I don't have an ID card anymore."

"Just follow the road," her father said, and in another

couple of minutes Lucinda spotted the O Club, a Spanish-style building with a long red awning half hidden in a stand of cottonwoods, which Lucinda drove past, taking the car onto a dirt road that wound through a creek bed and a desolate two-mile stretch of fenced-off prairie. As she drove across the prairie, Lucinda felt the words she needed to say to her father crowding into her mouth like panicked people pushing for an emergency exit. She would have preferred not to talk in front of her siblings, who had no idea about any of it, but it was time for the speech she had been planning. "Dad?"

"There it is!" her father said, pointing to a gravel parking lot on the north side of the road.

"Geronimo's grave?" Lucinda asked, turning the car into the lot. "This is your mission?"

"I thought a lot about this old SOB while I was over there," her father said, swinging open the car door. "Couldn't get him out of my head." He went around to the back of the car and asked Lucinda to open the trunk so he could get his duffel bag.

"We've been here," Erin said. "School field trip in seventh grade."

"Yeah," Jacob said. "I bet there are ghosts here, Lucinda. Lots of them."

Erin shoved him. "How can you be so weird?"

"On the field trip I tried to see them," Jacob said, addressing himself to Lucinda. "But people just wouldn't leave me alone."

"Don't mess with them," Lucinda said, slamming the car

trunk. From across the parking lot she made out rows of white tombstones glimmering with morning dew and she could see words across them, names, dates, even an occasional epitaph. For a minute she saw each stone as a story, as if the cemetery were a big library full of books nobody else knew how to read, and nobody else wanted to. "Jesus, it's getting hot," her father said.

They walked through the chain-link gate. A canopy of pecan trees threw much of the graveyard into shadow that grew deeper as the cemetery extended east to a creek where the trees were especially dense. "Shade!" Major Collins said, raising his face to the network of tree branches above him, leaning his body away from the duffel bag that hung in front of him from both hands. "What could be more civilized? A simple damn tree. God, I missed them."

There were no other visitors in the cemetery. Rows and rows of white marble graves stretched to the creek, but one grave at the front of the cemetery was a pyramid about six feet high made out of red cannonball-like stones. On the pyramid, a concrete sign announced it to be the grave of GERONIMO. The grave was flanked on either side with junipers probably as old as the tomb, their branches and the front of the tomb covered with bandannas, strings of Mardi Gras beads, pendants, a pair of dog tags, dream catchers, artificial flowers, American flags of varying sizes and conditions, and a black and white Vietnam POW-MIA flag.

Major Collins let go of the duffel bag and sat down in the dirt in front of the grave. He looked up at his kids. "You know, this old warrior spent his last years selling himself to sideshows for booze money?" He leaned back on his arms. "He said he wished he had died back in Arizona in the war that killed his family."

Jacob and Erin dropped to the ground next to their dad and sat cross-legged. Lucinda prowled around the grave, looking at the stuff strewn through the trees. Someone had left an OU hat. Lucinda pulled the cap off a branch.

"Over there it was me who was the old man," Major Collins said. "Nobody around me had ever seen combat. They kind of watched me, you know, to see what I did. If I panicked, they panicked."

Lucinda took a deep breath, draped the baseball cap back over the branch where she had found it. "You panicked?"

"Nah," he said, pulling back his shoulders. "Not really."

All morning Lucinda had envisioned scenarios where she spilled her flaming guts to her father, but none had them sitting at Geronimo's grave. If there was ever a setting to make her complaints seem trivial, this was it. It was getting harder and harder to find an opening. She was tired, and irritated at her father's sudden impulse to honor Fort Sill's famous dead man. He had never said much about the Native American experience, but if he had been in the Army and at Fort Sill a century earlier, Geronimo's Apaches would have been the enemy. Time made all the difference. You could even travel into East Berlin now.

She snapped a branch. "So what's up, Dad? You feeling like Geronimo?"

Major Collins unzipped his duffel bag. Reaching in, he pulled out a watermelon the size of a softball. He held it up.

"A little small," he said, "but not bad, considering." He cracked it open and pulled it apart, exposing the pink meat, shelved like a gun clip with black seeds. He handed a piece to each kid and kept one for himself. "Eat up, kids," he said. "You're holding history in your hands. The only watermelon ever grown in the Arabian desert."

Erin sniffed at the chunk of watermelon in her hand, nibbled the meat. Jacob buried his jaw in his piece and came up with a dripping smile.

"Gross," said Erin, looking at her brother.

Jacob widened his grin. "Tastes just like homemade!"

"It is homemade," Major Collins said. "I made it." He took a bite of the watermelon.

Erin held up her piece of fruit. "You made history, Daddy."

"That's right," said Lucinda. "Just like Geronimo."

Her dad chuckled, spit out seeds. "You can laugh, Little Miss History Major, but you're not far off. Those damn Indians made history, all right, but they were on the wrong side of it. They were going to lose, and they knew it." There was a trash barrel, painted green and chained to a peg in the ground not far from the shade tree. Major Collins walked over to the barrel, dropped his watermelon rind into it, and came back to the grave site wiping his hands with a handkerchief. He sat back down in the dirt. "Can you imagine that feeling? I sure as hell never could. But now . . ." He shrugged. "Sometimes I can."

"But we just won," Jacob said. "Right?"

Major Collins waved a dismissive hand. "I guess. But

everything else—everything I fought for all my life. My family. The Cold War. They don't exist anymore."

"We exist," Erin said.

"I don't remember you ever fighting for your family," Lucinda said. "And I remember you said once the Army was just a job."

He shook his head. "Honey, it was a life."

Looking down on him, Lucinda fought the urge to comfort him. "You're a young guy, Dad. You can do anything now. Dedicate yourself to peace!"

He lifted his head. "There won't be peace, baby."

"Peace seems like a stretch, and yet there's no other enemy. No other superpower. Who? This Iraq thing was just kind of random."

"Think of all those jobs," he said. "All those clerks and drivers and cashiers, all those radar techs and drill sergeants and snipers and engineers and nurses and doctors. Think of all the bullets and the uniforms and the buttons on the uniforms and the C rations and the tanks and rivets in the tanks, and think of all the people who make all those things. And the people who own the companies who make all those things, and the thousands of office workers running all the paperwork on all that stuff. No, baby. There won't be peace for long. They'll come up with a new enemy same as your mother found a new husband. For the same reason, too."

"Same reason?"

"Because it's a shame to let all those assets go to waste. Got to find something to do with them."

Erin smiled. "You miss her, huh?"

"I don't think about it much."

"I'm going to tell her what you said about her assets."

"Go ahead. I used to try to get my folks back together, too." The major looked at each of them. "You know me, kids. Better than anybody else. You know I've never questioned authority."

"Ha," Lucinda said. "You're always saying rules are for other people. If that's not questioning authority, I don't know what is."

"Well, yeah, but where it counted, it was Army all the way. I followed orders and never griped. I never questioned Vietnam. I mean . . ." He paused. "Jane fucking Fonda . . . I hated those goddamn protestors. My country, you know? Right or wrong? You know what I'm saying?"

Lucinda blinked at him. "I don't think so."

Her father shook his head. "I'm trying to tell you I was wrong. I've been wrong." He pointed to the palm of his hand as if the argument he was trying to make was written there. "This goddamn war was fought for oil. The greatest Army in the history of the world being used to secure a profit. It was bullshit."

Erin pulled her knees up to her chest. "That's what everybody's saying."

Major Collins sat back on his haunches, looking tired. Whatever confessional fit had gripped him was spent. He shrugged. "I'm just saying I was used. That's all."

Lucinda's own speech—about Shiloh, about the crime of sacrificing the young for the comfort of the old—where had it gone? Was she crazy, or had he just made her speech? Fat cats, indeed. Lucinda sat down shakily on the grass behind her brother and sister, looked up into her father's weathered face. Blood thrummed in her ears. He was a creature of war. All war sacrificed the young; it had been done to him and now he was doing it to her. He'd do it to Jacob and Erin when their time came. He had a dream of Shiloh and he would build it on her back; all the resources that should have kept a roof over her head would go to rebuild an old wrecked roof that probably nobody would live under, her needs deferred with the promise of inheritance. But his dream had been hers, too, all these years, and hadn't it, in a way, been a roof over her head all along? At least it had given her an answer when people asked where she was from. That was something.

Erin dropped her piece of watermelon and sprang at her father, embracing him. "Daddy!" Jacob joined her, and the three of them stood in a group hug next to the pyramid of stones that was the grave of Geronimo.

Lucinda sat on the grass and watched them, feeling numb. She had dropped her slice of watermelon in the grass next to her. Now she picked it up. "Here's to retirement," she said, and threw the rind toward the trash barrel anchored close to the shade tree. She missed by a good three feet.

"Here's to it, all right," the major echoed. "And here's to you kids. At least I have you. At least I didn't waste my whole life."

He stood up and dusted off his BDUs. "You know what? I want to go to one more place." He pulled Erin and Jacob to their feet.

"You're kidding," Jacob said.

"Come on," the major said. "The sooner we go, the sooner we eat breakfast."

"We're sleepy, Dad," Erin said.

"Go to sleep, then," he said.

When they got to the car, Major Collins took the wheel. "It's a five-minute drive." Lucinda climbed into the passenger seat. She couldn't imagine where they were going, watching as her father took the main highway through the Wichita Mountains Wildlife Refuge. In the early morning light, all the familiar landmarks looked strange, silvery with dew and deserted. She watched through the window without really seeing.

Her father was telling the twins something about the land they were driving through. It had to do with the days when he trained, long ago, on the Fort Sill firing range. But Lucinda couldn't focus on it. Instead, she found herself remembering with pinpoint clarity the last time she saw him before he went to the Gulf. He had driven up to the university from Lawton, but she had had to work, so he came with her to Liberty Diner and sat in her section drinking coffee and talking to her before the dinner rush. She had hoped he might ask her if she needed money for tuition or books or rent or car insurance, maybe leave a hundred bucks under his coffee cup. Instead he asked for change for a five and left a buck on the table when he shoved off.

That dollar bill alone on the table he'd vacated— anchored with a saltshaker—burned in her brain. But what the hell. Why fight? He was what he was, and he was right about one thing: she couldn't disown him. Wouldn't disown him. He was hers, as her mother was hers, and it didn't matter what they did. My parents, right or wrong. How ridiculous, how unfair that it was true, but, oh, was it true.

They had reached the foot of the Wichitas, and pink granite rocks the size of houses sprawled along the east side of the road. Major Collins pulled the car to the shoulder of the road at an undistinguished spot where the densely growing scrub oak, the cross timbers that had made the West so hard for settlers to cross, led away from the road, twisting among the rocks. There seemed no reason to stop.

Her father twisted in his seat and looked back at Jacob and Erin. "Back in a few," he said.

"Aww, crap," Jacob said. "We're going to starve."

The major turned to Lucinda. "Let's go."

Lucinda looked at him. What could he possibly have to show her out here in the middle of nowhere?

She pulled herself out of the car. In the backseat, Erin was putting on her headphones and Jacob was opening his comic book. "Just hurry up!" he said as Lucinda closed the door.

Her father walked up to what looked like an impenetrable wall of small, gnarled tree branches and pushed his way through, holding branches back for Lucinda, who followed behind him. They fought through dense brush for a few more yards before it gave way to a clearing of wide rocks that sloped gently up to the base of one of the Wichitas' small mountains. Desert willows grew between the cracks of the rocks and a thin waterfall ran down one side and dropped into a ravine behind the clearing.

Lucinda looked around. "How on earth did you know this was here?"

"Beautiful, huh?" Major Collins sat down on one of the flat rocks and started unlacing his boots. "I don't remember who first told us about this place. I'm just glad I remembered how to find it." He pulled off his boots and, one by one, poured sand from them onto the rock. "Iraq, meet Oklahoma," he said to the dust.

"Well, thanks," Lucinda said, puzzled. "Thanks for showing me. It's pretty."

Her father yanked off his socks and drew up his bare, white feet. "Cool air feels great," he said, wiggling his toes.

Lucinda perched at the edge of the rock where her father sat, his expression smooth and placid.

"Have you ever had a dream and realized it was set in someplace you know well, but it's different in the dream? A lot of times, in my dreams I'm here."

"Exactly here?"

"Yep. Right here." With the flat of his hand he dusted off the face of the rock.

"This," he said, pushing his index finger against the rock, "is where you were conceived."

"What?"

"Right here." He looked off at the pliant branches of the willows. "I was in basic training at Fort Sill. I got a pass and your mother and I came out here one weekend with a blanket and some beer. An auspicious rock."

Lucinda studied her father. The pale skin around his eyes looked almost translucent in the sunlight. She had never thought about the setting for her father's dreams, those most interior of rooms, or imagined that she existed there, her genesis at the root of his mind, like a haunting. She would never have believed it. "I'll be damned," she said.

Her biological conception was nothing she had ever wondered about, nothing she could use, but she looked at the rock. It was the two-second silence before the opening chords of the song, the beginning of history. Yet it was just a rock in the woods off the side of the road and she knew she would never find it again. She asked her father for her car keys and began scratching the surface of the rock. "That was the start of everything," he said. "You changed our world, Lucinda. You probably don't understand this, but a lot of people your age struggle."

Lucinda almost choked, bore down on the car keys. "Do they?"

"Your mom and I didn't know what we were doing until you came along." He shook his head. "We needed help. I know you'd rather die than take help from anybody, but we weren't like that. When you showed up, we had to figure things out fast and we wished like hell somebody'd show up with some kind of instruction manual."

"I struggle," she said, breathless with shock. Was that it? He thought she didn't need help? "And I don't mind help, either. I bet I'd like it."

He gave a short laugh. "Yeah, right." He craned his neck to see what she had scored into the rock. "What's it say?"

"Croatoan."

He pursed his lips. "Now, why?"

She couldn't explain. She wanted to mark another mute site where people had come and lived and vanished without a trace like unrecorded songs. This word that no one could understand seemed the best marker of all, inscrutable but holding the place of so many voices and stories.

And then the memory washed over her father's face. "You used to write that on your shoes. The damned Lost Colony—Lucinda?"

She looked in his eyes, the same shade of blue as hers. He was quivering on the edge of a point as he leaned across the rock and grabbed the keys from her. He stared into her face and spoke slowly. "You are not lost, do you understand me? You never have been." His gaze lingered on her for a second, but he looked away, grabbing his socks and boots and pulling them on, cinching the boots tight as he laced them up. Then he stood, stretched his arms over his head, and yawned. "You know, I've heard they think it might be the name of an island. Whoever carved 'Croatoan' might've been trying to say they were moving."

Lucinda brightened. "I've read that, too. If it's true, it means they weren't all killed."

"Yeah," he said. "There was some good reason they couldn't stay there."

Lucinda looked up at him. "It was like a forwarding address." She stood up, too. It made sense. What else could they have done, after all, those weary travelers, but pick up and leave again even though they thought they'd found home? They couldn't just stay there and wait on somebody to save them. They had to do it themselves. They had to move on.

ACKNOWLEDGMENTS

I am grateful and honored by the unflagging support of my agent, PJ Mark, who got the ball rolling and kept it rolling, and by the energetic vision and advocacy of Megan Lynch at Riverhead, and for all the dedicated work of Sarah Bowlin, whose identification with this project made all the difference. Thanks to C. Michael Curtis at the *Atlantic Monthly* for publishing the story that began this project. Earlier forms of some of this material appeared as stories in *Bayou*, Identity Theory, *The Briar Cliff Review*, and *The New Delta Review*.

Special gratitude goes to my parents, Reba Glenn Squires and CWO-4 Richard C. Squires Sr., U.S. Army, Ret., for their love and their lives. In so many ways, this book doesn't exist without them. Love to Rick, Mandy, and all my family, and thanks to my friends for the experience, strength, and hope. For their time and enthusiasm, I'm grateful to my readers Betteanne Palmer, Kit Givan, and Michael Robertson. For her rare friendship and insight as a reader of the various incarnations of this novel, I thank Rilla Askew. Most of all, my thanks to Steve Garrison, my chief reader, editor, critic, tireless supporter, and husband, whose willingness to live with these characters in the house surpasses generous and made the whole thing possible. And for my daughter, Nora. Nora, Nora, Nora!

Constance Squires is an Army brat who was born at Fort Sill, Oklahoma, and an assistant professor of creative writing at the University of Central Oklahoma. Her short fiction has won a number of awards and has appeared in the *Atlantic, Bayou, Eclectica,* Identity Theory, and *New Delta Review,* among other publications. She lives in Edmond, Oklahoma, with her husband and daughter.